CW01648368

Deceit in Cornwall

Chrissie Thomas

‘A celebrity friend is dead and the news hits the headlines. Is it suicide, accident or murder? Mel sets out to discover what has happened to her notorious and estranged friend. Generations of families are entwined. Why? With a backdrop of Arthurian legend, paganism, the KGB and Voodoo, Thomas’s story vaults from Cornwall and Devon to Lincolnshire to New Orleans with fast-paced intrigue.’

Jan Moran-Neil

‘This is a compelling and intriguing read. The imagination is unfailingly gripped at every stage as the story unfolds.’

Colin Pearson

‘Thomas’s debut novel is an engaging narrative that moves between the wild Cornish coast and the deep south of the USA. Mel, the lead character sets out on a mesmerising journey to find out what happened to her friend. The themes of family, friendships, legends and magic make this book an original and intriguing read.’

Diane Marriott

‘Interesting characters and an unusual plot promise an intriguing and absorbing read. Well worth investing time in.’

Chris Extence

‘I loved this tale of two families and found out such a lot about Arthurian legends and Paganism. When I read a book, I like to enjoy the story but also learn about a subject I am not that knowledgeable about. This ticked both boxes for me!’

Jane Keightley

‘The story is captivating and full of mystery and intrigue – you won’t want to put it down until you’ve turned the last page.’

Vanessa Fretwell

‘Full of intrigue and suspense.’

Mary Fox

‘Thomas’s novel is rich with description and detail built into an intriguing mystery that you won’t want to put down.’

Tricia Seybold

‘Loved reading this book – excellent scene setting and left me wanting to read on.’

Barbara Maycock

Deceit in Cornwall

Chrissie Thomas

PISKEY

This is a work of fiction. Names, characters, places, and incidents either are the product of the author's imagination or are used fictitiously. Any resemblance to actual persons, living or dead, or to actual events or locales is purely coincidental. The historical references and settings have been adapted for creative purposes and should not be interpreted as factual accounts.

Every effort has been made to obtain the necessary permissions with reference to copyright materials, both illustrative and quoted. We apologise for any omissions in this respect and will be pleased to make appropriate acknowledgments in any future editions.

A CIP catalogue record for this book is available from the British Library.

ISBN 978-1-9192317-0-9

Main text typeset in Georgia 11/14

‘Man’s dearest possession is life. It is given to him but once and he must live it so as to feel no torturing regrets for wasted years, never know the burning shame of a mean and petty past.’

Nikolai Ostrovsky

‘The comfort of having a friend may be taken away, but not that of having had one.’

Seneca

‘To lose a friend is the greatest of all losses.’

Publilius Syrus

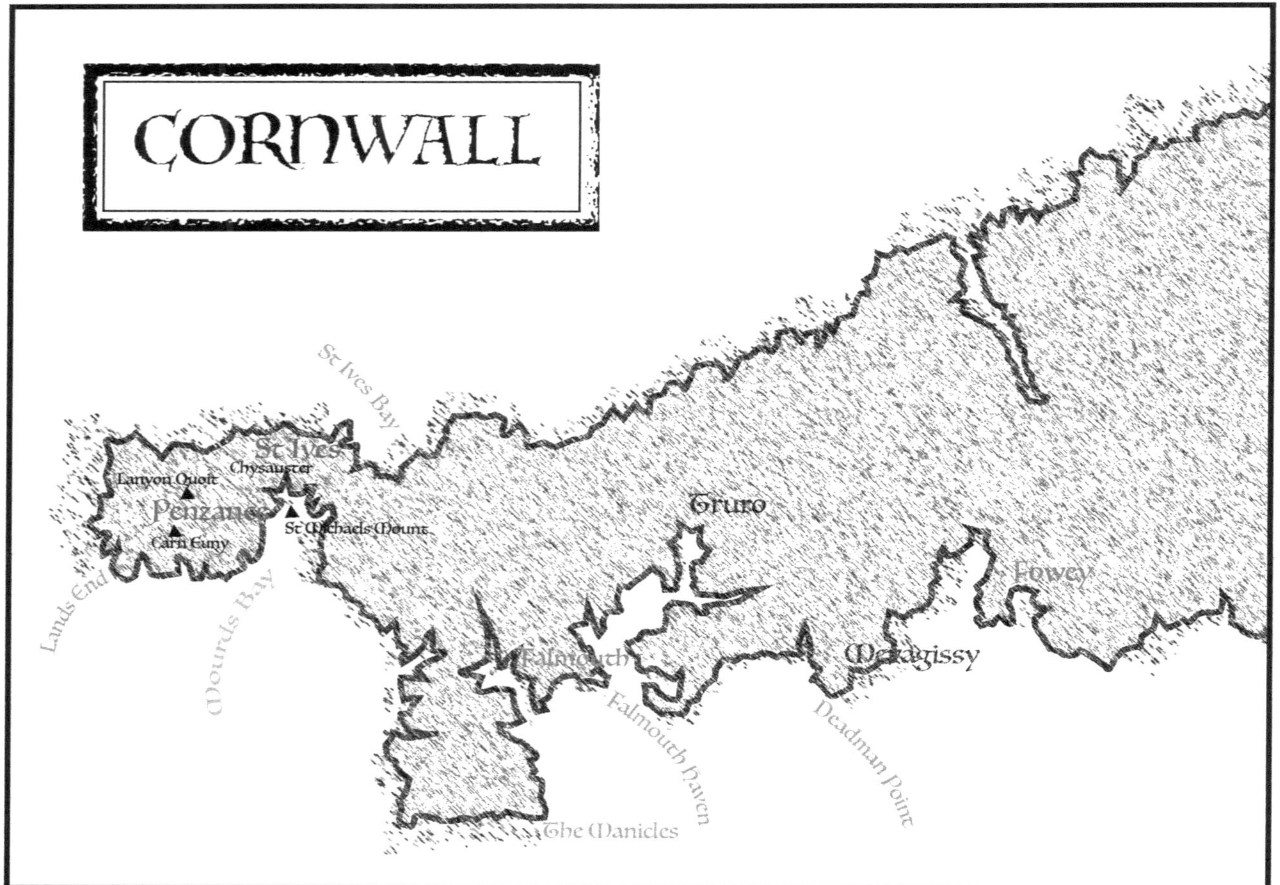
CORNWALL
St Ives Bay
St Ives
Chysauster
Lanyon Quoit
Penzance
Carn Euny
St Michaels Mount
Lands End
Mounts Bay
Truro
Falmouth
Falmouth Haven
The Manicles
Mevagissy
Deadman Point
Fowey

Periwad

'Twins run in our family, like pus from weeping boils.' This was one of our mother's most nauseating similes. However, despite the grotesque imagery, nowadays it is one I return to time and again as I ponder over our lives so far, and the trauma we have suffered. My twin sister, Mel, was the worst affected, for she bore the brunt of it all. Mel, at present, resides in what our mother refers to, as *the asylum*. Mel is often catatonic, interspersed with flashes of lucidity – we seize on the moments of lucidity and dare to hope.

As I sit above the cliffs in Zennor with Arthur and Jenny beside me in the warm Cornish sun, I think of others, also twins. Once, a lifetime ago, Mel was vibrant, witty, clever, resilient... but her words can reveal more than I could ever hope to explain? What follows is the story according to my twin. When the mystery was resolved, Mel inserted the Malory references which explained our Lawson friends' tortuous past and how Natasha came to be murdered. The tales were patched together from family history from our grandmother's and mother's recollections and some were from the actual people involved.

Kerensa Lowe

Limbo

September 2005

I am sitting in a wicker chair. Around me is an array of humankind: some elderly, some not. I see them staring, expressionless, into space, hands placed obediently in their laps. A few are agitated, continuously fretting with sleeves and cuffs, yanking at their hair; others pace up and down, mumbling obscenities or gibberish. A grey-haired woman sits across from me, cross-legged on the grass, a purple hat perched suggestively over one eye. She has a florid complexion. From time to time, she belches loudly. This is followed by raucous laughter.

In the flower beds, golden dahlias glare, whilst the cedars encircling the lawn and the mullioned windows of the building beyond threaten to engulf me. The building is at once forbidding and comforting: forbidding in that those windows are gazing down on me malevolently in judgement of my many wrongs; comforting because for now it is a haven where I am protected and cocooned, far from the cruel world beyond.

Presently a woman approaches. Her hair, peppery grey, is beautifully coiffed. She smiles, wanly, her pace quickening. I sit immobile, unsure how to react. I catch sight of a man, very tall, broad of shoulder, imposing; he is just behind her, beaming at me. His attire is bizarre. A children's entertainer, Merlin, the Magician, – what, here in this place – surely not? He is clothed in a long kaftan of oriental silk, orange in hue, silver threaded through it, which sweeps the grass. His snowy hair is clutched at the nape by a wide, black ribbon. I glimpse incongruous, black boots peeking out from beneath the kaftan as he bears down on me. He and the woman are now abreast, hands clasped, united in purpose. Heart pounding, I rise from the chair. They stop.

'It's alright, darling, calm yourself.'

She must be talking to me. I slump back down and wait. The woman moves forward, cautiously this time. The giant remains a few paces behind, no longer smiling. Marguerite appears, spruce in spotless tunic, hair smoothed back, the tiniest of gold studs in her ears. She waves cheerily.

'Look, you have visitors again, Mel,' she calls.

I am safe, for the moment. The grey-haired woman is now inches from me; she proffers a gentle kiss, brushing my forehead with delicate fingers, light as a whisper, cool as summer wine. I accept, silently, waiting for clarification. There is none.

'So, darling, how are you?'

I know not how to respond. Marguerite comes to my aid.

'Well, Mrs Lowe, Mel had a bit of a wobble yesterday after you left, but generally, things are stable.'

So, Mrs Lowe, whoever she might be, is a regular visitor? To assist my memory, she says, hushed, 'Don't worry, darling. Ren sends her love. She'll try to drop by tomorrow.'

'Wren?' I ask, pondering the strange name; bird doesn't compute. Patiently, the huge man comes to Mrs. Lowe's rescue.

'Ren's your sister, Sweetheart. I'm your dad and this here is your mom. We came by yesterday?' This question remains unanswered as I have no recall. who are these people?

The man's voice is a deep, bass drawl. The words slide, like molasses, from his tongue. Marguerite looks at me encouragingly but I feel a rising panic. I am struggling to remember. I hear myself scream, hurl abuse, try to get up, but Marguerite is by my side in an instant, placatory hand on mine. 'Mom' and 'Dad' exchange a horrified glance and I feel abashed, temporarily.

'You'd better try again tomorrow,' suggests Marguerite turning towards my unwelcome visitors.

'Would it help if we brought Jennifer and Arthur?' *Mom* is talking to Marguerite who shakes her head.

'Best not. Mel is seeing Dr Ridley tomorrow. The session with Dr Drislane had to be abandoned so we've changed tactics.'

Mrs. Lowe glances at the man who claims to be my father and nods. She bends to kiss me once more but I avert my cheek. As she walks away, the man's arm around her shoulder, I see she is shaking.

The sun bludgeons through the glass unbidden. Its yellow glare offends my eyes. I want to hide, to curl up foetus-like, become invisible. Across the desk, peering myopically over spectacles with minute frames, sits a slim blonde. Her hands are clasped in front of her and she exudes an aura of inner tranquillity. She reminds me of someone I seem to have known long ago. There is a crisp tang in the air around her, like newly laundered shirts, pristine and business-like, and I recall another time, another place. Then, all was well in my world. Now things are askew, awry. Why? I cannot say.

I focus on her face. Her gaze is gentle. She is Dr Emma Ridley. She wears a bright, lemon-yellow, sleeveless blouse. It is open at the neck, revealing a subtle, silver chain on which hangs a single black pearl. Pearls are creamy white, aren't they? The black pearl fazes me. Ridley touches the gem and smiles.

She speaks: 'I loved its uniqueness. I bought it on a whim.'

I strain to remember another woman long ago.

My attention returns to my surroundings. To the side, on the desk, slightly on the diagonal, a weighty tome is visible. It is 'leather-bound', indigo, with gold lettering embossed down its spine. I struggle to decipher the title. Perched atop, at a jaunty angle, I glimpse a far less grand paperback. I note it is one I recognise: Malory's, *Le Morte D'Arthur*. The cover shows the king's corpse recumbent on a wooden barge. King Arthur is clad in full armour which shimmers and sparkles in the light reflected from the water. A woman, Guinevere, is gazing adoringly at him. Behind the barge, three grieving women. In the foreground, a white swan. A swan... my throat catches. White lilies float on the water, symbols of purity or death. It is a tranquil scene. I know this book. I have read it many times. The doctor, aware of my gaze, begins to speak.

'You have psychogenic amnesia...' a condition frequently induced by severe trauma'

I stare at Ridley, uncomprehending.

'Yesterday your parents came to see you, as they do every day. I am going to lead you very gently through what I have discovered about your life, pieced together from your family and your own account.'

Her fingers caress the indigo, gold-embossed book on her desk.

'These books are, of course, here, not by fluke. The Malory, I know you are very familiar with. The other is your work.'

I croak feebly, 'I am a writer?' The room is distorted; Dr Ridley's face a melting clock.

'The book has been assembled by your father, Mackenzie Lowe. It is a history of your family and another with whom you all have close ties. It will be something significant to hand down the generations, for your children and for your children's children. But more than this, it gives us, your physicians, an insight into the occurrences that have caused you to become amnesiac. Although you evidently recall certain aspects of your life, the Malory volume for example, other more personal matters, continue to be shrouded in mystery – simply too painful to recall. It is this that we are trying to redress. It is apparent that chords have been touched; forgotten images and facts have resurfaced. So, let's make a start.'

She takes up her pen.

'You remember Malory and his tales of King Arthur and the Knights of the Round Table. I am confident that in time, you will be able to recall the extraordinary life you have led. Our journey together will be painful but I will support you through it. There are two young people out there who need you very much.'

I raise my hand to my cheek. I am weeping soundlessly. The room is silent but for the buzz of a distant chainsaw. I look again at Malory's cover. There is a tree-trunk, sturdy and broad, stretching into the heavens beyond. I close my eyes: a willow, lush and green, drooping into a lazy river, a gentle soughing and the *plish-plash* of riffling water. A man holds my hand; dark-hair, piercing, blue eyes, like cornflowers. Two swans glide by on an invisible tow-line, their snowy feathers converging. Their plumage mutates to black. An echo in my brain... *They pair for life.*

'Mel?'

Dr Ridley stretches a slender, beringed hand across the table. I discern a beryl on the index finger. Beryl is for long-lasting union, for purity, the stone of the seer and the mystic. There is a wedding band of Celtic design rose gold with intertwined knots.

Her voice is barely audible.

'Let's talk about Lancelot... about Guinevere and Tristan. Do you remember Natasha?'

The room swims. I put my head in my hands and sob.

Footnote:
My sister's reminiscences are blurred. She kept a diary of sorts. She began our strange tale two years earlier.
Kerensa Lowe

Blood Red Ink

December 2003

Some events are imprinted on the brain: for some, 9/11; for others, the assassination of JFK, November 1963. For me, Natasha's death. I recall precisely where I was when I heard the news that the woman I had worshipped all my life was dead. It was one of those granite-grey mornings, the bleak midwinter of Christmas carols when Oxford Street had gone into overdrive. Shops were bedecked with baubles and tinsel, crowds milling everywhere, bags stuffed to bursting. People were jostling their way along the glistening pavements. Children were screaming and taxi horns blaring.

Shoving my way forward, I stumbled into a shop doorway. There on the TV screen was BJ Lawson. He and Natasha were celebrities nationwide. It cut to Natasha, then a shot of an elderly couple, clearly distressed, pointing towards a cordoned-off wooded area... barely a minute of footage but already a throng was gathering around. Heart pounding, I hailed a taxi and threw myself into the back seat.

What to do? Call my mother? I had been down to Cornwall only three times in the last few years, usually staying with Grandma.

Should I call my twin sister? No, I would get little sympathy there; Ren did not share my obsession with Natasha. I could call Vin, maybe? No, we weren't on speaking terms since Saturday's argument.

'You gonna decide where to, luv?' barked the driver. I blurted out Felicia's address in Bayswater: it was a moment of madness.

I scrambled up the steps and hammered on the door. Felicia stood before me. Taking one look at my face, she ushered me in without a word.

'Can I get you some strong coffee? I have Jamaican Blue Mountain beans. They're rather fine, actually.'

Felicia's plummy tones were momentarily comforting. Then the stark reality of where I was hit me full on. Felicia was my boss. Why on earth had I ended up here?

I muttered that something had happened to Natasha and I didn't know what to do.

'Natasha? Do I know her?' she enquired.

'Felicia, I'm sorry I didn't know where to go.'

Words were inadequate to describe Natasha. I got up to leave.

'Look my dear, please stay, and take some coffee. Jamaican Blue Mountain - the best! I am rather concerned about you.'

'No, I'm sorry. I shouldn't have bothered you. I'm not thinking straight.'

A while later, I found myself on a bench in the Princess Diana Memorial Garden and howled out my grief. Passers-by glanced my way and walked on, averting their gaze as if I were a leper.

My mobile buzzed against my thigh. It was my mother.

'Natasha has been murdered.'

'W...w...what?'

'Yesterday, it was the winter solstice – so very appropriate for Natasha. Mel, please come home. I love you.'

The line went dead. My mother had always had a penchant for the dramatic.

Natasha – murdered? I pictured her: exquisite, heart-shaped face; feline, emerald eyes, black rimmed with impossibly long, silken lashes; chiselled cheekbones; alabaster complexion, flawless; tinkling laughter; restless, slender fingers topped with scarlet nails and encased in rings while silver bangles kept up a constant jangle as she turned her hands expressively. Her gaze would often fall on me, as if we two shared a secret nobody else was entitled to know. Natasha was forever young; I believed her immortal.

When my father left, my mother became morose; the relationship between Mum and Natasha strained and her visits rare. After my grandfather's funeral five years ago, they stopped altogether.

Three years ago, I dared to ask my mother, 'Why don't you tell me what went on between Natasha and you?'

A stony silence ensued. Eventually she said, 'I never want to hear from, or about that woman ever again. Do you hear me?'

Dabbing my eyes, I considered what to do. Should I drop everything? My mother had sounded desperate and alone, despite the rift between her and Natasha.

I called Felicia and told her I would be taking a break to go down to Cornwall to deal with a family tragedy. What else could I say?

Then I called Vin and spoke into another answering-machine.

Two hours later I was standing in line at the ticket office at Paddington Station. Natasha was high-profile. Headlines were screaming out the news:

> 'TRAGIC DEATH OF NATASHA LAWSON.'
> 'BODY FOUND IN WOODLAND'
> 'OH, NAT! YOU WILL BE MISSED!'

Murder had not been mentioned. My mother's wild imaginings?

A cup of steaming espresso was thrust into my hand.

'I'm sorry about yesterday and even sorrier about Natasha. It's all over the papers, of course.'

'Vin, you scared me.'

He looked as if he'd had a night on the tiles.

'I knew you'd be here. Get that coffee down you. I'll get your ticket. Take these.'

'Oh, Vin...'

I was touched by his thoughtfulness: I stared down at the latest Sebold and an almond croissant. Our relationship had been in the doldrums lately. Yet Vin was so dependable, so sweet, so thoughtful. Maybe in time I would cease taking him for granted and put an end to this pointless hankering after someone utterly unreliable and my mother's bête noire.

'So how did she die? Bit sudden, wasn't it? Was there some underlying illness?' Vin thrust a ticket at me.

'My mother says she was murdered.'

'Your mother called?'

I nodded meekly.

'Blimey! Not that dastardly husband in the ballroom with the candlestick?' He grinned.

'I wouldn't have BJ down for a murderer – he's a Lothario, full of his own importance and thoroughly disreputable... but no... not that... Never!'

'A high proportion of murders are committed by family members.'

'Look, Vin... let's not jump the gun... my mother was always prone to flights of fancy. In any case, surely the papers would have picked up on it, if there was foul play?'

He nodded, 'Yeah, I suppose so.'

The train left on time and soon Vin was a mere speck at the end of platform ten. I fell to reflecting about our decade-long relationship, my reluctance to commit. We had first met over a cup of espresso. He had plonked himself down at my table, pulled a medieval English dictionary out of his jacket-pocket and announced, 'So you're going to be studying Gawain and the Green Knight, too, huh? What have we let ourselves in for?'

I explained about my family, Natasha and Gramps and their fascination with all things Arthurian.

'I'd heard your family practised paganism – how weird is that?'

I rose abruptly.

'Oops, sore point?'

'You could say that,' I barked.

I had hoped by coming to London that I might have escaped the past.

After our initial encounter, I had gone out of my way to avoid him but Vin was dogged. Inevitably, we drifted into a relationship, despite the incessant taunts from my twin about him being, 'ginger.'

My thoughts returned to Natasha. Her husband's fame as a Fenland landscape artist had been eclipsed by his wife's, exacerbating the discord between them. Not enough to prompt him to murder though, surely?

Prior to *the schism* (as my sister wryly dubbed it) between our mother and Natasha, I couldn't recall a time when Natasha had not been there. She and my mother had been friends since the 1950s, just as my grandparents and Natasha's parents had been before that. Every school holiday Natasha and her four children, Kai, Lancelot, Guinevere and Tristan, would tumble out of the car: young Lawsons and Lowes would career off around the garden at Pen-Towan, or head off to the local beach, a frantic dog or two on our heels. Natasha and Mother would sit for hours talking over BJ's latest exploits: a never-ending saga of dalliances involving blondes, brunettes and redheads of every shape and size, the intricacies of which liaisons we were as yet blissfully unaware.

In the evenings before bedtime, Natasha would tell us tales of King Arthur and his knights just as my grandfather had to her, my mother and Aunt Lamorna. Like Natasha, we were captivated and we would act out those stories of derring-do: Guinevere, Ren and I and, were damsels in distress and our brothers hurried to our rescue on trusty wooden steeds. Little Tristan refused to play. Rough and tumble was not for him. He would sit close to his mother, looking up at her adoringly as she absent-mindedly stroked his hair with her long, slender fingers.

Everyone adored Natasha – or hated her. I stared through the window, lost in bleaker remembrances, to a dark time when all the laughter stopped. Kai was dead. Lance became sullen and Natasha seemingly blaming him for Kai's death. She spoke to him in clipped monosyllables, creating a chasm between them. Lance would look at her with a simmering rage in his eyes. Enough to murder?

I jolted myself out of the misery of the past into the present sadness. Glancing at my watch, I realised I had day-dreamed away the journey. The almond croissant remained untouched and Sebold lay unopened on my knee.

As the train pulled into Penzance station, I saw Mother on the platform, waving two-handedly, like a wind turbine in a force nine gale, Trelly beside her. Growler was straining frantically on his leash, yapping excitedly. As I struggled out of the carriage, I was immediately engulfed in a cloud of patchouli and deafened by the clang of innumerable silver bangles as my mother's tears soaked through my coat. She was clothed entirely in purple and her dark glasses were indigo-framed. I assumed it to be one of her colour therapy healing rituals. It was clearly not working, because she was as gaga as ever.

'Oh, darling... poor, poor Tash. What will become of her?'

I extricated myself and scrutinised her for a moment. Her grasp of reality had always been tenuous. Rivulets of blue-black mascara trickled down her cheeks, pooling at her chin before dripping onto her purple cloak. She was clutching a huge amethyst.

'Natasha is dead, Mum,' I said, with as much tact as I could muster. 'She will be interred or cremated – that's what will become of her! Or do you mean is she with the Great Goddess? Will she be reincarnated as a snow-leopard?'

'This is no time for levity, Mel. I was musing on the funeral arrangement. You can be sure BJ will have scant regard for Natasha's beliefs. In any case, a snow-leopard is far too aggressive a reincarnation for Natasha. A deer, maybe... something more flamboyant, a gazelle, graceful, majestic, a little exotic...

'Hello, Demelza,' piped up a small but precise voice. 'It's nice to see you again, only not under such tragic circumstances, obviously.' I resisted the urge to giggle and bent to kiss my baby brother lightly on the cheek.

'Squid says, "Hello," but you mustn't touch him because he's got a bandaged finger. He injured it in the door.'

There was still no sign of my sister.

'Where's Ren?' I enquired.

'We had a falling-out over Neil,' was the terse response.

This came as no surprise. Neither of us had warmed to Neil Macbeith, whose name alone had connotations I wasn't altogether comfortable with! He had a Chihuahua named Inez, on whom he doted. Neil was the latest in a long line of brief liaisons and marriages on which my mother had embarked post-separation from our dad.

'I blame BJ entirely. If it was suicide, which I doubt, that husband of hers drove her to it. It was just the final straw. Although...' Her voice became lower, conspiratorial, and she leaned towards me, her pursed lips forming a 'moue' of disgust.

'Although, what? And who said it was suicide? You said it was murder!'

'Natasha was totally against drugs, of any kind.'

I stared at her, wondering how to respond.

'I'm referring to anti-depressants, tranquilisers, Die... Sitty – something... She'd been prescribed them months ago. BJ insists Natasha's death was an accident – not that you can believe a word that man says. Izzie says it was suicide. Tris is usually very sensible but obviously he is distraught and quite evidently not thinking logically. Natasha left BJ three weeks before she died.'

I considered the facts. Izzie was partner to Natasha's youngest, Tristan. I'd last seen Izzie at Tris's birthday party last year. He had seemed measured and calm and if he felt Natasha's death may have been suicide, this was worth considering, although would she have chosen woodland for such a deed? Debatable! I recalled the footage I had seen in London. Since the split with Mum, Natasha had been increasingly distressed – this much I had gleaned from Tris. Citalopram or Diazepam might be considered appropriate by the medics. So, was it murder, suicide or accidental? I considered Mum's latest snippet of information. If Natasha had finally plucked up the courage to leave BJ, would it have provoked him to murder?

'Natasha has met a cruel fate, and the information I have so far corroborates this,' declared my mother, exploding into my thoughts like a ten-tonne truck.

'My dear Sherlock, what has led you to this hypothesis?'

'Why is flippancy your immediate response, Demelza? I have evidence, recent letters-written by Natasha in which she voices her fears. The ink is most bizarre... but I suppose Natasha tended towards the flamboyant.'

I could scarcely contain my exasperation. 'And how pray, can ink be bizarre?'

'It was a dark, magenta colour – it looked like blood. Natasha was convinced people meant her harm. She even suspected her own family.'

'Oh, for God's sake Mother, get a grip! To write a letter in blood she'd have to be haemorrhaging, I'd imagine.'

My mother pursed her lips.

'How's Vincent?'

I replied that he had come to the station with me and left it at that.

We climbed into Mum's VW, affectionately named Loulou. There was total silence. Mum concentrated hard on the road and Trelly was immersed in a book. Dusk was falling rapidly. I gazed out at St. Michael's Mount, enveloped in a delicate haze of wispy, pewter-grey cloud and contemplated Mum's *evidence.* A few letters voicing imagined fears of mysterious individuals, *out to get her* sounded feeble. Logic persuaded me that Mum's hint at, *blood-written* script was out of the question.

'When's Grandma home?' I enquired.

'Tomorrow, 9.45, Heathrow. Apparently, she's made a friend in Rio – Zeus! I'm picking her up from Exeter at some point. Lamorna is off the radar. She's never around in a crisis.'

Mum and her sister didn't have a close relationship. I wondered how Grandma would take the news of Natasha's death. Gramps would have been devastated; he had always been fiercely protective of her. Like Natasha, I had adored my grandfather, but it would not be long before my adoration would morph into disgust and disillusionment.

Arthur

'Now put me into the barge," said the king. And so they rowed him from the land... Comfort thyself, said the king, for I will unto the Vale of Avilon to heal me of my grievous wound; But ever the queens and ladies wept and shrieked, that it was pity to hear.'

Le Morte D'Arthur by Sir Thomas Malory

Arthur Trelawney was a Cornishman through and through. The Duchy was in his blood; he lived and breathed her essence. Arthur understood her history, her geography, her language, her customs as timeworn as the rugged tors, as ancient as the undulating, heather-strewn moors. Each time he abandoned her for the cold confines of his London college lecture theatres and the world of academia within its hallowed halls it was like a wrench to the heart. When the yearning became too much, he would head off to Paddington Station and stand gazing forlornly at the platform, tallying the days until the next break. Then Arthur would trudge sadly back to his seedy 'digs.'

1950s Finchley, comprised substantial houses, the provenance of a bygone era of Victorian grandeur. It was in such a house that Arthur rented rooms, overlooking the busy Finchley Road. The accommodation was basic but it suited Arthur.

The view from the window was uninspiring, particularly for Arthur who was steeped in the beauty of the rugged cliffs of Zennor. It numbed your soul this place, sucked out the life force like an incubus: menacing, steel-dark clouds, the roar of traffic along the North Circular, dilapidated front gardens where neither hydrangeas nor rhododendrons would ever sprout; those hues of amethyst, rose-pink, magenta and cerulean, to which Arthur was accustomed, the harbingers of warm, Cornish summers.

But every cloud has a silver lining. One day, into Arthur's life, came Angharad, a young, bird-like girl who lightened those dismal, monotonous days with her tinkling laughter and merry eyes. They met, quite by chance, one of those fortuitous occasions with which life is replete. Arthur happened upon them as he exited the tube on that morning; squinting at his watch and noting his tardiness. They were scrutinising the map and talking animatedly in their native tongue. He didn't know what made him do it, especially considering he was already late for classes, but he stopped and enquired politely, 'Are you lost?' It snowballed from there. Arthur pointed them in the right direction and offered to show them the sights. Tomorrow was Saturday; he was at a loose end and he'd be more than happy to take them round, *his city*. Arthur had to smile to himself as he reflected on that encounter later that day. 'Arthur Trelawney, you're becoming a city-slicker,' he thought to himself. *His city*, indeed! And him, a Cornishman! But there was something about that young woman.

So, Arthur discovered the city he'd inherited, by default. He showed them around because Annie was eager to see it all. Her enthusiasm was contagious. She was the tonic he so desperately needed, the antithesis of those pompous professors with their po-faced, interminable ramblings and political debates. It seemed an unlikely alliance: Annie was no scholar. But with Annie, Arthur could live a little again.

He regaled her with yarns of life in Zennor and she would listen, mesmerised.

For Arthur was a born teller of tales, passed down by family, through the mists of time. Naturally reserved to the point of timidity, some would say, Arthur came alive in the lecture hall. His students, glad of the chance to deviate from the tedious complexities of the Russian language, would encourage Arthur to diverge from the traditional, to distract them with re-enactments from Tolstoy and Pushkin; he made them tangible. Sometimes, he would draw parallels between Russian folk tales and Celtic myth, ideas and beliefs which intertwined. His unorthodox methods of teaching drew him a faithful band of followers.

Years later Arthur's audience, although smaller in number, would still sit spellbound listening to his tales. For Natasha, though, they became much more. They were her passport into another world, a world where she felt secure, treasured and content.

But for now, Arthur had Annie – Annie who took him back to her native Wales with its sing-song, lilting tongue where Arthur was able to revel in the Celtic-ness of the land. In reciprocation, Arthur took Annie to Zennor. When Annie, with a mischievous twinkle in her mahogany eyes, said gently, 'Now just, Arthur Trelawney, when are you going to pop the question?' and, as an afterthought, she whispered, 'cariad.' Without hesitation he answered, without hesitation. 'Angharad Davies, will you be my Guinevere, my true love, my soul mate through life?' And so, it was settled.

After their wedding, Annie agreed to exchange life in the valleys for the sandy coves of Zennor. For now, though, Arthur kept his tiny room in London, but every alternate Friday, after lectures, he'd rush excitedly to platform five to catch the Western Belle to Penzance, where Annie would be waiting. They settled into a comfortable routine, until Ivan entered their lives.

Ivan Rodomski was of a similar age to Arthur, a Russian immigrant who had arrived in London shortly after the turn of the decade with barely a penny to his name. He found a position at the local factory almost at once. He spoke little English but Ivan was a grafter and the factory was desperate for post-war hands. He trudged to work every morning and wearily back home again every night. If any overtime was available, then Ivan was first in line. He needed the money. He desperately needed to fill his days to blot out the pain of life without Galena, left behind in a Yaroslavl cemetery along with their still-born son, Dimitri.

It was a bitterly cold night in late November when Ivan emerged from the Golden Lion. It was his birthday, so he'd decided he could afford to push the boat out with a couple of vodkas. He turned up the collar of his well-worn coat and shivered as he made his way down the dreary street. He must be getting soft; surely Russia was far colder than this? Unused to alcohol of any sort these days, he staggered slightly. Two *bobbies* were strolling towards him. One of them glanced at him as they passed. He heard one murmur, 'Looks like he's had one over the eight, George.' Ivan wasn't familiar with the term, but he gathered by their accompanying gestures the implication was that he'd had too much to drink. He felt indignant. He tottered on. With a sudden jolt, he realised he'd strayed from his usual route. He was now in a side street bearing no resemblance to the familiar broad avenue that took him past the park and eventually up the hill to his lodgings in Solent Close.

How did I do that? he wondered. He was livid with himself. He'd sobered up and longed to be back in the comparative comfort and warmth of the place he called home.

Better turn back and get my bearings, he thought.

As he turned, he became aware of three young men walking towards him. There was something purposeful in their stride which uneased him. He looked around nervously. The street was deserted.

'What 'ave we got 'ere, boys? Not that little Yid from down the road, is it?'

'Nah,' responded his companion. 'Don't look like it but he looks a bit foreign, don't 'e? Don't like the look of that beard one bit.'

The man was close enough to tweak the source of his displeasure playfully. He pulled again - this time harder. Ivan winced.

'What's up, mate... you deaf and dumb, or sumfink?' The man pulled a maroon scarf up to his face, evidently feeling the bitter night air.

The third youth surveyed Ivan without a word. The first character scratched his head. His curly mane of black hair was bare of any covering but his thick overcoat was buttoned tight to the neck.

'Well, now then, boys, seems to me he's not being very polite. Not said a word yet, 'as 'e? Least he could do is say sumfink. Respond to our little bit of fun, eh?'

'I don't have any money,' Ivan began to protest.

'Ooh, ve don' 'av eny monny,' mimicked Red Scarf. 'Don't ee spekee English, matey?'

Ivan suddenly found himself shoved against the wall. One of the thugs held him there; he was pinned, unable to move a muscle. Another of the youths was busily fumbling through Ivan's overcoat pocket whilst the third stood a little to the side, leering at him.

'Smells like you bin drinkin', mate... that means you gotta have some dosh... what d'ye think, Jack?'

Jack leered at Ivan once again and muttered, 'More than likely. You'd better keep looking, Tommy, ol' son.'

Jack brandished Ivan's wallet, triumphantly in the air.

'There ye go, lads. What'd I tell you?'

'Please don't hurt me; it's my birthday.'

All three youths laughed uproariously.

'Well, blimey, we'd better give you a present – what d'ye reckon, boys?'

So, they gave him a special gift, one each: blows to the stomach winded him so that he doubled over; another to the side of the head sent him reeling; a final vicious kick in the lower back left him groaning in agony. He dimly heard gales of raucous laughter. A window opened nearby and a voice bellowed angrily, 'Oy, you lot – what the bloody 'ell's going on? There's some of us tryin' to get a bit o' shut-eye.'

'Sweet dreams, Grandad!'

A parting shot at the nameless voice above and the three were gone. The window slammed.

It was serendipitous that Arthur Trelawney was unable to sleep. Annie was pregnant and he couldn't wait to get back for Christmas. He had essays to mark to keep him occupied. He'd be doing it now but he'd left the damn things in his office. It seemed to have addled his brain, this pregnancy. He'd go out for a quick walk around the block... it'd clear his head and then perhaps he could settle down again and get some rest. As it was, he had been walking for over an hour.

As he rounded the corner, he nearly collided with three young men. They seemed to be in one hell of a hurry. He quickened his pace. God, it was freezing tonight! Turning into Carlisle Street, he heard a faint groaning and made out a dark shape sprawled across the pavement. Arthur approached the figure cautiously, wondering if this was another vagrant in his cups. They seemed to be an ever-increasing breed these days. He bent over the figure. It groaned again. Arthur kneeled beside the man.

'Are you injured?' he enquired.

The man mumbled faintly, 'Puzhalsta...'

Arthur was alert at once. After a few minutes, he was able to ascertain that the man's injuries were not life-threatening. Arthur carefully helped the man struggle to his feet and they made their way back to Arthur's home.

Arthur settled Ivan in an armchair and gathered warm water, cotton wool and antiseptic. Ivan had sustained a nasty cut above his left eyebrow, his beard was matted with congealed blood and angry-looking bruises were forming on his lower back but, that aside, he'd got off lightly, it appeared. Arthur chatted amiably to Ivan about Russia, the factory, life in England. He patched him up as best he could and prepared a pot of tea.

'I've only condensed milk, I'm afraid,' he admitted, reluctantly, 'but the tea will warm you and sugar is good for shock. You look as if you're in need of a hearty meal.'

Ivan was exhausted but eternally grateful. Arthur insisted he spent the night on the couch and Ivan take his bed. Too tired to protest, Ivan's last thought before sleep overcame him was that some English folk were human after all.

The following morning was Saturday. Ivan opened his eyes, groggily, and peered around the unfamiliar room. It gradually dawned on him that he was in Mr. Trelawney's house, the latter had given up his bed for him and best of all he could speak his language. He could hear the Englishman moving around; there was the clank of crockery being laid out, drawers being opened and shut. Ivan got to his feet. The linoleum was icy-cold. He padded to the door. Across the corridor was the kitchen and leading off it, the sitting room.

'Good morning, Ivan,' said Arthur cheerily. 'I hope you slept well. How are you?'

Ivan began to thank him profusely, stumbling over the difficult name.

'Oh, please, I insist you call me Arthur. How about some breakfast?'

It was strange how the two of them settled into a companionable chat, partly Russian, partly English, over bacon and eggs. It was as though they'd known each other all their lives. Ivan, the shunned foreign factory-worker, and Arthur, the admired university lecturer-linguist.

'You have been very kind to me, Arthur,' murmured Ivan, gratefully. 'So far, my experience of English people has not been good. Sometimes I've almost wished myself back in Russia, but it's not possible.'

Why did you leave Russia?' Arthur enquired, politely.

For several moments Ivan said nothing and Arthur was concerned that he had offended the man. Then Ivan said very slowly, 'My wife and baby son died over there and... and there were bad things I needed to escape from.'

Arthur could see that whatever was troubling Ivan, was a private matter. Tactfully, he changed the subject. He started talking about Cornwall and invited Ivan to come and stay with him and Annie after the birth of his baby. It would give Ivan a chance to see another side of England. Surely, he was entitled to some breaks from the factory?

Ivan beamed with delight. As he stood to leave, he scratched his head and falteringly enquired, 'Arthur, would you, if I pay you... would you teach me some English?'

Arthur Trelawney grinned from ear to ear.

'Ivan, my dear fellow, I'd be delighted; you don't have to pay me one penny.'

So began a friendship which would last through three generations. Sometimes Ivan would invite Arthur round to his tiny room and they would share blinis and a couple of glasses of cheap vodka. Arthur would notice the little table in the corner, a sepia picture of a smiling young woman heavily pregnant perched on it surrounded by votive candles. In front lay an ancient prayer book with heavy, gold lettering engraved, Russian script on its cover. To the right-hand side of the table, stood a rather grand, wooden chest, with gold, Cyrillic letters etched into the lid: 'ГаПеНа РаДоМСКаЯ – Galena Rodomskaia.' Arthur made a mental note. It was dark, possibly ebony, and incongruous amidst Ivan's meagre surroundings. Arthur enquired whether this was all Ivan had managed to salvage from his former life. Ivan nodded mutely and turned away. Evidently the key to Ivan's life would remain a mystery, perhaps until his death. But by then, Arthur would be gone.

Some months later, Ivan took Vera as his wife. A meek, submissive girl, orphaned since the war and alone. Vera was only too glad of the security Ivan provided. She was happy for a while and learned to cope with Ivan's strange moods and erratic outbursts. Arthur would visit the couple from time to time, but often felt uneasy at Vera's evident reluctance to engage in conversation. He thought her shy, at first, but it became apparent that she was anxious not to displease her husband.

Then Arthur was invited, quite out of the blue, to visit Ivan's little flat. It was shortly after his first daughter, Lamorna, was born. Arthur surmised that Ivan and Vera wanted to help him celebrate the happy event. It transpired that the motive was of an altogether different calibre. At the door, Vera beckoned Arthur inside with a shy smile.

As the years went by, Annie and Vera became firm friends and their children too. On summer visits to Cornwall, Arthur's two daughters, Lamorna and Ruth, and Natasha, Vera's daughter, would race around Zennor church or scramble over the beach screaming with delight. An intense bond grew between Arthur and Natasha. When the time came for her to return to London the child would weep bitter tears yearning to return to this wonderful man whose comforting voice calmed her wounded soul.

The year Arthur died, floods came to Cornwall. The sky wept for Arthur. Arthur's ashes were scattered over the Zennor cliffs, where they tumbled into the waters below and were washed out into the great, green expanse beyond. It seemed appropriate somehow; Arthur was on his way to Avalon. Four women cried bitterly at his passing, for it seemed to them that the world had lost an integral part of itself. There on those rugged cliffs overlooking the Atlantic Ocean, Annie, Ruth, Lamorna, and Natasha, knew they would never see his like again, but in Natasha's life there was an unfillable void.

Pen-Towan

Our family home, Pen-Towan (literally, sand dune on the headland) nestled in a grove of trees, at the end of a narrow lane some distance from the beach. In her typically asinine way, our mother had alighted on the name because it had, 'good vibes.' When we arrived, Ren's cobalt Renault was on the drive. It amused my twin that her car and her name bore a close resemblance. As Mum narrowly avoided the hydrangea, the front door opened and Ren emerged, arrayed in a fluorescent pink jogging suit. A tearful reunion ensued as Growler hared into the house in hot pursuit of Janis, the cat who had appeared to welcome us. Anguished yowls and excited yelps echoed down the hallway and up the stairs, as we piled inside.

'Nice frock,' said my sister nodding at me, as our mother prepare a pot of lavender tea.

'Nice... er... fluorescence,' I muttered back.

The kitchen was bedecked with wreaths of evergreens: ivy, holly and mistletoe, it being Yule. In the corner, an altar was awash with candles. The scent of sage, rosemary and pine cones permeated the air. Atop the ancient Aga was an enormous pan of soup which would be set bubbling when guests arrived. Even the momentous news of Natasha's suspicious death could not thwart our mother's plans for her usual pagan celebrations.

Ren pointed to a package wrapped in brown paper with my mother's name written on it.

'Shall I open this?' she enquired.

Mother absent-mindedly nodded assent. Inside was a large bottle containing a blood-red liquid. Mum screamed.

'It's not blood, Mum,' I said quietly. 'It's got a cork in it.'

Ren shook her head in disbelief. I shook out the rest of the packaging. A piece of tatty paper materialised on which was scrawled in a shaky hand:

'I thort you mite like this. It's alderflows berries from are garden. Missus Lorson liked it. Thirza.'

'Ah, that explains the colour,' Mum said with a sigh of relief.

Having established his book was more interesting than a bottle of wine, Trelly disappeared, helping himself to a handful of biscuits before he went and I began to question our mother.

After a brief rummage in the kitchen drawer, she withdrew a piece of paper which she placed carefully on the table.

'Read!'

'Mum thinks Natasha's been murdered, Ren,' I whispered.

It was dated June 25th, six months ago. It was written in an unusual, dark red, script.

Ruth, help me! If I die, it is murder.

N.

Ren sat open-mouthed.

'It's not blood Mum. It's blood-coloured,' I declared gently.

Ren snatched the slip of paper.

'Surely you can't believe that's blood? Are you completely barking, Mother?'

Mum produced another smaller envelope addressed to Ruth Trelawney. It was smeared with a tawny substance. Ren and I regarded it mutely for a second. Inside in the same script was a reiteration of the initial note, apparently penned three months later.

'Mum,' I asked, 'Is this the first communication you've had from Natasha since the rift?'

She nodded.

Ren asked. 'Do you think Natasha was of sound mind when she wrote this? What grounds are there for suspecting foul play?'

'I have no idea, but there are enough people out there who hated Natasha.'

'Should we go to the police with this?' I suggested.

'I'm afraid there's more.' From her handbag, Mum withdrew another note. 'This arrived two days before her death.'

Ruth,

You are my only hope. I can trust no-one. Not even my own family. Ginny is hateful after the Lara business. Keep this under wraps if you value your own life and that of your family. Oh, Ruth, I have betrayed you...

A torrent of questions poured out from us both. Was Ginny gunning for her mother? Who was Lara? How had our mother been betrayed? Why did Natasha believe we were in danger?

'This has all come completely out of the blue. All I have, are these three notes.' Mother's voice trailed off.

The shrill ring of the telephone, split the air.

It was Natasha's husband, BJ. His tone was brusque: his wife's funeral was to be held in Boston, Lincolnshire at twelve noon on 3rd January. The service at St. Botolph's Church would be followed by burial in the nearby cemetery. There was to be no mention of that occult nonsense by *any* of our family. Then he was gone having given no indication of how Natasha had died.

I needed clarification.

'So, Mum,' I began, 'let's get this straight. Tris called to tell you Natasha had died and he thinks it's suicide? But BJ thinks its accidental.

TV footage showed her body was found in woodland. What – a heart attack whilst walking in the woods?'

'Tris said his mother called before she died, totally incoherent. He told his father who ignored him.'

'Natasha is high profile – the media must be speculating,' I protested.

'Tris told me his mother had left BJ prior to her demise but offered no reason.'

With that she burst into tears.

'Natasha would not have wanted a burial – it's against our beliefs.'

I wondered how BJ had engineered this funeral service so quickly in what was a fairly prestigious parish church. Wouldn't there be an inquest and investigation?

I voiced my thoughts to Mum.

'Friends in high places I'll be bound,' she replied, 'and if there are mysterious circumstances even more reason to hush it up.'

'Ah… lovely,' remarked my twin. 'Quirky handshakes and baring of the bosoms type friends?' She gave a huge wink and tapped her nose conspiratorially.

Barely had she finished speaking, when another call came through.

This was brief, punctuated by Mum's sniffs, strangled gulps and soothing platitudes and ended with, 'No, of course not, Tris; I wouldn't dream of it.'

Natasha's youngest lived in Devon remote from his two siblings. All three had distanced themselves from Lincolnshire. Natasha's pagan beliefs, her obsession with Arthurian legend and much-publicised relationship with her husband were not well-received. The accident which had claimed Kai's life had added fuel to the flames. Did it have any bearing on her 'death?' I wondered.

'Mum, was the rift between you and Natasha linked to Kai's death?'

Mother's eyes misted over.

'You know we were like sisters. Then one day she told me she had to distance herself. I asked her to explain. She refused. I was devastated. For me it was like a bereavement. I called, wrote letters. She refused to engage. To this day, I have no idea what I could have done. I spoke to others who knew her. Nobody knew why she had deserted me.'

'When did it all start?'

'About the time your father disappeared to the US. On top of the pain of that separation, it was one more heartache for me - those were dreadful days.'

I recalled mum's sudden launch into frantic liaisons with a plethora of men – it explained a lot.

'Let's get back to what we know,' I began. 'Shall we give Ginny a call? See if she knows anything?'

'Let's wait until the funeral.'

Ren's suggestion made sense.

'If Ginny is the murderer, she's hardly likely to *fess up*! she added.

Mother seemed to be reflecting.

'Then there was that awful incident with Faye,' she announced suddenly.

'Faye?' we said in unison.

'Your sister-in-law's mother. She hated Natasha.'

Joodee, our brother Sam's wife, was persona non grata with our mother. Mother took exception to the spelling! But Joodee was a tricky customer and we all gave her a wide berth.

'So, she had some grudge against Natasha?' I asked.

'Yes. We never understood why. She joined our coven. Came over from the States, said she had links to Abigail Williams.'

'Who's Abigail Williams?' asked Ren

'Implicated in the Salem Witch trials,' I informed her.

'Faye tried to stab Natasha at Beltane. Luckily, Wenna and Iris were on the ball and grabbed the dagger before she did any damage. She left the coven soon afterwards.'

'So, she could be a suspect?' asked Ren.

Mum stared into space, tears rolling down her cheeks.

'I was always jealous of Natasha. I took a back seat whilst she pursued her various career paths. Her cruel dismissal of my own ventures took its toll. Maybe I let my tongue get the better of me and that caused a rift between us... I simply don't know, but if only we could have resolved it all.'

'But Mum,' I said, 'if Natasha was mentally unstable it may have contributed to her behaviour.'

'We reconciled fleetingly at your grandad's funeral but then things were as before.'

'Why don't we leave it Mum?' I suggested. 'You don't owe her anything.'

'I can't, Mel, she was my best friend.'

'What happened to Kai?' I ventured.

Mum inspected her teacup for a while.

'Kai was found dead in a local church near to Natasha's home. He'd tumbled down stone steps into the flooded crypt and drowned. Natasha was convinced Lance had pushed him. The coroner recorded accidental death and no blame was apportioned.'

'Did Natasha have proof it was deliberate? They were kids – blaming a little boy is harsh.' I reasoned.

'Nevertheless, Lancelot is an emotionless individual – always has been.'

'Could it be a motive for murdering your mother? He and Ginny as partners in crime?" Ren mused.

'Kai's death led to a severe decline in Natasha's mental health. From then on, she was convinced that her family was re-enacting Arthurian legend due to a fatal flaw. It was quite preposterous, as I told her.'

Mother stood up. 'I'm going to the temple.'

The temple was a grand edifice in our garden which held the pagan regalia and was the venue for coven meetings. It was where she retreated in times of stress.

Ren and I reflected on what we had just learned.

'I still wonder if we should contact the police, if only to protect our family,' I said.

'Given the press interest, they'll be baying for blood if they get wind of possible murder. Knowing the local cops the last thing they'd agree to do is protect a load of weirdos like us, with no concrete evidence!' Ren replied.

'Let's investigate the possibly 'blood-stained' envelope; that's can be proven conclusively, surely? Then we can take it from there.'

'There could be an innocent explanation,' responded my twin. 'I'm on excellent terms with the pharmacist in town – I'll take it in tomorrow.'

Ren and I spent the next few days quizzing our mother. As we absorbed the full extent of the Lawsons' tragic history, Ren and I agreed that if Natasha had been murdered, there were plenty of suspects.

Yuletide came and went.

It was now the 27th December, six days since Natasha's death. Grandma had been surprisingly calm at the news. Despite our protests she insisted she had everything under control and her Brazilian friend, Zeus, would *'help Ruth get over that nasty business with Natasha'* by the laying on of hands. At this point, Mother had placed a lump of something in grandma's hand.

'Protection – black tourmaline,' she barked. 'You barely know the man!'

Ren's pharmacist friend, James, had discovered that human blood – Type A – was on the envelope. But whose? The pharmacist pointed out that it could be as innocuous as a paper-cut. I asked if Natasha was type A. Mum had no idea.

We had learnt more about Faye, our sister-in-law's mother. We were informed the woman was as demented as a tree-load of chimpanzees just like her daughter and, as far as Mum was aware, had returned to the States so was out of the equation.

Ren and I decided to pay a leisurely visit to Zennor and Grandma and then call in on our brother to see if he knew of his mother-in-law's whereabouts.

'Oh, how wonderful to see you, cariads! Come in. I have that carrot and karaoke soup you like. There's Welsh Cakes and home made strawberry jam.'

The place was crammed with ornaments and knick-knacks. I sidled past the narrow, wooden shelf in the hallway. An enormous donkey with a naff sombrero perched above his ears, crashed to the floor despite my best efforts. A hefty suitcase graced the kitchen floor, its contents spilling out onto the quarry tiles.

I took the bull by the horns.

'Gran, we wondered if you could shed some light on a few matters to do with Natasha.' I ventured tentatively.

Ren bulldozed in, 'We need to find out if Natasha was murdered.'

Grandma collapsed into a chair. 'Oh, cariads, surely not!'

I glared at my sister. 'Her death was a bit mysterious, Grandma. You see Natasha wrote to Mum before she died.'

'Were they friends again?' she asked tremulously.

'No, but Natasha wrote when she thought she was in danger.'

Grandma was appalled.

'Surely you need to call the police?'

'Mum wants us to investigate by ourselves, Gran.'

She shook her head in disbelief.

'Those two were inseparable, shared all their little secrets. When Arthur was dying, she and Ruth started talking again, just like old times. Then a few hours before he passed away, Arthur asked to see Natasha. Just her, mind, alone, like. I never knew what passed between them. Whatever it was, Natasha was upset by it. At the graveside, I truly thought she was going to throw herself into the earth. Then we never saw her again.'

What on earth could have been divulged by our grandfather to have unfixed Natasha so badly?

The soup bubbled away in the pan, the kettle sang loudly on the hob and the delicious smell of Welsh Cakes pervaded the room. From afar, I heard Grandma's voice, soft and lilting.

'I wondered if it was to do with Ivan,' she continued. 'He and Vera... well, their marriage was difficult.'

'How, Gran?' I prompted gently.

'She just did as she was told – always. Arthur said Ivan was unkind to her. He had a nasty temper and was unkind to poor little Natasha too. He would hit her; sometimes she had bruises. Or he locked her up for hours.'

'Couldn't you and Gramps stop it? The physical abuse I mean,' asked Ren.

'It wasn't for us, cariad. It was private, between those two. Arthur felt the same.'

'But if a little girl was being beaten and Vera too?' my voice was getting louder. 'The police could intervene.'

'Gran, you had a moral duty.' Ren was as horrified as I.

Our grandmother shook her head sadly and repeated, 'It was none of our business – your Gramps agreed.'

'But Gran,' protested Ren, 'it had a major effect on Natasha, ruined her mental health. Mum said she was damaged all her life and that Kai's death made matters worse.'

'It must be dreadful to lose a child, look you, but Gramps and I well, we had our own family and Vera didn't want us to interfere.'

My sister seized the nearest object to hand and hurled it across the room. It landed with a deafening crash and shattered into a thousand pieces.

'Fuck the pair of you!' With that, she slammed out of the room.

Grandma burst into tears. I threw my arms around her.

'I'm sorry Gran, Ren will calm down. I know you did what you thought best.' After a while, my grandmother's sobs subsided.

'There's terrible language, look you, Demelza; you'd not hear it in chapel. Just like your mother, that girl.' She fetched the dustpan and brush and mechanically began to sweep up the fragments of porcelain from the floor.

Grandma sat down and collected her thoughts again.

'It was just as well Natasha had your grandfather. He showered her with affection. Arthur was a kind man. They had so much in common those two.'

For a while she lapsed into Welsh. Unable to comprehend the words, I allowed her to ramble on before I gently interrupted.

'Grandma I suppose you don't happen to know what blood group Natasha was?'

'I don't know, my dear. Mel, you're usually so sensible. Surely you don't believe the poor girl was murdered?'

'Could be, Gran.'

'Arthur was A; I think most people are 'O',' she said sadly.

I took my leave and went in search of Ren, slightly regretful that neither Welsh cakes nor karaoke soup had been offered. She was where I knew she would be, perched on the cliff's edge gazing out to sea.

We both stared in silence at the waves below which had, five years ago, taken the ashes of my grandfather and swept them out to the great ocean beyond.

'How can you be so calm?' her voice was a whisper.

'Different times, Ren.'

She shook her head, 'I cannot tolerate cruelty to women and kids. Somebody should have done something.'

'Maybe if the police had got involved the abuse would have got worse for her,' I suggested.

Changing the subject, I added, 'Shall we go and see Sam?'

'No, I can't face that bitch of a wife of his right now,' she replied.

The following day we went to Marazion. The beach was empty. Trelly tore off after Growler in a rare moment of childlike joy. We strolled behind. I inhaled deep lungfuls of sea-air. We agreed to visit Sam as soon as possible and get the low-down on Faye. At least then we could eliminate her or not from our list of suspects.

The steady stream of paparazzi had at last given up the ghost and left the environs of Penzance, unable to glean any more about Natasha's demise. The couple who had discovered the body had become minor celebrities. They had apparently lost their dog shortly after their gruesome discovery. The poor creature had died having devoured several chocolates that had been discarded near where Natasha had been found.

Our mother had returned to work at Ruth's Remedies in Penzance High Street. To our amazemen,t the place was inundated with customers all wishing for help with a plethora of ailments and disorders. There had been a flurry of enquiries after Yule and mother's supply of crystals had been exhausted. The cynic in me put it down to the locals wanting to quiz her about Natasha's death rather than a sudden viral epidemic.

Felicia Galsworthy had generously allowed me leave of absence until after the funeral. Tris had called to say his sister was not answering her phone and he was quite concerned. Having discovered Ginny would be taking on the role of Blanche Dubois in the West End on 19th January, and knowing she often stayed with friends in London when she was on stage, Tris had tried to track her down there but to no avail. I volunteered to contact Vin. He ran a missing persons agency in London and although he'd been rushed off his feet for several weeks now, (Christmas always seemed to be a bad time) he promised to try to locate her. Ginny's decision to be incommunicado at such a time set alarm bells ringing for me.

It was now New Year's Eve, and at 7.30pm Ren headed off into town. She was meeting James, the pharmacist; their relationship had blossomed! I retired to my room to read. My mother was baking cakes and preparing a bed for our father, who had been summoned, from New Orleans.

Mackenzie Lowe, our father, is a larger-than-life character. He stands six-feet-six in his stocking feet and dominates the room entirely. His voice booms out, interrupted by guffaws of laughter. His eyes are the colour of mud-brown puddles, flecked with moss. His hair, grey for many years, is tied in a long, straggly pony tail and his garb of choice is a cross between ageing hippie and country bumpkin. Never without headgear, attired completely in black, today, he was sporting a Fedora worthy of Al Capone. He filled the room like an enormous grizzly bear and gathered both Ren and I up in a hug, which took my breath away.

'You grow more like your ma every day and just as beautiful. Has she put a spell on you?'

We smiled politely. Our father's capacity to treat us as if we were still toddlers never ceased to amaze.

Trelly and Growler arrived and were subjected to a more subdued scrutiny. Our mother turned to the Aga, slightly flustered.

'So, Trelawney, how is life treating you?'

'Squid has been a little under the weather,' said my brother, solemnly.

'Oh, I'm sorry. I hope your mother has been able to concoct something to alleviate his suffering.'

Trelly seemed unsure whether Dad was mocking him. After a brief moment, he volunteered more information.

'Neil was very unkind to Squid who is rather fragile.'

'Who is Neil?' queried my father.

'The latest ex.' Trelly's retort sounded wise beyond his years.

Mum wheeled round, kettle in hand.

'Trelawney, show some respect. You know perfectly well Neil was only having a joke with you.'

She banged the teapot down onto the table and threw herself into the chair with a grunt. Dad stared at her. Nothing could be heard but the sound of rattling chinaware and the tinkling of cutlery.

'For God's sake, can we deal with our grief instead of casting aspersions about my bloody love-life?'

'Calm down, Ruth. You're upsetting the kids.'

'Two of *the kids*, are grown women and well able to bear the upset!' she retorted indignantly.

Trelly bowed his head and marched towards the door. His parting shot was, 'And Neil hated Natasha – so there!'

Trelly tore upstairs with the dog yapping at his heels.

'What does that mean? I asked.

'Neil got irate whenever Natasha was mentioned and I mentioned her frequently,' confessed Ruth.

Could Neil be a murderer?

'So, Squid's a teddy bear, huh?' enquired Dad, in a feeble attempt to restore the peace.

'He's an imaginary friend.' Ren gave a wry grin... 'damp squib, overheard by Trelly as *damn squid* - we dropped the damn!'

I wondered if Mum had broached the subject of Natasha's concerns with my father. In the intervening days, there had been a call from Vivienne, dad's new wife, unbeknownst to him, as far as we knew. She had demanded to know what had gone on between Natasha and our dad. My mother had informed her that they had been good friends and asked what she was insinuating.

I was about to pose some questions to my father when the doorbell shattered the silence. We all leapt from our chairs. It was Jim Davy.

'Sorry, I couldn't make it afore now but Mother was taken bad. She's in the 'ospital. At 'er age, the shock is too much. I'll be going in to see 'er again tomorrow but she seems to be as comf'able as can be espected. Missus Lawson will be sadly missed, me dears. Mother and I was very fond of her, y' know and 'er death affected Mother more than I'd've believed possible. Takin' yer own life... well, Mother didn't like the idea at all. She did take on alarmin' and Missus Lawson, Lord love 'er, 'aving them kids an' all.'

'Thank you, Jim. However, as yet we are unsure of the cause of Natasha's death. I am so sorry to hear that your mother is ill. It was so nice of her to send the wine. How old is she now?'

'She'll be a 'undred an' four in two days' time.' Mr Davy looked crushed.

Mum urged him to have some tea with us.

'No thankee, my lover. I'd ruther be in the garden. I'll go direc'ly if you don' mind.' At which point he remained in the kitchen for a further fifteen minutes talking about his mother and how she had 'taken on so.'

Eventually, Mr Davy wandered outside and we mooched off to sit in the comfort of the living room. It had got considerably colder in the last hour and we felt the need of the log fire. Mum bent down and set a match to the kindling. She and Dad sat on the couch opposite, Growler lumped between them, and it looked just like your typical suburban family.

Mr Davy took his leave as soon as darkness began to descend, amid many reiterations that he hoped Mrs. Lawson's suffering was at an end, and that God would grant her a place in his kingdom.

'For God's sake, stupid old bugger, muttered Ren. 'Can't he give it a rest?'

'Calm down, Honey. These ol' boys are steeped in superstitious garbage.'

Dad, who never failed to call upon the spirit of Aleister Crowley in times of trouble, saw no irony in our humble gardener believing in 'superstitious garbage.'

'He knows it could be suicide?' I enquired.

'Cornwall is not a complete backwater, retorted my mother. 'We DO read newspapers.'

'The Cornish can read?' guffawed my father. Mum scowled.

The following day my mother broached the thorny subject of Natasha's revelations and our need to keep our counsel. There had already been speculation in the media. No definite cause of death had been released so far.

'If you guys have suspicions then you should take this to the cops,' boomed Dad.

Ren and I nodded vehemently but Mum was adamant.

A bright blue sky greeted us the following morning. Ren and I nibbled our way through Gran's 'bara brith.' Mum had gone to Carn Euny to engage with the fogous. When Dad appeared Ren launched into him, like an Exocet missile.

'Vivienne called. She asked Mum why Natasha had phoned you in December.'

'As I told my wife, it was a private conversation between Natasha and me.'

'Does it have relevance to her possible murder?"

'Leave it, Kerensa!' he shouted angrily. With that he rose to his feet shutting the door firmly behind him.

'Christ, what's got into him?' muttered Ren.

2nd January arrived. 'Hunt the murderer' was on hold. The entire family, Mum, Dad, Ren, Sam and I, set off in Sam's camper van around midday in order to begin the long journey from West to East. Joodee had custody of Growler and Trelly.

Dad was subdued. He and Ren had barely spoken since yesterday's altercation. My mother was completely impervious. Ren and Sam were keeping up a witty repartee. As dusk fell, a few miles short of Leicester, we parked at a cheap motel, little imagining the chaos that would ensue next day.

Merlin

'And it fell so that Merlin fell in a dotage on the damosel... And ever she made Merlin good cheer till she had learned of him all manner thing that she desired;'

Le Morte D'Arthur by Sir Thomas Malory

It was the coldest day of the year: December 3rd 1945, New Orleans. In a pocket-sized back room in the heart of the French Quarter, a baby boy uttered his first lusty cries. His mother, Maria, died within hours of his birth. His father, Grant, aged 41 was already beginning to show the ravages of age, having dabbled in cocaine. He was a hardened toper. He sent a wire to his friend, Aleister, residing in Torquay, England. It read:

SON BORN 6 AM STOP MACKENZIE GRANT ALEISTER STOP IN RECOGNITION OF HAPPY TIMES SPENT WITH YOU STOP YOURS GRANT LOWE STOP.

Grant swaggered down the steps into the deserted street. He wore a thin, cotton shirt and a grubby cravat, ruffled around his scrawny neck. Sauntering into the first saloon he could find he slapped seven shiny coins on the counter.

'When the money's used up, I'm outa here. Get me a glass of your finest bourbon.'

Rarely does New Orleans suffer freezing temperatures. That night Grant Lowe was out of luck. They found his body in the gutter a few yards from Sol's Bar on the following day.

Mackenzie Lowe's unpropitious start in life did not augur well. He spent his first five years in the Van Diemen's Home for Orphaned Boys. One day a woman came to claim her only nephew. Staunchly Baptist and firm of purpose, Eliza Lowe ran a no-nonsense ship in Des Moines. Mackenzie's life was rigidly conformist. His days followed a strict pattern of prayer and readings from the Holy Book. Meals were simple, furniture utilitarian, laughter rare.

Aged sixteen, Mackenzie packed a bag and kissed Iowa goodbye.

First things first, he decided. 'California'll suit me.'

Mackenzie hung out with all the long-haired guys around the Bay. When that palled, he high-tailed it up to Yosemite, living a hand-to-mouth existence, picking berries and begging the odd dime for a hot meal. He helped the Park Rangers felling trees, picking up garbage. They let him fish where he wanted; some of them even stood him a home-cooked supper.

When late September finally came around and Mackenzie was nearing his eighteenth birthday, it was time to move on. Back in Des Moines he discovered Aunt Eliza had died last March. Very sudden, they told him. Mackenzie trotted obediently up to her grave the following morning with a bunch of chrysanthemums, purloined from a neighbour's back yard.

What to do next? Mackenzie rifled through the papers Aunt Eliza had left in a strong box at the local bank. There he discovered the old lady had left him a meagre sum and some fading letters of his father's. Mackenzie was resourceful: here was his opening. His father had known a notorious occultist, Aleister Crowley. Mackenzie pored over the endless newspaper cuttings of the man: his links with the Hermetic Order of the Golden Dawn; his sorties into the nether world of drugs and paganism; bisexuality, liaisons with countless prostitutes, syphilis, adding an aura of mystique and sending tremors down the spine - a source to be tapped, for sure. Mackenzie developed an obsessional thirst for knowledge about his father's tenuous links with this dubious character, Crowley.

He set about looking into the world of 'magick' and pagan ritual. Hitching a ride back to his native Louisiana, Mackenzie resolved to set up in business. He rented a shop in the heart of New Orleans and sold artefacts, purporting to be relics and memorabilia amassed from his father's friendship with Crowley. The locals spread the word and people flocked to learn more. It became hard to keep up with demand, so he hired a couple of helpers. He saw a market in making cassette tapes telling Crowley's story and his supposed link with Mackenzie's old man. Louisiana swallowed it all, hook, line and sinker. Mac became rich and famous overnight.

One day in the late Fall, near All Hallow's Eve, a woman with emerald eyes and long chestnut hair entered his shop. She flashed him a brilliant smile. Bewitched, he asked her name.

'Natasha,' she responded. 'My friends are outside. Would you like to meet them?'

For a fleeting moment Mackenzie saw wickedness in her eyes – it was not something he could warm to.

Minutes later a young blonde and her sister hurled themselves through the door, laughing excitedly.

'Ooh, can we browse, kind Sir?' enquired the blonde, grinning broadly. He nodded mutely. They chattered animatedly about a double-edged dagger in his glass cabinet. Mackenzie approached, offering assistance.

'It's ceremonial - an athame,' he told them. He related its history in witchcraft and its provenance. He held it to the light, where the rubies and emeralds within its black handle sparkled and shone. The girl with the mane of golden curls gasped with delight as she looked up at him.

'I love your cloak,' she said, simply. Mackenzie glanced down at his midnight-blue robe which he invariably had draped around his shoulders, in an attempt to add veracity to his lineage. He gave a sheepish grin. Mackenzie couldn't bring himself to lie to this woman. There was a frankness about her that seeped into his soul and destroyed all pretence at source. The glamorous Natasha was nothing in comparison.

'Well, Ma'am, I bought it out in San Francisco some weeks back when I was visiting some old buddies.'

'Oh, I thought it must be something you'd inherited from your father's association with Aleister Crowley,' she smiled sweetly. 'Your reputation is considerable, you know!'

'I'm Ruth and this is my sister Lamorna,' she announced.

A week later, Mackenzie Lowe was on a plane to England. In his wallet was a rose-gold Celtic wedding band studded with rubies. At an ancient quoit near Lanyon in Cornwall, at the autumn equinox 1973 Ruth Trelawney became 'Ruth Trelawney-Lowe.' Twenty-four hours prior to the hand-fasting ceremony, Mackenzie had been initiated into the Gulval and Marazion Coven under the name of Merlin, his midnight blue cloak flapping around his ankles as the south-westerlies blew in from the sea.

One day, years later, Mackenzie made a serious error of judgement. When his world collapsed around him, he returned to his roots in New Orleans where Vivienne was waiting for him, like a black widow spider enmeshing him in her wicked web.

A Consummate Performance

'St Botolph's Church dates back from 1309. Archaeological evidence suggests...

Ren had acquired a pamphlet from the local tourist office. Despite the longevity of the Lawson-Lowe relationship, we had never set eyes on Boston before.

The church failed to inspire me but Ren was bewitched. She stood gazing up at the tower, shrouded in mist, as if praying for a miracle reveal.

The market square was a sea of milling fans. Microphones were rammed into our faces as we tried to beat a path to the church door. Banners proclaiming 'Gone but never forgotten' and 'Oh-Nat, we love you!' wafted like gigantic items of laundry above our heads.

We filed inside. Before us, was an immense nave bedecked in crimson roses. Dad looking younger than his sixty-two years, wore a voluminous tunic, embroidered at the cuffs with gold and green brocade, over loose-fitting ivory pants. To complete the ensemble, slightly dipped over one eye, a Stetson. Mum's greying hair was loose and flowing. She had forged a coronet of white daisies within a circlet of braided, gold wire. She sat, stony-faced.

Atop a catafalque, was the casket, draped in purple. The organ plodded out Chopin's *Marche Funèbre*. BJ had gone to extraordinary lengths to negate his wife's pagan past.

As the vicar stood to begin the address, BJ Lawson strode purposefully to the coffin and placed a single blood-red rose upon it. The church was crammed. Many coven members were there: Iris, her Titian hair cascading in ringlets around her shoulders, turned momentarily. Dad grinned broadly. Since his taciturnity during the journey yesterday, he had perked up and was his usual, jovial self. I recognised Athena O'Shea and Levant Cooper with Morwenna Perran to their right. Wenna's head was bowed. Tamara Killick and her cousin, Abel Menheniot, were whispering conspiratorially.

I searched in vain for Ginny, but could see no sign. Lance was seated next to BJ at the front of the church. In profile, his handsome, aquiline features reminded me of Natasha. He turned, caught my eye and looked away – a mask of indifference. Ren, who had evidently followed my gaze, nudged me, 'You still got the hots for that pillock?'

Natasha's father, Ivan, was in a wheelchair hunched over a hymn sheet. A tartan rug was cast loosely about his wizened frame.

'Did you read the latest pile of crap your hero's written? A load of bollocks about the history of Marxist-Leninism in literary criticism,' she goaded.

'He writes for a quality paper – polysyllabic words out of your range!' I snapped.

An uninspiring cleric was standing in the pulpit. His black cassock contrasted forlornly with the surroundings.

'I would like to invite Natasha's husband, Barry John Lawson, celebrated Fenland landscape artist, to say a few words on this very sad occasion.'

His voice echoed around the sacred walls.

'Oh, for goodness' sake!' My mother sounded exasperated. Her intrusion was noted. The vicar cast a stern look in our direction.

BJ took centre stage. Displaying his usual sartorial elegance, he approached the lectern, adjusting his spectacles. He was still dashing; charisma oozed from every pore. He took a moment to grace us all with a laconic smile. Mum's hands were clenched into fists of ill-suppressed rage. Dad had removed his Stetson and was rubbing his chin from right to left with his index finger, his mouth set in a grim line.

BJ smoothed an imaginary crease from the lapel of his exquisitely tailored, charcoal jacket. His voice reverberated confidently around the ancient church.

'I know Natasha would have been overwhelmed by the support demonstrated by your presence here today,' he began.

The clearly enunciated speech was mesmerising. I could see how easily he must have woven his deadly web around the myriad 'nymphs' who had succumbed over the years. Natasha had been easy prey at fifteen.

'Natasha had not been well over the last few years. I, along with our children, had to witness her heart-breaking decline in mental stability.' BJ's voice sank dramatically. 'Sadder still, we were all powerless to alleviate Natasha's mental torment. However, I must put the record straight.'

There was a brief hiatus.

'Natasha did not take her own life, as has been suggested by some…' (he glanced coldly at Tristan, whose head was resting on his partner, Izzie's shoulder.) 'She did not, I repeat NOT, wander into the woods drugged and wanting to die.'

He allowed his audience to digest the import of his words.

'It was a tragic accident.' Did I imagine or did he cast a fleeting glimpse in my mother's direction?

'This will be a great shock to you all but I have asked the vicar's permission and he has agreed, that it is in everyone's best interest, as well as in my wife's, that I reveal to you now, here in this church, the true facts of the situation, however painful this might be.'

The entire congregation, taut as a bowstring, held its breath.

'Natasha's death was due to a miscarriage. She…'

My mother stood up and yelled, 'For crying out loud, you imbecile, she was fifty years old!'

BJ was undeterred.

'Unbeknownst to me or my family, Natasha had been carrying on an affair with a man half her age. In her weakened state over the past years, the poor girl was easy pickings for the likes of him and she carried on this illicit liaison under my very nose. This was not her first dalliance. However, now is not the time nor place to dwell on such matters.'

The silence echoed around us. There was more.

'I do not for one minute blame my wife. I have to confess to not being the perfect husband.'

He coughed gently at this point and glanced downwards as if at a painful remembrance.

'A few weeks ago, Natasha left me to live with this person...' (this last word was hissed out) '...until her untimely death. The doctor had confirmed that she was several weeks into a pregnancy. After a bitter argument, Natasha left their squalid bed-sit and took her car to the woods seemingly to walk off her anger. She became disoriented and when she was discovered she had gone completely off track. She stumbled over a fallen tree trunk, bringing on a miscarriage. Her body was discovered several hours later. Although I have no doubt that my disclosures will cause untold media frenzy and consternation among Natasha's many friends and acquaintances, the Reverend Proudfoot and I are agreed that my decision to speak to you at this particular venue was vital. It is always wise to allay unnecessary speculation and given my position,' (a dramatic pause) 'I hope my wife can now rest in peace.'

Before mayhem could ensue, the Reverend Proudfoot arrived at the lectern and, patting BJ discreetly on the shoulder, he held his hand aloft for silence.

'Let us pray for the soul of our dearly beloved sister...'

An excruciating keening could be heard. Natasha's father sagged, his body shaking uncontrollably.

The prayers and hymn-singing seemed interminable but at last Reverend Proudfoot uttered his final requiescat in pace and we were a bedraggled group standing outside in a bleak January mizzle, trying to assimilate the astounding revelations of the man who had been Natasha's husband for almost thirty-four years. The Press was ecstatic.

Flashbulbs exploded around us like firecrackers and I could hear the banshee screeches of my mother as she let rip at BJ.

'How could you, BJ? It's totally preposterous. Do you really think that Natasha would not have confided in me?'

Reporters were now clamouring for more and there were shouts and screams from the surrounding masses. Suddenly, Lance joined the fray.

'Look, Ruth, firstly this is a family matter. Secondly, our mother was already fragile enough without you plying her with all that mumbo-jumbo witch crap over the years. In the end she thought we were all trying to do her in! The two of you hadn't spoken for years and now here you are at her funeral! I told Dad not to even give you lot the satisfaction of an invitation.'

He looked daggers at Ren and me and then, casting a withering glance at my father, he took BJ firmly by the arm, steering him towards a waiting limousine. My mother opened her mouth to explode but was stopped in her tracks by a sickening thud. Lance's head struck the cold, hard ground as a brutal punch hit him full force in the stomach and he doubled over, stumbling onto the ancient gravestone of a Bostonian worthy. Reddish-purple ooze seeped ominously across the sodden grass and wound its way onto the path. Amid screams and gasps, my father sprang into action. He marshalled the three of us away from the immediate vicinity whilst barking out orders to call an ambulance. Having established that his own family was reasonably compos mentis, Dad walked calmly across to Tris, who had landed the punch.

I caught sight of a stranger standing next to Tris. Her age was hard to determine. She had short, spiked-up black hair tinged with purple at the tips, putting one in mind of a porcupine. She looked curiously at me as though trying to place me. I returned the gaze unflinchingly. Within minutes we heard the wail of sirens. Reverend Proudfoot came out of the church at a rate that belied his doddery frame.

'Mr Lawson, I must urge you and your relatives to spare a thought for the shades of those around us.'

He gestured grandly at the crumbling tombstones. Cameras whirred excitedly; the crowd surged forward; things were in danger of careering out of control.

'I believe you should be making your way to the Crematorium to prepare for the interment,' muttered Reverend Proudfoot as he vanished back into St Botolph's.

Lance's eyes were beginning to flutter open as paramedics placed him carefully on a stretcher.

Two policemen arrived in separate vehicles. My father was attempting to explain the situation as placidly as possible and Tristan was taken away for questioning. The rest of us were encouraged to 'carry on with the interment,' although it was stressed that we might need to be available at some future date to make statements. The two cops turned their attention to the crowd and urged them to disperse peacefully. One of them acknowledged BJ who was standing helplessly staring at the disappearing ambulance.

As we elbowed our way through the melee and piled once more into Sam's waiting van, Mum announced in acerbic tones, 'He had it coming to him. Natasha deserved better for a son.'

There were fewer people at the burial. The occasional camera flashed but it seemed the Press had given up, having had enough headline news for one day. As we stood silently under an old yew tree in the crematorium grounds the rain came down in torrents. As the coffin was lowered, BJ made an ostentatious show of crossing himself. Natasha's father bowed his head and his carer, Leigh, who had not left the old man's side, sprinkled some sweet-smelling herbs. My mother was fumbling in her handbag. I saw a silver pentagram on a chain slither into the pit. My parents held hands chanting softly, 'Oh, sister Tanith, you have been dear to us and will be again. May the spirit bring you peace, peace in the East and in the West, peace in the South and in the North.'

'Jesus H Christ,' muttered my sister.

As we began to wend our way back to our various modes of transport, I glimpsed a young man leaning against some railings. He was clothed in a pale blue denim jacket, a turtle-neck sweater pulled up, obscuring the lower part of his face. Realising that he had been spotted, he ducked behind a tree. I went to nudge Ren but he was gone. The wake was held at Plumtree Hall, the Lawson family home. Shortly after two thirty, we drew up outside the palatial residence, just as the sun began to peek out from behind a cloud, and were ushered into an enormous entrance hall by a bespectacled individual oozing a mix of verbal diarrhoea and sycophantic outpourings regarding Natasha. Eventually Mum interrupted him still in full flow and enquired to whom she might be speaking.

'I am Reginald Ferguson, Madam, and I have been butler here since....'

'Natasha never mentioned you,' said Mother. We moved away, leaving Ferguson standing open-mouthed with a tray of canapés in hand.

Ren had struck up a conversation with a good-looking stranger. I wandered off to have a peek around the house. To the left of the hall, where many mourners were still gathered in cliques, talking in hushed tones, there was another room with the door slightly ajar. As I approached, I discovered it to be a library, stacked from floor to ceiling with aged tomes. Tiptoeing nearer, I glimpsed Cicero's entire collection. Livy, Horace, Vergil, Catullus. Natasha's? They didn't seem Natasha's style.

I moved across to the fireplace, above which there was a landscape painting, showing a dull, grey sky and flat, barren mudflats. BJ had captured the atmosphere entirely: not one tree nor plant broke the monotony. In the far distance was the sea, reflecting the dull steel of the sky above. In the foreground a gull stared straight ahead, wings primed, contemplating flight. I started to retreat, when suddenly I caught sight of another picture – a portrait of a young Natasha, her essence perfectly captured. She was seated on a bench, fronded by trees, sunlight playing on her exquisite features. She was clad in a dress of pure white, a silver bracelet gleaming on her slender wrist, which rested in her lap. A half-smile hovered around her mouth and her other hand was raised as if to brush away a lock of hair. Her eyes fastened eerily on mine, a deep emerald, gentle and wise. A portrait of a woman, lovingly painted. BJ's initials were scrawled across the bottom right-hand corner.

A huge circular table, inscribed with the names of King Arthur's knights stood in the middle of the room. Strewn across it was a collection of paperbacks. I picked up Malory. Various passages had been highlighted in orange felt-tip. Clues to the murder suspect?

I leafed through *Idylls of the King*, also with highlighted passages. 'The King is sick and knows not what he does.'

I could make no sense of it. On a whim, I seized both books and thrust them into my capacious shoulder bag. It wasn't stealing; it was necessary research. Aunt Lamorna would understand their significance.

To the right of me were French doors leading out to a massive walled garden. The key was in the lock begging to be turned. The rain had stopped but a chill wind issued from the east. At that moment I caught movement out of the corner of my eye. It was my sister with the guy she'd been with earlier. She waved cheerily and called me over.

'Mel, this is Mike Mills. He's a friend of Ginny's.'

He held out a hand.

'Where is Ginny?' I asked, abruptly. 'It seems she can't be contacted.'

Mills looked puzzled.

'She can. She called me. She said she couldn't face the funeral. So, I'm here in her stead,' adding apologetically, 'there was never much love lost between those two. I liked Natasha. Ginny was influenced by that husband of hers - Richard, Rick, wasn't it?'

Ren and I exchanged a look. We had met Rick Morrison once or twice. We had taken an instant disliking to him. At Tristan's birthday party last year, he had insinuated himself into everybody's conversation. Offensive remarks to Ginny about Tris and his partner that we had overheard had alienated him from us even more.

'I'm not keen on Richard,' Mike was saying. 'He and Natasha hated one another's guts.'

That was no secret but Mike's next statement was a bombshell.

'Natasha had suspicions – she had become quite paranoid of late – that Richard was trying to harm her – that her life was in danger.'

'How so?' Ren fired at him immediately.

'Ginny said her mother's dislike of Rick was connected to animal welfare. I didn't know the bloke was remotely interested in animals, let alone their welfare. Turns out, he was involved in vivisection. Not quite legit, I gather.'

'I understood he was involved in financial affairs in Switzerland,' I ventured.

'Yeah, that's what he told us, but not so, as it turns out. He kept going over to Geneva, didn't he?'

I thought it was Zurich but I didn't contradict him.

'Mike, where was Ginny when her mother died?'

'No idea, why do you ask? Ginny can't have killed her mother, along with Richard, even supposing Natasha's hypothesis was correct. BJ seems to think it was explicable – an accident.'

'And you believe BJ?' asked Ren.

'No evidence to suggest otherwise! I know Ginny. She's no murderer I can assure you. Rick – who knows? However, I think it unlikely. If he has a passion for slaughter, I think he reserves it for small rodents.'

Mike wandered off to inspect a shrub drooping languidly in the centre of the walled garden. We followed. I looked back at the house and felt that someone was watching my every move. I gazed at the windows above. Had I become as paranoid as Natasha and in so short a time?

'Do you know The Wash?' Mike asked, fingering a withered branch. 'Just beyond that wall. Pretty interesting, if you're not used to this kind of terrain. Sometimes, the sunsets can be stunning.'

'Not today, given the collection of nimbus clouds above,' I muttered.

Nevertheless, we agreed to follow since there seemed little else to do apart from eat and drink. He walked us over to the wrought-iron gate in the corner of the wall. There was a greenhouse to the right, containing the remnants of plants, long deceased. Two of the glass panels were cracked. We filed through the gate and trudged along a dirt track. In the distance I spotted a raised bank. Mike turned and announced loftily, 'Over there is the sea.'

Ren murmured, 'Mike, I don't think this is such a good idea. It's starting to get dark and we've got no coats.'

The sky was already flecked with indigo. What little sun that had emerged sporadically earlier that afternoon, was long gone.

'Where's your sense of adventure?' he laughed, but he turned and we gratefully retraced our steps.

'Maybe some other time? There's a very strange old girl who lives over there. She has an enormous Mastiff. Natasha used to go and visit her occasionally.'

'She's not called Lara, is she?' I asked him.

'Rachel, I believe,' he replied, matter-of-factly.

Was this another red herring? Possible suspects seemed to be accruing by the minute. Back inside, we bumped almost immediately into my parents. Mother was engrossed in another animated discussion with BJ.

'But you know perfectly well Natasha was totally against anti-depressants.'

The situation was getting out of hand. Ferguson, aka Uriah Heep, was hovering nearby. Dad was tentatively stroking Mum's elbow. To my surprise, Mike strode up to BJ and said, 'I've just been conducting these young ladies around the estate, beyond the perimeter walls.'

BJ's relief was evident.

'Excellent. Are they persuaded that Lincolnshire's not half bad?'

'I'm working on them.'

'Splendid, splendid. Are you intending to come back soon?' he enquired pleasantly. 'Only, I'm going to be away for a while. I need a holiday...'

It struck me as odd that BJ should be making a point of telling us his immediate travel plans. I blunder-bussed in.

'Do you know why your daughter's not here? Mike says Ginny couldn't face it. The rest of us have coped and it hasn't been easy.'

There was a flash of annoyance before he barked, 'Look I have no idea; that young woman is a law unto herself and always has been.'

'Where were you, BJ on the night your wife died?' I tried again.

'Home here, as it happens. What is this? Turned detective now, have you?'

Mike coughed politely. Whose side is he on? I wondered.

My sister chimed in, 'It's weird, don't you think, not to attend your own mother's funeral? Do you have an alibi?'

'I do not need to answer to you lot as to my whereabouts and as for my daughter's failure to appear to wave her mother off...

He turned away.

'Wave her off!' screeched my mother.

I was not about to let Natasha's husband off the hook.

'Why wasn't there an inquest, BJ?' He didn't flinch.

'Because it wasn't necessary. The cause of death was obvious. Just butt out, will you, Kerensa?'

'She's Demelza,' retorted my sister. 'It's a perfectly reasonable question. There's always an inquest.'

Sam approached, 'We ought to be getting home. It's a long drive and it's already getting dark.'

BJ, more than eager to see the back of us, said, 'Your brother's right. The roads are narrow and flanked with dykes. When the fog comes down, well, I'd hate you to have an accident.'

There was menace in the tone.

There ended the memorable life of Natasha Rodomski-Lawson. She had lived out her days on the public stage. Why should her death be any different? Her youngest son was charged with assault and ordered to pay a hefty fine. Lance recovered but retained a discernible scar just below his right temple.

It seemed we had a thousand possible leads to follow up. All the while I could not slough off the impression that my every movement had been observed.

The Sybil

Our father had returned to the States. He and Mum had grown closer, brought together by their joint grief over their friend's death.

We were sitting in the study at Pen-Towan. Janis was on my lap, purring loudly, and Piskey, her brother, at my feet.

BJ's response to my queries were disingenuous and inadequate. If Natasha's death was through natural causes, this would surely nevertheless need to be verified? I expressed my thoughts to Ren.

'Well, she's been interred and can be dug up, if necessary,' she responded.

'You're a complete stranger to subtlety, aren't you?' I barked.

She shrugged. We decided on a plan of action: we would chase up Faye, Joodee's mother, Rick Morrison, Ginny's husband, and the mysterious figure at the crematorium. Who was the stranger with purple hair, outside St Botolph's Church? Neither of these latter two had been noticed by my sister. The purple-haired woman had not been at the interment. We also had a cranky female named Rachel, who lived, *over on The Wash*, to whom Mike had alluded at Plumtree Hall.

I was uneasy about Mike Mills. His interruptions to divert attention from BJ unnerved me. Ren was adamant he was harmless.

I recalled Ginny and her absence at the funeral. Vin had tracked her down, and she had agreed to see me. Should I call on Lance? I realised I could well be rebuffed given his insolence on 3rd January. Then there was Neil MacBeith who wanted Natasha dead.

When the phone shrilled Ren got up to answer it. It was Morwenna. She needed to see us and we were to come alone.

Two birds with one stone, I mused, since Sam lived within a half a mile of Wenna's home. We could interrogate him about his mother-in-law and maybe mention our grandfather's funeral.

Wenna's house was not easily accessible. A ramshackle old cottage, it stood in splendid isolation at the bottom of a steep cliff path in Zennor. Leaving the car near the church, we wound our tortuous way down the steep cliff path, slick with rain.

Zennor was shrouded in swirls of thick fog. It lent the place an other-worldly aura. As witches go, Wenna was the stereotype. Her hair was unruly, tumbling over her face and shoulders in scraggy tendrils. She was constantly scraping it out of her eyes with long, pointed finger-nails. Her face was remarkably unlined, despite her age. Wenna seemed to maintain an all-year tan, living outside for much of her time, gathering shells and seaweed and foraging for berries in the hedgerows along the cliff roads. She was standing on the doorstep as we rounded the bend. Despite her slender frame, she hugged me in a bear-like embrace all the while squeaking with delight. Her eyes twinkled with merriment – like little stars in a swarthy brown firmament. Within seconds we were surrounded by an army of felines of all shapes, sizes and hues.

'Come on in, dears. Shall I put the kettle on? I think a sage tisane would be appropriate...'

Wenna gave one of the most vocal of the moggies a gentle nudge with her foot and it sidled over to the fireplace where a roaring pile of logs was blazing ferociously. Some of the other cats joined their sister and Ren and I made our way gingerly across to the old beech table which was hidden under a scattering of pine cones, acorns, dried lavender, sea-shells and assorted flotsam and jetsam.

I pulled out a chair and another cat emerged. It arched its back, and jumped to the floor with a loud mew.

'Oh, never mind her, Ren, dear.'

'I'm Mel,' I murmured.

Wenna ruffled my hair affectionately as though I were one of her cats.

'Well, you're so alike.'

I looked at her dubiously.

Wenna chuckled mischievously, 'I thought BJ's performance at the funeral was superb, didn't you?'

We both grimaced.

'I don't believe all of what he said.'

'You mean you do believe some of it?' I asked.

'I believe Natasha was pregnant, yes.' Wenna was surprisingly composed.

'She came to see me shortly before she died. I couldn't help noticing that she had a definite radiance about her. I'd had a vision beforehand: some highly unusual formations in the tea-leaves. I connected it to Natasha because it was her favourite brew, jasmine.'

Ren snorted derisively.

'Is that why you wanted to speak to us, Wenna?' I asked softly.

'Did our mother know?' Ren asked.

'Ruth isn't as attuned to the leaves as I,' Wenna answered. 'Crystals are her speciality.'

'I meant about the visit?'

'In view of the argument between them, I thought it best not to mention it.'

Wenna seemed to go into a trance. I coughed politely. The old lady gave a start and picked up her story.

'Natasha wanted some information about the properties of wolf's bane, belladonna and a whole host of others. I knew something was wrong. She begged me to tell nobody that she had come. She was wrapped in a woollen shawl. All I could see were those extraordinary eyes of hers. She told me she was being followed. I asked you both here today as I suspect foul play? Natasha's death is certainly not clear cut. To suffer a miscarriage and bleed to death is not a common occurrence, even though the risks to an older pregnant woman are considerable. You must discover the truth, my dears. I suspect there are matters in which Natasha should not have dabbled.'

Wenna's button eyes gazed at us sadly.

'I have tried to make contact but nobody is coming through,' she added.

We made no comment and made excuses to leave. As we made our way to the door, a large, grey Tom jumped up and followed us.

'Greymalkin, you haven't had your tea,' Wenna announced with concern. 'Come back soon.'

There was an answering miaow suggesting she had been speaking to the cat. As we slogged back up the cliff path, Ren remarked, 'Nuttier than a fruitcake. Total claptrap!'

Greymalkin turned and trotted back down the path, his tail in the air.

'I think we have to accept the *claptrap* if we are going to help our mother solve the mystery of Natasha's death,' I admitted somewhat ruefully.

'What if there IS no mystery. What if she topped herself?' Ren persisted.

'It's a strange way to choose to die... take yourself into the local woods and deliberately fall over something in order to bring on a miscarriage? If she had access to medication, that would be a far easier way to die.'

'I reckon we need to keep an open mind, Mel. But say I'm wrong, dear sis, God knows how you'll cope if old Lancey turns out to have murdered his mummy?'

'It's more likely to be Ginny,' I responded. 'She was the one who couldn't face her mother's funeral!'

'In that case she wouldn't be agreeing to meet up with you.'

She'd got a point.

'Why was Natasha quizzing Wenna about poisons? If Natasha was so keen on animal rights, she'd hardly be contemplating getting rid of a little human... it just doesn't fit! So, she must have suspected others of trying to poison her.'

It was time to investigate Faye. When we reached Sam's, Joodee opened the door. 'Oh, it's you two. Sam's out back with Bryony.'

I smiled politely. It was always pot-luck with Joodee whether you'd find her in a good mood. Ren and I privately felt sorry for our brother, who tried his best to make a living out of his Wendy House business. Invariably, it would be left to him to deal with childcare whilst Joodee travelled half the country buying up vast quantities of beads to make jewellery.

At that point, Sam and Bryony both emerged from the garden.

'Oh, hello, I thought we heard the doorbell.'

'Yeah, we've just been to see Wenna so we thought we'd pop in,' said Ren in a flat tone.

Bryony leapt on Ren with obvious glee.

'Auntie Ren, come and see what Daddy made for me.'

My sister scurried off to see what new construction Sam had erected. Joodee announced harshly, 'He's been using half the local log supply making a gingerbread cottage. He's got a load of orders pending meanwhile.'

Before I could voice an opinion, there was a frantic rush for the phone.

'What's up, Jood, you expecting a call?' Sam looked perplexed.

She passed the phone to Sam, 'Tris wants to speak to you.'

Sam wandered off into the sitting room. Bryony had just hurtled back into the kitchen with Ren, and the baby had been woken by the racket.

A few minutes later he re-emerged and passed the phone to me, 'Tris would like a word.'

Tristan sounded agitated and furtive.

'Look, I need to see you and soon. When can you make it?'

'What's the matter?'

'I need to see you... just you. It's about Mum.'

'How about I try to get over next week? I need to go back to work.'

'Can't you get time off?'

'I've already taken time off. I'll let you know.'

'I want you to come alone. Clear?'

'Why all the cloak and dagger, Tris?'

'Look, Mel, don't be difficult.'

There was a click and he was gone.

Why couldn't he have spoken to me at the funeral? If it was that urgent, why hadn't he arranged to meet up before? They all looked up expectantly as I entered the living room.

'What was all that about?' asked my sister.

'Oh, just Tris, venting his spleen over BJ and Lance,' I retorted.

'Yeah, that was a rum do, wasn't it?' muttered Joodee.

'What did you make of the pregnancy confession?' Sam asked. 'What did Wenna think?'

I muttered vague comments about Natasha's age being against her.

'I'm amazed Morwenna had nothing to say,' announced Joodee. 'She's always coming out with outrageous bollocks, mostly down to consulting the tea-leaves or some such.'

'Bollocks,' mimicked Bryony loudly.

'For God's sake, Jood, not in front of the kids.' Sam glared at her.

'Joodee, we were wondering whether we could ask your mother a few questions about Natasha? Mum said there'd been a problem between them?' I asked.

'What the hell for? She hasn't spoken to any of that lot for years. In any case she won't talk to YOU.'

'Mel was only making a polite request, Jood. Give it a break.'

'Butt out, Sam. It's none of your fucking business. The whole family is deranged. Especially that precocious, little idiot brother of yours. I've had a belly-full of his crap, bloody *Squid* and the like.'

Bryony burst into tears.

Sam picked her up with a sigh.

There was absolutely no chance we could get our brother alone to discuss private matters. I resolved to call him at some point and arrange to meet up.

When we walked into the kitchen at Pen-Towan, Mum's face was ashen.

'Natasha's friend, Adam, called from Boston. He wants me to go up to see him.'

Ren ignored her.

'We spoke to Grandma. Interesting, what she had to say about Natasha's childhood?'

Mum's hackles were up immediately.

'You needn't adopt that tone with me, Kerensa! What about Natasha's childhood?'

'Just the small matter of her being knocked around by that bastard father of hers.'

'What could I have done about it? She met and married BJ and in some ways that was her salvation. Adam says he is being watched and that he is in fear of his life. Not exactly reassuring, is it?'

She marched resolutely out of the room.

Was this the man to whom BJ had alluded at the funeral – the father of Natasha's supposed baby? Or was he the mysterious stranger I had spotted at the cemetery – or were they one and the same?

I sat contemplating for a while. I decided to call my dad.

'Vivienne?' I enquired affably.

'Speaking - who is this?'

I told her I needed to speak to my father.

'Well, Demelza or Kerensa, whichever one of you this might be, anything you need to say to him, comes through me. Got it?'

I gave up on diplomacy.

'Look, Vivienne, it's private.'

My sister, who was hanging at my elbow, snatched the receiver.

'Look you annoying bimbo, butt the fuck out!'

The phone went dead.

'FOR CHRIST'S SAKE, REN!' I yelled. 'We need answers. That's not how to get them.'

'Don't worry, I will get them if I have to take a plane to do so,' she muttered through gritted teeth. 'That woman is the absolute pits!'

As soon as I heard the front door slam, I picked up the phone again. This time I was in luck. A warmer voice said,

'Hi there, Lowe Residence, Marie-Ghislaine speaking.'

Hesitantly, I told her who I was and asked to speak to dad.

'Honey chile, your pa is allas talking 'bout y'all – how wunnerful to make your acquaintance. He's outta the house right now but I can get him to call you right back.'

'Marie-Ghislaine, you don't remember a friend of ours, Natasha, calling my dad in December, do you?

'The lady that died? She an' your dad were real good friends. But no, honey, I don't recall no phone call.'

'Ok well, thanks, anyway. And, Marie-Ghislaine, please don't tell Vivienne I called.'

'Understood, Ma'am.'

Then I called Sam. Fortuitously, Joodee was out.

'I have a meeting to go to tomorrow so I thought I'd ring. What do you know about Faye?' I asked getting straight to the point.

'What do you want to know?'

'Where she lives, how can I contact her, whether she could have murdered Natasha?'

'No idea, you can't, and possibly, if murder it is.'

'Presumably Joodee knows where she lives?'

'Are you insane? I can barely mention our family and Joodee goes ape-shit.'

There was silence and then he added thoughtfully.

'Joodee has a half-sister/cum half-wit.'

'Political correctness is alive and kicking,' I sighed. 'And where does she live? Is there any point my contacting her?'

'None whatsoever. Faye hated Natasha and our family too. I met her once. Caught a brief glimpse of the half-sis at the funeral. She seemed to be an acquaintance of Izzie but I didn't get the chance to enquire. As far as I'm aware, Joodee doesn't ever see her sister, and her mother, rarely.'

'With purple hair, this sister, right?'

'Yeah, how do you know?'

'Well, she stood out just a tad at the funeral but apparently only to me! Where's Joodee's father?'

'Long gone.'

'Her half-sister's name? Her half-sister's father's name? Any clue?'

'Father is persona non grata and never mentioned. Sister's name is Morgana. They used to live in the US. Not sure where they are right now or even if mother and daughter are living apart. Last I heard the girl was so incapacitated she could barely function although she seemed relatively with-it at the funeral.'

I digested this information. It appeared I had reached the end of the road with Faye, but what about Morgana? I voiced my suspicions.

'Nah, I doubt it and if murder is what we're looking at, that girl would be incapable of doing anybody in,' replied my brother. 'She didn't know Natasha.'

'So, if she'd didn't know Natasha, it's curious she was at the funeral,' I replied.

'Guess so. But she def has a screw loose.'

'Sam, you went to Gramps' funeral?'

'Yep. What about it?'

'Gran said he spoke to Natasha privately right before he died and she was upset by whatever it was he said. Do you know what happened?'

'No idea. I have never understood your hero-worship of Natasha, Mel. She was a complete bitch. Evil. Cruel to Lance. A vamp – preyed on men. I never liked the woman.'

I sighed and put the phone down.

Mother left early the following morning. Ren had an interview at a local gym for a job as a fitness instructor and I had an appointment to keep in Devon.

Discord

The sun was just coming up when I set off. Faint and waxen, it matched my mood. Yesterday's call with Sam had unnerved me and I had a nasty suspicion about Vivienne. In an effort to put myself into a better frame of mind I cranked up the stereo. I had a desire to reconnect with the woman behind the myth that was Natasha. Some ancient, hippie songsters, blared out. The Grateful Dead, Jefferson Airplane – another bunch who put me in mind of a trio of solicitors, singing about Guinevere! I recalled happier times when Natasha and Mum would be singing at the tops of their lungs in our kitchen. In tune with each other at least!

I arrived at Ringmore Heights around two o'clock. It was Gothic in appearance and dated back to the fourteenth century with a maze of underground passages, smugglers' tunnels and a couple of oak panels in walls which opened up to reveal labyrinthine corridors. It belonged to Tristan's partner, Izzie, gained from his lucrative trade in antiques. He gave the furniture he sold an air of authenticity, or so he said, by faking woodworm holes. The location was idyllic. Perched atop a hill, it commanded magnificent views over the Teign estuary. It boasted a couple of turrets, and inside, a minstrel's gallery. In the walled courtyard that led to the main entrance stood two massive, stone dogs. Tris called them the hounds of the Baskervilles. I rang the doorbell; a stranger stood before me. He proffered a pale, slightly freckled hand and said with a wan smile,

'Hi, you m-m-must be M-M-Mel. T-T-Tom and T-T-Tris are expecting you. I'm M-M-Mark.'

'Hi, pleased to meet you.' I shook a hand that felt like limp lettuce, clammy and lifeless. 'Who's Tom?' I asked, politely.

He looked stunned. His sandy hair was infused with pink stretching from his chin to his forehead.

'Well, he's b-been T-T-Tristan's p-p-partner for the last z-z-zillion years or so, so I thought you w-w-would know him.' There was a discernible pouting of the lips as though he found the liaison distasteful.

Thankfully Tristan appeared at that moment. His annoyance at me on the phone had dissipated and he seemed pleased to see me. He glanced at Mark.

'Izzie is Tom. Natasha named him Izzie since he's Tom Isaacs and she thought it hilarious that we should be the Arthurian lovers, Tristan and Iseult!'

'Ah... and now there's Mark... King of Cornwall,' I said.

'What c-c-c-can I get you?' stammered Mark. I noted the irritation in his tone.

'A fruit juice would be great,' I replied.

As he disappeared, Tristan looked after him speculatively and whispered conspiratorially,

'He's not the sharpest tool in the box. Actually, he's an old school chum of Izzie's who has resurfaced. He has just acquired a little studio down the road. He hardly sells anything – but we feel sorry for him. Added to which, he has this gorgeous friend, Dora.'

Before I could ask about Dora, Izzie appeared, a pair of secateurs in his hand.

'Just been pruning the roses and cutting back overhanging branches. Well overdue, I'm afraid.'

Mark reappeared with a tray of drinks. He took his leave rather peremptorily, muttering, 'Catch you later.'

Tristan became immediately business-like. Izzie, picking up on the moment, took his hand sympathetically.

'Mel, I have some shocking things to tell you about Mum.'

Walking over to the chiffonier, he handed me an envelope.

Tristan's name was capitalised in black on the front.

'Open it,' he directed.

It was the same script in the same red ink as the notes Mum had given me at Pen-Towan.

December

My Darling Tris,

If you are receiving this, then we will never see each other again, at least, not in this world.

Your father is Mackenzie Lowe. I do not want to depart this life without divulging your true parentage to you.

I know I should have confessed my terrible secret before now. Call it cowardice. I couldn't bear to lose your love. I hope you will find a way to give Ruth the enclosed letter. She and Mac have been in ignorance of the situation – I alone have shouldered the guilt. It will perhaps explain why I chose to distance myself from Ruth, unable to bear my feelings of shame.

I have now confessed to Mac that you are his child. I hope you will find it in your heart to forgive me. I know I am asking a lot of Ruth and her family.

I felt as if I had just been landed a hefty punch in the solar plexus. I could neither cry nor vent my anger.

Natasha's call to dad at the beginning of December now made perfect sense.

Why had I never noticed? The muddy brown eyes, flecked with green, just like my father's. I managed to stammer out,

'When did you get this, Tris?'

'The day after the funeral.'

'This arrived AFTER your mother's death?' I asked, incredulous.

Izzie joined in.

'Yes, it was hand-delivered – there was no stamp or postmark.'

I had a sudden thought.

'Izzie,' I ventured, 'there was a woman at Natasha's funeral - Sam said she is a friend of yours and half-sister to Joodee. Did she know Natasha?'

Both men were immediately on the defensive.

'I think anyone can go to a funeral; she's a friend, as Sam said,' said Izzie, angrily. 'Natasha must have given the letter to someone she trusted and knew. She and Morgana never met.'

I felt duty-bound to disclose what I knew.

'Natasha wrote to my mother; she feared she was being targeted and her life was in danger.'

'Tris and I are painfully aware that Nastasha became paranoid and suspected us all of wanting to kill her. It was utter nonsense. BJ admitted she was unstable at the funeral, hence the medication.'

'I agree with Izzie, Mel. She was delusional. Having heard what my da... BJ said at the funeral I now believe her death was a tragic accident.'

'Tris, hard as this is to hear, your mother made herself very unpopular with some people. She's what you might call *marmite*.'

Izzie smiled, 'Marmite's good for you, Mel.'

His feeble attempt at a joke angered me. 'That's not funny. Murder is a serious matter.'

'It would be if it were murder. As we have said, Tris and I are ruling that out.'

'Can we return to your mum's letter, Tris?' I asked. 'What else can you tell me?'

'It was in a large brown envelope with two letters inside, onc addressed to me, and another for your mother.'

'Do you still have the envelope?' I asked

Izzie rose obediently, at a glance from Tristan.

'I'm not sure what that'll prove other than corroborating what we've said, which you seem determined to tear down in flames.'

Izzie disappeared.

'Tris, Natasha seemed to believe Ginny could be capable of murder.'

'Impossible! If my mother was murdered by ANYONE, it couldn't be disguised; there would have to be an investigation.'

'The absence of an inquest bothers me, Tris, I thought it was a given in such circumstances. Could BJ be guilty of a cover-up?

Or even be responsible for her murder, having found out she was pregnant? My mother says he has contacts in high places.'

'But those contacts would not be able to hide evidence of murder, Mel. Be sensible! Do you have one of the letters Ruth received with you?'

I had to confess that I didn't.

'Your mother's death is very strange – surely you would agree? Could BJ's account of pregnancy be correct?'

'How the hell should I know? On the scale of possibilities and given my mother's age you would think it's hogwash, but women do get pregnant later in life and this is not the first time she's committed adultery.'

I got up and paced the room. I cast my mind back to the incident in the churchyard immediately after the funeral. It all made sense: my father taking command of the situation; that leap into action to try and placate Tris.

Izzie had returned with the envelope.

I stared at it: **MR.T. LAWSON**. The letters were strong and bold and bore no resemblance to the script, either in colour or design. The second envelope was identical in style: **RUTH**.

'So, this was written by someone else?' I mused.

'Not necessarily,' said Izzie thoughtfully. 'Capitalised script can look entirely different.'

'And it's not in red ink,' I said.

'Probably written afterwards with whatever colour came to hand? However,' Izzie began again. 'Most British people do not put a full stop after Mr. That is American.'

Are you sure?' My mind flew to my father. Could he have delivered the letters?'

'This will be a terrible blow to your mother, Mel,' Tristan remarked.

'She's in Boston, visiting a friend of Natasha's – Adam.'

'Never heard of him.'

I was still not satisfied with Izzie's relationship to the mysterious friend at the funeral.

'Could I just ask how you know Morgana?' I began, trying to muster as much diplomacy as I could. 'Where did you meet her? Is she American?'

'For Christ's sake, Mel. She's the daughter of our friend, Dora. She'd come to visit, so we brought her to the funeral.'

'So Faye, who is in a relationship with Dora, is Joodee's and Morgana's mother, correct?'

'Yes, Morgana sees both her parents, even though they no longer live together – is that so odd? And since you ask, both Faye and Dora lived in America for many years.'

'Sam told me that Joodee's half-sister is severely mentally impaired. What made you think that going to a funeral would have any meaning for her,' I persisted.

'Your brother is way off beam.'

'So why couldn't Dora have his daughter for the day or hey, even better, come too,' I asked.

Izzie's eyes were blazing.

'I've had enough of your insinuation, Mel. You have a letter for your mother, so go!'

Tris reached for Izzie's hand, 'Let's calm down. Mel, there really is nothing untoward here. Dora was abroad on business. We didn't like to abandon Morgana; she was at a bit of a loose end, to be honest.'

'At a loose end!' I was incredulous. 'And so, you thought she'd like to go to the funeral of a woman she didn't know, because she couldn't amuse herself for the day? Really?'

'YES, REALLY!' he retorted angrily.

I shook my head in disbelief.

'Look Mel, lets go for a walk and clear our heads and the air.'

I got up to go. Tris grabbed my arm.

'Please, stay, Mel, I don't want you to leave so abruptly.'

We donned our coats and ventured out. As we strolled down the driveway, I noticed Izzie look anxiously to his left. Mark seemed to be gingerly donning some gardening gloves.

'I thought he'd be long gone,' muttered Tris, catching Izzie's gaze.

'I asked him to examine those plants for fungus. I'm not sure how to deal with them.'

There was a slight edge to Izzie's voice.

'What does he know about plants and fungus?' asked Tris, irritably.

A discernible tension had arisen between the two men. I made a sudden decision.

'I'm just going to have a brief word with Mark. I was a little off-hand with him earlier and I don't want to create a bad impression.'

I marched over determinedly with Izzie right behind me.

'Hi, Mark,' I called out cheerily.

He looked up at once, evidently thrown off guard. We all stared down at the dark green and purple leaves Mark was holding in his gloved hand.

'That's an unusual looking specimen,' I remarked, trying to sound innocuous.

'Yes, that's why I got it,' blurted Izzie. 'It adds colour in the winter, It's a species of euphorbia.'

'I'm surprised you couldn't have found something more colourful if you wanted to brighten up the dullness of winter,' I threw back, 'And what do we have here?' I nodded towards a large evergreen with palmate leaves and purple berries.

Izzie burst out laughing.

'*Fatsia japonica*, my dear. Another firm favourite of mine. But let's quell your fears, shall we and improve your knowledge of botany. Euphorbia doesn't flower at this time of year but when it blooms it has beautiful purple flowers. I'm not cultivating toxic substances with which to murder Natasha – she could have administered her own without my help.'

'M-m-maybe you'd like s-s-some c-c-cuttings to g-g-grow at home, M-M-Mel?' Mark's invitation had a malicious edge.

'I'll pass, thanks.'

I resolved to add euphorbia and *Fatsia Japonica* to my list of items for research.

The sky was hyacinth blue, as we strolled along the riverside. Dotted here and there were tiny, cirrocumulus clouds that were tinged with a quiet, salmon pink. The Teign was gently lapping the shingle and far in the distance I could discern the rolling hills of Dartmoor. A teenage girl was dragging a young, and obviously reluctant, Border Collie along the beach. He was whimpering pathetically. The tide was coming in rapidly now and the waves were creeping up the dark wooden poles supporting the landing stages of the nearby jetty.

'Let's have a drink.' suggested Tris.

We retraced our steps, eventually arriving at a beautiful, old pub which was reputedly the home of a former smuggler who had met an untimely end. Tris, grinning broadly, asked the landlord whether anything had been heard of Old Snowy Westlake lately. The wrinkled old gent behind the bar frowned clearly intuiting he was being teased.

After a couple of rounds, we decided to wend our way back and by the time we reached Ringmore Heights the sky, a deep indigo, was speckled with twinkling stars. Izzie turned the key and the huge, oak, door groaned, as if in some Radcliffian novel.

Around midnight we all turned in. Tristan had allocated me a room on the river side of the house. Beyond the courtyard, I could just make out the murky waters of the Teign. Muffled whisperings seemed to come from behind the walls. Every creak of a floorboard unsettled me. I imagined the spirits of previous owners, immured bodies, mouldering bones in the cellar below, corpses floating on the waves in the distance. I climbed wearily into bed. Sleep evaded me. I tossed and turned and every moan of the wind set my nerves jangling.

I heard the unmistakeable rasp of a door opening. I listened intently. Someone was descending the stairs. A key was being turned in the lock downstairs. I got out of bed and tiptoed to the window. Looking out, I discerned a shape striding across the moonlit courtyard. Hurriedly, I hauled on a sweater and jacket, determined to follow. I tiptoed silently down the stairs. Gentle snores could be heard in the room to my left. I heaved open the huge oak door, closing it carefully behind me and hastened across the courtyard, past the Baskerville Boys and down the hill towards the river. As I reached the road, the hooded figure was just rounding the bend. I quickened my pace trying to keep close to hedgerows.

I followed for about half a mile. The golden glow of the moonlight illuminated the seaweed-fringed shore of the Teign.

I could distinguish the church spire ahead. Suddenly, the figure turned to face me. Then he strode towards me.

'What the hell do you think you're doing?' Izzie demanded, grabbing my wrist in an iron grip.

'I could well ask the same question of you,' I countered. 'It seems an ungodly hour to be traipsing around all by yourself. Does your partner know of your little tryst?'

'What little tryst? I suffer from insomnia so I get up and walk. Unlike the peerless Natasha I do not rely on opiates.'

He let me go abruptly.

'I will escort you back home. There is to be no further meddling in our affairs. Your outrageous speculations about the death of a woman who was evil, self-centred and pernicious are beyond the pale. I refuse to be subjected to this ridiculous harassment. You will leave in the morning.'

I was frogmarched back to Ringmore Heights. The house was in total darkness and as quiet as the grave. I could still feel Izzie's vice-like grip around my wrist and hear his icy words. Did Tris know he bore such animosity towards Natasha?

I fell into an uneasy slumber interlaced with nightmares of seedy smugglers, cheerless graveyards and collie dogs which morphed into phosphorescent hounds. A soft, pastel light was creeping into the room, when I was awoken by Tris who entered with a mug of steaming tea.

'I was beginning to think you'd met an untimely death,' he joked. 'It's ten o'clock.'

I stared at him. He looked so like Natasha, long lashes, a mane of dark hair but he had my father's mouth. The lips were full; he had Mackenzie's infectious grin. He was tall and slender, just like his mother, but deceptively strong, as the punch he had landed his half-brother at Natasha's funeral had proven. Then I recalled Izzie and shuddered.

'Did you sleep well?' he asked.

'Fine. Where's Izzie?' I asked.

'He's gone off to St Ives.'

I dressed swiftly and went downstairs. I was about to take my leave when something caught my eye. I noticed a large rectangle of wall, a faded green, out of kilter with its surroundings.

'Has something been taken down, Tris?'

'Yes, a painting Mum gave Izzie and me as a gift. It depicts the legend of Tristan and Iseult. Do you know the story?'

'They were lovers. Iseult, the Fair, and King Mark of Cornwall were to be married until Tristan, Mark's nephew, went to collect Iseult from Ireland. On their way back Tristan and Iseult drank a magic potion and they fell deeply in love.'

Tris continued the story.

'There was a second Iseult, Iseult of the White Hands. She too was in love with Tristan but she played him false. After Tristan had decided he couldn't live without Mark's wife, Iseult the Fair, he returned to take her back with him to Brittany. Iseult of the White Hands promised to raise a white sail as Tristan was approaching the shore, if Iseult, the Fair, was still alive. If Tristan saw a black sail, it would mean that Iseult the Fair had died. Iseult of the White Hands was duplicitous. She raised the black flag and Tristan died from grief.'

'Ominous,' I remarked, 'but just the one Iseult in your life?'

'Yeah, but strangely there's Isadora - Dora. You know the gorgeous one I told you about and Morgana's father.'

How could I forget?

'What's with the name?' I asked.

'His trademark is scarves – Isadora Duncan, you know?'

'Why have you taken the painting down?' I asked.

'Izzie couldn't bear to look at it after Mum died. He was fonder of my mother than he'll admit.'

I was disinclined to contradict him. I stored the anecdote for future reference.

'I guess we should repaint the walls really. Looks a bit out of place, doesn't it?'

We said goodbye and I headed off towards the Teignmouth and Shaldon Bridge. If I had not had to stop the car to avoid a little old lady crossing the road, I wouldn't even have noticed... but she took her time, inching her way forward tentatively, peering from right to left. I glanced towards the bridge. Then I saw them – three men in a line all facing up-river towards Newton Abbot. One, small-framed and sandy-haired had his arm around the other's shoulder. Izzie was definitely NOT in St Ives. The third had to be Dora – the tell-tale, woollen scarf, wound around him, the surplus falling almost to the ground. Had the midnight tryst been between three people? Perhaps, they'd had to postpone their meeting due to my interference? Furthermore, what was the purpose of the rendezvous? Had I compromised the entire situation now by recounting what I knew about Natasha? I found first gear and moved on.

Feeling in desperate need of an injection of caffeine, I pulled into a roadside diner from where I called Aunt Lamorna. I told her about the purloined Arthurian tales.

'Will you take a look at the high-lighted passages and see what you make of it?' is asked.

'I'm up in London next week. We could have lunch?' my aunt suggested.

'Perfect. I'll meet you at the Hussar, Tuesday at 12.'

It was 1.30pm when I walked into the hallway at Pen-Towan to be met by my mother's former partner, Neil Macbeith, and a red-eyed Trelly. I was astounded to see him. The man had the decency to look as though he had no right to be there.

'Hello, Mel,' he muttered. 'I just dropped by to pick up a couple of things. Sam's in the kitchen. I'll see you again, I expect.'

As he made his way to the front door, I peered anxiously at Trelly.

'You alright, sweetheart?' I asked.

'Isambard let me sleep at his house with Growler,' came the subdued response. Trelly wandered off unhappily.

Sam appeared.

'Where's Ren?' I enquired.

'Some bloke called Mike summoned her to Boston. She got the job at the gym by the way. She starts next week.'

'Blimey. Mike is the guy she got friendly with at Plumtree Hall after the funeral. I thought there was a spark or two between them.'

'Whilst I was trying to get Trells sorted, that character arrived. He frightened the living daylights out of me. When I heard the key, I thought it'd be you or Mum.'

'Yeah, he gives me the creeps too. And as for that bloody Chihuahua...'

'Poor Inez died a couple of weeks ago. Sudden heart attack, I gather.'

'Comes from living too long with him,' I snarled. 'How come he's still got a key?'

'I'm surprised Mum hasn't taken it back but you know what she's like. The number of lovers she's had it's a wonder half of Cornwall hasn't cleared us out of house and home by now.'

'Sshhhh,' I hissed. Trelly had just reappeared.

Trelly was definitely looking peaky. 'You sure you're ok, Trells?' I enquired again.

Trelly looked at Sam and me dubiously and then he said, 'I hate Neil. He's horrid.'

With that, he burst into tears.

Between us, we calmed Trelly down. I sat him on a chair beside me.

'Is there something we need to know about Neil?' Sam's voice had an edge.

'He's nasty to Squid. He shuts him in doors. That's how Squid got his last bandaged finger.'

We all knew Squid was only make-believe but shutting a little kid's imaginary friend in doors was cruel. I was about to voice my thoughts when Trelly blurted, 'And he hated Natasha. He said awful things about her.'

'What kind of things, Trelly?' I asked.

'He said she was evil and that he'd be glad if she dropped off the face of the earth and given half a chance, he'd make sure she did.'

'Do you think Neil could have done any harm to Natasha, Trells?'

Trelly responded soberly.

'He said Natasha was the reason he and Mum weren't together anymore and that he would never forgive her. He said Mum wanted to marry Natasha not him. But that's just silly – girls can't fall in love with girls.'

Trelly was still very much the innocent child. He was now in full flood.

'He said Squid was stupid and all the children round here thought I was a weirdo and it was no wonder nobody played with me and that he supposed that if he didn't have any friends then he'd have to invent Squid too...'

Another fit of sobs wracked him. Sam put his arm around him at once.

'You keep Squid for as long as you need him,' he said, soothingly.

I added, 'Neil's wrong. You have friends – Nathan's your friend.'

Trelly seemed reassured and trotted off to his room.

I told Sam about my visit to Tris, but left out the revelations about our father and Natasha.

'I'm convinced Natasha's death was murder, Sam,' I confided. 'Mum thinks so too. Natasha wrote letters recently, declaring she was going to be killed by someone, possibly Ginny.'

Sam was unimpressed.

'Natasha was devious and malevolent. When it suited her, she left our mother bereft and for no apparent reason.'

I felt deflated. In her letter to Tris, Natasha had disclosed her reasons for deserting our mother but I wasn't about to let that cat out of the bag.

Sam got up to leave.

'Sam, Izzie... well he's not all he's cracked up to be. There's something going on.'

'Like what?'

'Izzie is behaving very strangely. I followed him last night at midnight. He was going to meet someone in the graveyard.'

'MI5?' he enquired caustically.

'Sam, please. He was meeting a man or men, I think.'

'Well, it's not against the law. He's clearly not averse to two-timing!'

'But a picture has been taken down from the wall,' I spluttered.

'Oh my God… they're changing the décor… that has GOT to be suspicious, right?'

'It was all out of kilter. Izzie couldn't bear to look at the picture after Natasha died.'

'And that is relevant because?'

'Because Natasha bought the picture for the two of them and it pertained to the legend of Tristan and Iseult.'

'Not with you, sorry!'

I recounted the story.

Sam remained totally impervious.

'Sometimes you are as unhinged as our mother, Mel.'

'Do you think Natasha could have been killed?' I persisted, desperate for someone to share my thoughts.

'Who knows? Certainly, that loon Macbeith is a fishy bugger! But frankly, my dear, I don't give a damn, to coin a phrase.'

He gave me a peck on the cheek and left.

It was now dark and I realised, with surprise, how quickly the day had disappeared. I made some sandwiches which Trelly and I downed with some hot chocolate, topped with marshmallows, a rare treat, left over from Samhain – and my mother's only nod to Halloween. I packed Trelly off to bed, and a little while later, I followed. The last twenty-four hours had been gruelling.

'Tomorrow's another day,' I told myself, taking a literal leaf out of Sam's book. I longed to see Vin again, my touchstone to normality.

The last thing I remember was hearing Growler's soft padding as he came into the room and a contented grunt as he jumped up on the bed next to me. It was comforting to feel the warmth of another body next to mine, even if it was that of a slightly befuddled dog whose breath left a lot to be desired.

Growler's name was a family joke for Growler was misnamed. Growl was never what he did – he whimpered, when he was unhappy; he whined when he couldn't get his own way; he yelped when he was excited; he yapped when somebody came to the door. So, I was immediately awake, and on my feet, when Growler growled.

Tristan

' "Sir," said Sir Tristram, "... I will desire.... that ye will give me La Beale Isoud, your daughter, not for myself, but for mine uncle, King Mark, that shall have her to wife, for so I have promised him."'

Le Morte D'Arthur by Sir Thomas Mallory

Once upon a time in the West, Mark Banks loved Tom Isaacs. They met at break-time on a drizzly September morning. The village school had a playground a quarter of the size of Tom's back garden. Whereas his parents had well-manicured lawns and perfectly-shaped flower-beds, the school yard had hard, grey concrete, emblazoned with a white-painted hopscotch ladder. Tom's mother came from wealthy landowning stock in Connemara and his father's antecedents had owned several Cornish tin mines. Aside from his well-heeled provenance, Tom wasn't like the other boys in his class – his waif-like expression, slender frame and halo of golden curls provoked taunts from his classmates. If their games became too riotous, Tom would sneak away, fixing his eyes on the estuary. He would stare longingly at the soft waves rippling the wine-red shingle and sigh, with pleasure. Sometimes his gaze would shift towards the distant purple crags of Dartmoor.

On occasion, Mark would approach the older boy, a little shy, and offer him some treasure he'd discovered near his tiny cottage a mile down the road. Like Tom, Mark was a loner. He had a stammer and the other boys would make fun.

'Hey, M-M-M-Mark, w-w-w-wanna p-p-p-play f-f-footie?'

And the boy would flush up – a deep scarlet suffusing his neck – creeping, until it reached the ginger ringlets that framed his chubby face. Mark's family was as dirt poor as Tom's were rich. His mother was wheelchair-bound and his father took on odd jobs around the village. But Tom, always a sucker for a hard-luck story, took Mark under his wing and the two became firm friends – a further source of amusement to their peers.

Aged sixteen, Tom went to a grand college in a town upcountry to study Art History and Mark took up odd-jobbing, mowing lawns, pulling weeds, pruning bushes.

After graduating, Tom bought a gallery in St Ives and set up a thriving business. He soon added on an antique emporium. Tom asked Mark to help him, instructing him slowly in the day-to-day necessities of running the place. Their friendship grew into a tender love, which was the scandal of the village.

A couple of years later Tom opened a second gallery. He and Mark would stand gazing over the golden sands of St Ives and the cold, grey sea and sky with its strange reflections like mirages. Sometimes they would peer across the water below or through the haze to the tranquil village of Shaldon, revelling in the pure joy of being alive.

One day a tall youth came to the gallery, a beautiful woman on his arm. He smiled his infectious smile at Tom who was immediately captivated by the stylish couple. The woman, entrancing with emerald eyes and lustrous dark hair, smiled too.

'I'm Natasha,' she announced, 'and this is my son, Tristan.'

'Tom Isaacs.' He proffered a slim, white hand.

'Oh,' she said, laughing gaily. 'I must call you Izzie – Tristan and Iseult – you must know the legend.'

There was mischief in her eyes which Tom found unnerving. They went to lunch, her suggestion. She needed a new handbag – she'd seen one in the shop just down the road – so would they excuse her for a little while? She was gone for over an hour. By that time, Mark was history; Izzie was making plans for a brand-new life.

Mark, heartbroken, took off for the continent. In Paris, he slept under bridges, around the slopes of Montmartre, where he'd wander aimlessly around the Place du Tertre, peering enviously at the colourful paintings and remembering Tom. With no money in his pocket, he became easy prey, an itinerant, living in the shadows, a hand-to-mouth existence. So, he offered his body to an assortment of low-life for pennies or a square meal.

Gustave, an artist who scraped a living from the hordes of tourists, eager to take gaudy mementoes back home, took pity on Mark. He set him up with a few pastels, an easel, some brushes, some oils, just the basics. After two months Mark's luck changed – he met Robin and his half-sister, Faye. Accompanying them was a young girl her hair, heavily gelled. Her eyes were expressionless behind steel-rimmed glasses. Faye asked about his paintings. Then she quizzed him about the local area. Did he like it here in Paris? Where was he living? Did he have family?

He answered her questions as truthfully as he could. Then she said: 'Would you like to make some money? You seem a little down on your luck.'

Mark nodded, dumbfounded but willing to do anything to enable him to climb out of this morass of unseemliness, poverty and filth.

Mark discerned a faint burr in her speech – American perhaps?

'We need to find someone who has connections to a small village in Devon, England and we've heard that you know something about the area and the people who live there.'

How they had happened upon this information, he had no idea but he sensed this would be his passport to a better life. He packed up his things and said *au revoir* to Paris.

He told her everything: Tris, Tom, their business ventures, their domestic arrangements. The woman seemed delighted. She intuited that he was no friend of Tristan and that she could rely on Mark. She outlined her plans and suggested that maybe he could win Tom back? Robin, needed someone for important work...

Mark didn't question. He wanted Tom back, more than he'd ever wanted anything in his life before. He would stop at nothing to achieve his goal. The die was cast.

When the four of them boarded the boat across the English Channel on a chill February day the sun was beginning to set; a smile played about Faye's painted mouth. It had been a very successful trip. Everything was panning out nicely. She glanced across at her daughter whose face was as fathomless as the sea beneath them. Faye purred with contentment.

On deck, Robin stared moodily ahead, a voluminous, multi-coloured woollen scarf wound around this throat to combat the bitter chill of the Channel. His hands were thrust deep into the pockets of a navy trench coat that came almost to the ground. It would only be a matter of time and they would both be avenged.

Back on the banks of the Teign, Mark was no more than a memory that Izzie had eradicated from his thoughts. Now he was cocooned in a deeply satisfying and contented love. After their first year together, Natasha had come with a gift.

She placed the parcel, wrapped in brown paper, on the kitchen table. It was large and rectangular in shape.

It was a watercolour of a wide expanse of pale grey sea with little, white, scudding clouds in a perfect sky. In the foreground, two sailing boats stood side by side, one with a black sail and one with a white. Izzie was delighted.

'It's your story,' said Natasha. Izzie looked perplexed, but Tristan, steeped in the tales he had learned as a boy, knew it well. He recounted the story of Tristan and Iseult.

'A sad tale of betrayal, to be sure,' murmured Natasha, her eyes clouding over.

'I will never betray you,' murmured Izzie.

Some years later, Izzie removed the painting from the wall, hid it away in the attic – out of sight, out of mind. It spoke of treachery and hinted at deeds to which he could never admit.

An Intruder

'What the hell are you doing?'

Without thinking, I picked up the brass-stemmed lamp next to the bed. Growler was by my side, fur bristling, a low rumble coming from his throat.

'That's not much of a welcome.' Neil's voice was soft and menacing.

'You come any nearer and I'll hit you, you creep.'

'Now that's not very polite, is it? Especially considering how we were once nearly related.'

The prospect sickened me. I raised the lamp above my head. It was very heavy and I felt comforted that any blow with this would knock him out temporarily, allowing me time to summon help.

Neil's voice was barely audible now.

'Natasha came between your mother and I. She was evil. Now, my little Chihuahua, Inez is dead, I have no-one.'

'Where's Trelly?' I heard the panic in my voice,

Macbeith changed tack. 'Why do you and your siblings hate me so much? What did I ever do wrong other than love your mother to distraction? You know, Mel, I could kill you if I wanted to, with my bare hands but I'm not the murdering kind.'

I raised the lamp higher.

'Come, come. Let's calm down, shall we?'

'You have no business being here,' I stammered.

He ignored me. 'Put the lamp down. I need to talk to you.'

I found myself staring into steel-grey eyes, icy with loathing.

'I have nothing to say to you. Get the hell out of here!' I yelled.

His gaze was unflinching. I had visions of my family finding me in a pool of blood, as dead as a dodo and Trelly and the dog likewise.

It was then that Growler sprang. He leapt with full force at the man in front of me and seized his leg. Macbeith stumbled and cried out in pain. He struggled to release the dog's grip but to no avail: Growler was clinging on for dear life. I struck with a ferocity I didn't know I possessed. The lamp engaged with Neil's skull and he crashed to the floor shards of multi-coloured glass spattered like mosaics around him. Trelly wandered in sleepily, a rug wrapped around him and stared in disbelief at the scene.

'What's happened?' he asked, wide-eyed.

Grabbing him by the elbow and calling to Growler to follow, we staggered downstairs. My fingers prodded the telephone keys with an insistence I could barely muster.

'Get me the police, now!'

The voice on the end of the phone was annoyingly calm. I wanted to yell that we'd been in mortal danger, that we were still in mortal danger and here was this woman probing into who I was, who was with me, the name of my second cousin's mate's cat, etc.

'Look, for Christ's sake, we're all going to die. There's a complete nutter upstairs.'

I yelled the address at her and slammed the receiver down. Wrapping Trelly snugly in a blanket, I opened the front door and screamed. I reasoned that anyone hearing that would get to me faster than the police and at least we were out of the immediate clutches of that maniac when and if he regained consciousness.

It was incredibly cold. The night air knived my cheeks. The full moon cast eerie shadows on the driveway. Growler was now yapping fit to burst and in a matter of seconds, half the neighbourhood had emerged from the bowels of their cosy little homes, still in their nightclothes, demanding to know where our mother was and what was going on. I felt more than a little hacked off that, as a thirty-something woman, I should be chastised for being alone in the house without my mother.

'Someone's inside my house and he has tried to kill me,' I stated, blandly.

I heard someone allude to my mother as that *coven-woman*, implying that this sort of thing was to be expected in our family.

Shivering with cold, and angry at the neighbours' apparent indifference I turned my back on them and stepped back inside, where I sat on the icy flagstones with Trelly, door open, until the law arrived. They duly screeched to a halt outside Pen-Towan and two young chaps emerged. My cries for help vindicated, I glared at the assembled crowd and pointed mutely towards the stairs. Growler had decided that since help was at hand, he need play no further part. He plonked himself down and fell asleep. A few minutes later the two hefty heroes returned to the ground floor.

'No sign of him. What did he look like?'

I informed them that he had most decidedly been there a few minutes ago and had been unconscious, to boot. Furthermore, he was my mother's former partner, Neil Macbeith. They appeared somewhat uncertain what to do next. Then one of them said,

'We'll just look round the back. Maybe he's run off.'

'Well, he can't have got far. He must have one hell of a headache,' I retorted, tersely.

They were gone a few more minutes and when they returned their manner was far more appropriate.

'Yes, there are certainly footprints under the kitchen window, madam. We'll put out a call for reinforcements. There's no sign of broken glass. Have you any idea how he managed to get in?'

This was the taller of the two who looked about as old as Trelly. He had the beginnings of a large pimple on the end of his nose.

'I... he... he had a key.'

My words were practically inaudible.

'And why was that, Madam? I thought you said he was your mother's former boyfriend? Do all her former boyfriends have keys?'

He was certainly on the ball, this guy. His mate turned to the assembled crew outside.

'Now then, all of you let's get back to bed, shall we? The small but by now noisily vocal, gathering ambled off, muttering sagely, as if they knew this family was touched and this latest occurrence, and at such an inopportune hour, only proved the point.

Whilst the younger of the two cops ushered us back inside the house to the relative warmth of the kitchen where a residual heat came from the Aga, the other called his buddies for help.

When the four of us were all gathered together again, I repeated my tale, recalling precisely how Growler had saved my bacon and recounting how I'd belted Macbeith with the bedside lamp. They seemed impressed. Trelly certainly was and kept butting in with stuff about Neil and Squid. Reinforcements turned up and prowled around outside for a while. Having ascertained that the coast was clear the two men, Police Constable Youngman, fittingly enough, and Police Constable Whitehead (perhaps Blackhead would have been more apt) took their leave, taking their reinforcements with them but telling us they would be back and were taking our allegations very seriously. This was good news considering the lameness of my replies concerning Neil and the keys. Nevertheless, I can't say I felt greatly comforted. When they'd gone, I bolted every possible ingress leaving the key firmly in the lock of the front door. A little more reassured, I got straight on the phone to Vin.

Groggily, he answered. If I hoped for sympathy, I certainly didn't get it.

'Well, darling, this is the price you pay for getting involved in such utter twaddle. This is the first time you've actually bothered to check if I exist for aeons and now you choose this hour! Given the lunatics your mother associates with, it's hardly any surprise that this has happened.'

'Thanks a bunch!' I yelled.

'Oh, and by the way, Ginny says you need to get in touch pronto.'

He slammed the receiver down.

Mum got back about two that afternoon. She looked exhausted. I had to tell her about Neil; there was no choice since the police were there again when she arrived home.

Mum was apoplectic. Why couldn't she be a better judge of character? She was too trusting, that was her trouble. After a while, she sat mutely gazing at Trelly and me, as if eternally grateful that she still had her family alive and breathing. Every so often she patted Growler's head. He appeared bemused by all the sudden attention but revelled in it, realising it would be short-lived. Eventually the police had statements from us all. Was the suspect acting out of character or true to form? Did he have a history of violence, to which Trelly burst in with, 'Of course he did. I told those other policemen what he was like with Squid.'

Sergeant Dawes smiled politely. Fingerprints were taken of all the family.

Macbeith had vanished without trace. His house was surrounded, but so far, he had not returned home. Give him time, they assured us. Eventually they took their leave. Mum mechanically lit a fire. Now was not the time to hand Mum her letter from Natasha.

The next morning, was Monday and I slept late. Yet again I had to call Felicia and tell her there'd been an incident. Her response was terse. After breakfast I broached the subject of my visit to Tris.

'I think you'd better read this, Mum',' I muttered bleakly, handing her Natasha's letter.

She regarded me for a second, then, she tore open the envelope. She said nothing for several minutes. She seemed neither angry nor sad.

'I always knew your father and Natasha had a very strong bond. But I trusted them both.'

She proffered the letter whose contents I had already guessed at. I skimmed through the by-now familiar script. Natasha was apologetic, of course, seeming to suggest that because she and Dad had had a mere 'one-night-stand' that was less reprehensible.

'Look Mum, I understand if you want to forget all this detective work now,' I said, quietly. 'You owe Natasha nothing.'

'It all makes sense now: Tris's supposedly premature birth, your dad's departure, Natasha breaking off our friendship. In many ways, it's comforting.'

'But they betrayed you, Mum. Right now, I hate them both.'

'Mel, we make mistakes. Natasha was vulnerable. She says they both had immediate regrets after that night.'

'So, you still feel loyal to that woman and there is no rancour towards Dad?'

She nodded.

'When did Tris get this letter?' she asked.

'After the funeral.'

'Who delivered it? It has no postmark.'

'Izzie has a theory that the name on the envelope which was not in Natasha's handwriting must have been penned by an American.'

She looked alarmed.

'Your father delivered it? How was he in possession of the letter?'

'I don't know, Mum. Tris and Izzie know Faye and her partner, whose name is Dora and he's Morgana's father. They all lived in the States.'

'How can Dora be anyone's father? Who is Morgana?'

I explained everything I'd learned.

'I knew Faye was American but I haven't seen her for years. I had no idea she was back in England.'

'I'm not sure she is mum, but her former partner is and has a very close relationship, I believe, with Izzie.'

'Oh goodness, is he two-timing Tris?' she enquired, picking up on my tone.

'I suspect so, Mum. I guess the logical conclusion is that Natasha asked that in the event of her death, her confession was to be handed over to you and Tristan by somebody, either Dad or Faye.'

'It can't be Faye. Natasha would never confide in that woman. It has got to be your father. It would make sense.'

She collapsed in a chair with her head in her hands.

'Oh Mum, I'm so sorry. It's such a shock for us all.'

After a while she calmed down again.

'It seems your dad was unaware of fathering Tris.'

'Mum, It's betrayal – your best friend and your partner.'

'I know Mac; he will be tortured by regret. He was so kind to me at the funeral. He told me he had never realised what he'd lost and I was still very special to him.'

'He was too cowardly to 'fess up,' I retorted angrily. 'Frankly Mum I want nothing more to do with all this. Sam's right... Natasha was evil! There's already been one attempt on my life. I'm through.'

My mother's voice was shaky.

'Natasha needs us. I was her best friend. As for your dad, yes, I'm hurt – but it was one night – a mistake with terrible consequences.'

'Mistake!' I bellowed. 'One hell of a mistake, Mum. What do we tell Ren?' I asked.

'That will be difficult,' she admitted.

I thought back to Ren's reaction to Natasha's childhood abuse.

'I will deal with Kerensa when she returns. I can't do this alone, Mel,' she pleaded.

'Mum, I need some air.'

I walked for miles along the sea front, mulling over all that happened. I was furious with them all: Mum for being so calm and reasonable, Dad and Natasha for betraying her, even Ren for not being around when I needed her.

When I got home, Mum was sitting in the kitchen surrounded by crystals, a large pot of lavender tea and coloured unguents in bottles of varying shapes and sizes.

I put my arm around her shoulder and she smiled up at me weakly.

'Look Mum, I won't abandon you. I can't pretend to like this and Ren may like it even less but for the time being I'm in. I know what Natasha meant to you. Where do you want to start?'

'Adam thinks this is murder,' she announced decisively. 'He's a private detective – hired to follow Natasha's would-be killers. Natasha did not leave BJ to live with him. That is a lie.'

'And what has he discovered?' I asked.

'There was a tenuous link to the political underworld in Russia. Adam believes Ivan may have done something to upset the apple-cart over there and had to leave.'

'Like the KGB?' I enquired.

'Well, it's a possibility,' she replied.

'I cannot believe that. This is the stuff of Le Carre and not petty factory workers, surely? Why would they target Natasha rather than Ivan?'

'Adam thinks it may be tit-for-tat. Vendetta for Ivan's father's past misdemeanours. His first wife died – maybe it was murder? And now they're out to get his daughter?'

'Really? After all this time? It seems unlikely.'

'Adam was investigating further when Natasha's death was announced. Now he fears for his life.'

'Comforting. Anything else?'

'Yes, Rick Morrison, Ginny's husband, Adam has evidence that he has connections with Russia.'

I wasn't surprised that Morrison might be involved, given the mutual dislike between him and Natasha but could he have murdered her? Was Ginny in league with him?

I voiced my thoughts to Mum.

'On the day Natasha died, she was meeting Ginny at Tunman Woods where her body was found.'

'Does Adam know why Natasha and Ginny were meeting?'

'Natasha was attempting to reconcile with Ginny – their relationship was always fractious – and they were meeting up to have a friendly chat. Adam went to the interment, by the way.'

The mystery man who dodged behind the bushes!

'Vin told me Ginny wants to see me,' I told her. 'Only hope I'm not next in line for the chop, in case I know too much?'

'Oh, God Mel, don't say that. Shall I come with you?'

'I'd better take the risk, Mum. No point both of us putting ourselves in danger and probably Ginny will be happier confiding in me.'

'I'm glad you and Vin are getting on so well. He's such a nice man.'

'He's not as nice as you think, Mum.' I retorted.

She rose from her chair and rummaged through the kitchen drawer. She took out a dark red crystal and placed it in my hand.

'Red jasper: it's for stamina and courage. You will be facing tough times ahead.'

I started to protest but she announced, 'I need to go to Chysauster,' and disappeared.

Chysauster was the site of an ancient Iron Age settlement. There was a particular 'fougou' within the settlement, where my mother claimed to feel definite vibes. I examined the crystal sceptically. It looked like something you might pick up on the beach.

The phone rang. It was Ren.

'I found some interesting info about Rick Morrison,' she announced triumphantly. 'He and Ginny are estranged. He's moved out and living in Switzerland permanently.'

'Would this info have come from Mike by any chance?' I ventured.

'Yep! And there's more. Natasha was in an animal rights group in Lincoln, the Lincoln Animal Rights Association to give it its full moniker and they held a demo outside Ginny's house and pelted the place with eggs in protest against Rick's work in animal experimentation. Rick stormed out and grabbed Natasha by the throat, yelling that he was going to kill her. Ginny threw him out.'

'LARA!'

'Seems so.'

'They went all the way up to London from Lincoln to make a point? There's dedication!'

'Well, these cranks do this sort of thing you know.'

'Oh, come on, Ren. They're hardly cranks. They are perfectly legit and have good cause. So how does Mike know all of this?'

'Ginny called him to ask about the funeral. He was going to question her further, but she hung up.'

'Why would Ginny divulge this information and why would she not tell the police if she has suspicions about Rick?'

'Who knows? I'm in love! I'm coming home tomorrow and starting my new job Monday.'

'Congratulations on the job! Felicia is getting hacked off with me, so I'm back in London tomorrow.'

'Where's Mum?'

'Talking to a bloody fougou!'

'Oh, Christ, no change there, then.'

I fell to reflecting on how quickly Ren's bubble would burst once she had been informed of Tristan's parentage.

When Mum reappeared, she was in loquacious mood. The stones had done their magic.

'Neil never got over my need for Natasha. One day we had a real set-to. He accused us of being "closet lesbians." He told me I was obsessed. True, I could never let her go. She was like a burr clinging to an Irish

Wolfhound. I wonder why he wanted to talk to you?'

'Cut up about the bloody dog so he said. After losing you, it was the last straw or some such piffle.'

'He was terribly close to Inez, Mel. He took her death very badly. I wonder if I should contact his sister, Daphne?'

'Should we change the locks? He still has the key.' I ventured.

'No, I think not. He might get desperate enough to come back... and then we'll turn him in.'

'What a wonderful idea! Then he can cut all our throats.' I retorted.

'You have to trust me, Mel. Neil is not a killer.'

'Where was he on the day of Natasha's death?' I asked.

'He doesn't ever leave Cornwall, Mel. He would never contemplate it.'

I wasn't convinced.

'Trelly said Neil announced he'd like to see Natasha off the face of the earth.'

'We all say extravagant things when we are irate, Mel. Trelly is an impressionable child.'

It seemed to me that Trelly was often the most prescient of us all. I told her about my suspicions regarding Izzie and Mark.

'I really don't know Izzie,' she mused.

'Mum. I suppose you don't know anything about euphorbia? Or fatsia japonica? Izzie was definitely spooked by my interest. They are cultivating it supposedly because it gives colour to brighten winter's drabness!"

'As a matter of fact, I do,' she replied. 'Euphorbia is used as a purgative. If ingested it can cause death so medical attention is needed immediately. The other plant, I am unfamiliar with. Possibly Jim Davy would know.'

'What does euphorbia look like?' I asked.

She walked off to our extensive library. Two minutes later she thrust a book on my knee, open at the specific page. The picture bore a strong resemblance to the plants, that were growing in the garden at Ringmore Heights.

I was triumphant.

'There you have it. Izzie is growing it!' 'What about Belladonna and Wolf's Bane?' I added

'He's growing those too?' she asked.

I remembered my promise to Wenna and muttered I'd been wondering about how to cure my headaches.

'For God's sake, Demelza. I have crystals. Belladonna is highly toxic and so is Wolf's Bane. I recommend Selenite. I'll bring some back next time I go to the shop.'

'If Adam's research has led him to Ivan's Russian connection, then euphorbia doesn't seem to be KGB tactics, does it?' she added. 'I know little about these things but I believe their methods are far more sophisticated than someone growing plants in his back yard. And why would Izzie be involved with the KGB?'

I toyed with the idea. Maybe Tris was in it up to his neck as well as Izzie, Rick and Ginny. Could I trust my half-brother? The phone shrilled. I picked it up. It was Ren again.

'I am such an idiot...' she began.

'I'm not going to contradict you.'

'This is serious! Mike took me to see that old girl out on the Wash. The tides turn very quickly and we had to be careful not to get stranded. She lives way out on an inlet that gets almost entirely surrounded by water at high tide. God knows how anyone could live there. It's not even scenic...'

'Get on with it, Ren,' I interrupted impatiently.

'There was a dog – Mastiff or something – it was gi-normous! If she was in there she sure as hell wasn't letting us in – so we gave up. Anyway, Mike is taking me to dinner – must dash!'

I felt uneasy. Had Ren divulged too much to Mike?. Could we trust him?

‘Why should Natasha have visited this woman?’ I asked my mother. ‘Is she a casual acquaintance?’

‘I’m not privy to the company she keeps these days,’ Mum said bitterly. ‘It’s unlikely that Natasha considered her a suspect because she’d hardly go to some desolate spot.’

Tomorrow I would be back in London and I intended to make a visit to Ginny my priority.

Fleetingly, I wondered why Dad had not returned my call? I needed to know whether, my step-mother, Vivienne, had any hand in all this. But maybe it was for the best. In my present angry frame of mind, I would inflame the situation.

However, things were about to get much worse. It began with an anonymous call, telling us that Adam had been found dead with copious bottles of pills and a bottle of whisky by his side.

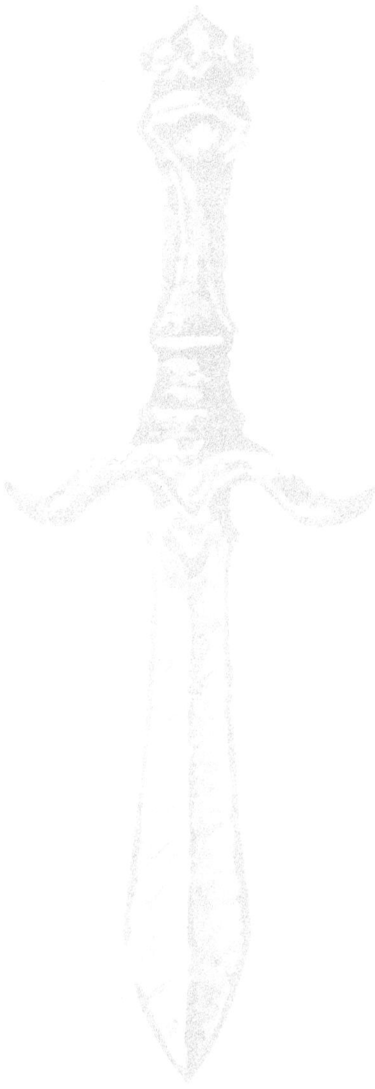

A Ritual Killing

Stunned at this latest development, Mum and I discussed Adam's death. Had he been bumped off because he knew too much as he feared? Should we contact the Boston police and ask if the death, was suicide? It seemed foolhardy to draw attention to ourselves; we decided to let sleeping dogs lie.

It was now Imbolc – the beginning of February – another pagan festival celebrated in our house. Mum had been making garlands since last night. Pieces of cloth had been placed around the well at the bottom of our garden where members of the coven would parade later in anti-clockwise movement. Thankfully I would be ensconced in my flat in Putney by then, but not without a ton of indigo potions for my headaches, along with an enormous tiger's eye to ward off evil which I was to place by my bedside.

Whilst sifting through Natasha's letters once again, I had been reminded of LARA - the Lincoln Animal Rights Association. I intended to go to Lincoln, find the woods where Natasha died and ask Reginald Ferguson at Plumtree Hall a few searching questions about his 'boss.' I would also seek out the mysterious Rachel with whom Ren and Mike Mills had failed to make contact – giant Mastiff or not.

We had made very little progress into our investigation: just an ever-increasing catalogue of 'could-be' murderers. I lugged my suitcase downstairs ready for the long journey back home.

My mother had cooked some megrim, a speciality of the area, for breakfast and I wasn't about to pass on that offer. I was about to tuck in when there was a ring at the doorbell. It was Mr Davy looking absolutely wretched. His snow-white hair was tousled and a stubble of grey beard sprouted from his chin. His rheumy eyes gazed at me forlornly.

'Good morning, Miss Kerensa. Where's Miss Trelawney?'

This was unlike him; he always referred to Mum as *your mother*, when addressing me.

'I'm Demelza,' I muttered.

He continued to stand there wringing his cap in his hands.

Oh God, I thought. His mother's died.

I told him to step inside but he refused to budge, shuffling uncomfortably from foot to foot. I walked off to find Mum, who was gathering coal into the scuttle from deep within the bowels of the cellar. At my call, she emerged, heaving the large, brass receptacle up the last step. It was full to the brim with nuggets; under her arm was wedged a log.

'Mum, it's Mr Davy; he wants to speak to you.'

'Well, tell him to come in. Maybe he'd like some megrim. He's quite partial to it, you know.'

'He definitely wants to talk to you about something important.'

Mum put the coal down, mouthing at me, 'Is it his mother?'

I spread my palms in a gesture of ignorance.

'I'm coming, Jim,' she called, 'I'll just go and wash my hands.'

I hovered anxiously by the door of the coal cellar, uncertain what to do next. She returned wiping her hands on a towel.

I heard her say, cheerily, 'Now then, Jim. What can I do for you? How's your mother? Is she improved?'

'Miss Trelawney, I think you'd better come outside.'

There was a fleeting intake of breath and then a piercing scream. I rushed to the door.

There on the bonnet of Mum's VW was the body of our cat, Piskey. He had been stabbed through the chest with an athame, the ceremonial

Wicca dagger that the coven members used during gatherings. The bejewelled handle was pointing skywards. Piskey's eyes were wide open. His legs were splayed, and visible, through each foot, was a stake which held all four legs in position. By his side was what appeared to be a small fetish or talisman – a replica of a cat: it had a nail through its heart!

Mr Davy stood gazing in horror.

It only took a moment for Mum to take charge of the situation. She said, 'Get back in the house, Demelza. Do not let Trelawney out of your sight.'

I saw her take the broken body gently in her arms whilst telling Davy to help her dig a grave in the garden. Meekly, I went in search of Trelly.

When she entered the kitchen half an hour later, Mum's face was grey. A space had been prepared, near the temple under the ash tree – Piskeys's favourite spot in the summer months.

We informed Trelly, matter-of-factly, that Piskey had died in his sleep because he was very old. He was in fact seventeen. Trelly took in the news soberly and walked over to Janis, who was lounging in the armchair, blissfully unaware. He sat down beside her and began stroking her. I knelt beside him while Mum gazed sombrely at us both. There was another ring at the front door. I felt sick. I couldn't take any more bad news.

'Lois, I wasn't expecting you. Is everything alright?' Mum's voice sounded relieved.

'I have some information. Can I come in?'

Lois Shaw was mother to Trelly's friend, Nathan. The latter, tore upstairs with Trelly, a book under his arm. It was the size of the Encyclopaedia Brittanica. Mrs Shaw caught the direction of my gaze.

'I thought it was about time Nathan got to grips with the intricacies of the Wiccan tradition. Trelly looks a little under-the-weather. Is everything ok?'

'Our cat just died, I'm afraid,' responded my mother quietly.

'Oh dear, I'm so sorry.' Lois was genuinely sympathetic.

'Nathan's a little young to be familiarising himself with Wicca, Lois – it's very complicated,' added Ruth, 'but I suppose it doesn't do any harm to start them early.'

Over a pot of lotus blossom tea, Mrs Shaw embarked upon the reason for her visit.

'Ruth,' she began, earnestly, 'I thought you ought to know there's a man who I think may be a warlock in Penzance. He was looking extremely furtive and attracting quite a few glances.'

My mother looked wary.

'And what exactly does a warlock look like, Lois?' she queried.

Mrs Shaw looked a little taken aback as if this was not the response she'd been anticipating.

'Well, you know, strange get-up, a long cloak, big black top hat, and, even more peculiar, he was white.'

Had she assumed because he was dressed strangely, he must be black? I felt my mother bristling. Mrs Shaw, married to a Jamaican was certainly not racist.

She seemed to realise what she'd said because she giggled nervously and added, 'I mean he was chalk-white, as if he'd been painted. And he was carrying a long cane; it had a lion's head on the top, so I noticed it particularly. It struck me as something warlocks might do… maybe he'd be a new recruit for the coven?' Her voice trailed off.

After studying her teacup for the best part of a minute, Mum looked up and said, 'I think we have enough members, to be honest, Lois.'

Mrs Shaw appeared crestfallen. An uncomfortable silence ensued and after draining her cup noisily, she got up to leave.

I blurted out, in an effort to patch up the embarrassing situation, 'I love the tattoos, Mrs Shaw. Were they painful?'

'Glad you approve. Elvish – *Know thyself.*' With that Lois Shaw called to Nathan, who appeared, still with his nose in the Wicca manual, and departed.

'Sounds like the circus is in town to me,' muttered Mum dismissively.

The megrim was consigned to the bin.

We discussed who could possibly have murdered our cat and what could be the motive? Would it have any link to the supposed 'murder' of Natasha? Could it be Lois's *warlock*?

My mother dismissed this at once.

'A total stranger to the area looking like that would have drawn a massive amount of attention to himself, if he had been the culprit,' she opined.

'Maybe it's some kind of ritual the likes of people like him indulge in,' I proffered pathetically.

'That's ridiculous, Mel. Nobody goes around slaughtering people's cats randomly.'

'Neil?' I suggested. 'He has access to the house. He's still at large and he has an axe to grind.'

'Neil may be many things but animal murderer he is not.'

'Well, who could have stolen the athame? It's always in the temple, isn't it?'

'I unlocked it for Imbolc,' she confessed. 'There's so little crime around here.'

'Trespassing is a crime, Mother.'

'Neil didn't *trespass* exactly – he had a key.'

'Yes, and he still has one!' I yelled.

She was silent.

'Rick?' I offered. 'He's into vivisection.'

'Demelza, this has all the hallmarks of a ritual killing. The use of a ceremonial athame, the talisman, the way...' her voice broke.

'Shouldn't we call the police?' I asked timorously.

'The police have never understood our pagan traditions,' she murmured. 'In my view, Piskey's murder is a cruel attempt to give the impression of witchcraft, for whatever reason. In any case isn't Richard in Switzerland? Vivisection is purportedly for experimental and scientific purposes.'

'Could it be one of the locals trying to make a point?' I asked.

'Hardly! They wouldn't waste their energy; they've lived with the fact that we practice Wicca for too many years now. It could be voodoo. I may give your dad a call and ask after Vivienne.'

'I can't see it, Mum. She's in New Orleans. And why would she do such a thing?'

'That woman is capable of anything! She's already suspicious that there is something going on between your father and me. And furthermore, we cannot rule out that she may now be aware of Mac's former transgression with Natasha. I'll call Iris. She knows about voodoo practices. We might discuss it tonight at the Imbolc gathering.'

'It seems a strange way to get back at Dad or Natasha – murdering our cat,' I said.

I was astounded Mum still wanted to go ahead with the Imbolc celebrations in view of the circumstances. However, Iris was always the voice of reason.

'I need to get back, Mum,' I announced.

I wanted to distance myself from this horror. I gathered my things and we set off for the station.

Back in London, my mother called to tell me Neil had been found. He had hanged himself from a tree near Lanyon Quoit. Was this yet another faked suicide aka murder? But why should Neil be targeted?

I was about to get into bed when Ren called. She was back in Gulval.

'So, it's good riddance to Neil – he's done himself in; tick him off the list of suspects,' she announced.

'Not necessarily,' I replied. 'Guilt could be a motive for killing yourself.'

She hadn't finished.

'Nah, his sister, Daphne told mum he was grieving over that bloody chihuahua and had been for some time and that was the final straw after the split from mum – he'd lost the plot! Iris says Piskey's death is definitely voodoo. She was here for Imbolc. It was good fun, to be honest and took all our minds off Piskey. All hell's broken loose here. Ivan has died - massive heart attack! Grandma is inconsolable. She even cancelled Zeus's visit! Oh, and Mr Davy has hung up his trowel. The Piskey murder was a step too far!'

'Oh, my God! Poor Ivan,' I said.

'Poor Ivan, my arse! He was a complete bastard, have you forgotten? Look how he treated Natasha. I'm still trying to absorb all this horrendous stuff with Piskey. Who would hate our family enough? It's got to be that bitch in New Orleans. I'm going out there with Iris to investigate. Do you wanna come?'

'I can't, Ren. What about your job?'

'I got fired... I insulted a customer in the gym... ignorant cow! She made some snide remark about my tracksuit. I gave her a mouthful...'

'Well, I need to hang onto my job, Ren, so you go off to New Orleans by yourself ... you might just make Mardi Gras. Have you spoken to Dad?'

'No, why?'

I wondered if Mum had neglected to tell her about the letter in all the furore of Piskey's death. I kept stumm in case.

'Iris spoke to him,' she said. 'We are pretending it's just a little holiday.'

'Oh great, a little holiday to investigate the slaughter of our cat. When are you going?' I asked.

'Ivan's funeral is being arranged for nine days' time – customary, apparently. It's in London - Russian Orthodox. We'll go after that.'

'Are the Lawsons coming?'

'JE-SUS Mel, can't you get that almighty prat out of your system!'

'I meant all the Lawsons, not just him,' I said somewhat untruthfully.

Ren grunted and hung up.

At work, I informed Felicia who told me tersely it would be unpaid leave this time, funeral or not.

The following morning, I awoke to the sun blazing through my bedroom window. I could hear the usual commotion in the street below: sirens blaring, people shouting. I glanced at the clock.

'SHIT!'

It was 9.30am! I gulped down some coffee, threw on some clothes and raced to the Tube. It was packed solid. I tore up the escalator, shoving past commuters. Outside I hailed the nearest cab. I barked the destination at the cabbie and slammed the door.

'You in a bit of hurry, luv?' he enquired.

I arrived, in record time, the driver having been sympathetic to my urgent pleas to get a move on and I'd pay him double.

I was greeted at the door by a furious Felicia.

'Don't bother coming in, Demelza – there is no longer a position here for you.'

I sat on the pavement and howled like a child, while pedestrians skirted around me. I had rent to pay, bills piling up and no job.

I trudged wearily back to my flat and immediately scoured the small ads. When Ren called, I burst into tears again.

'I thought you'd be at work; I was about to leave a message.'

I stuttered out my plight.

'Oh shit! Well, that makes two of us. But things are getting much worse. Mother's been arrested.'

'What? Why?'

'She's suspected of killing Piskey. News travels fast and the ritual killing was clearly a Wiccan tradition according to them.'

'Can't you do something, Ren? This is ridiculous.'

'They claim she may also be responsible for Neil's death.'

'But he hanged himself!'

'Yes, but maybe she strung him up?'

I laughed. I couldn't help it. I tried to picture Ruth, at five feet four and Neil, the beefy six-footer as she hauled him up to Lanyon Quoit, put the noose around his neck and strung him up on the nearest branch.

'Iris is at the cop shop, trying to calm the situation. I called her immediately.'

'How is Mum?'

'Not good. Iris says she flits between yelling abuse and sobbing hysterically. Iris has a solicitor on the case, but he's not that sympathetic to witchcraft and keeps making derogatory remarks.'

I sighed. 'Well, I could come down again I suppose,' I said tentatively, 'but I have to keep an eye on my money.'

'Let's leave it in Iris's capable hands and hope for the best. Good luck with the job hunting.'

I returned to poring over the small ads. At 12.30 I met Aunt Lamorna for lunch. She arrived bang on time.

'You look a bit forlorn,' she said. 'Not Vin, again?'

'No, he's history. I lost my job though.' Apart from her letter to Tris, I filled her in on everything concerning Natasha, the death of Ivan and my mother's arrest as we tucked into a huge plate of goulash.

'Hmm, well it all sounds melodramatic as usual with your mother. No doubt Iris will sort out Ruth's arrest. I never did see what all the fuss was about with Natasha. Ruth was completely besotted. Your grandfather too! It's sad she's died but she was self-centred, a ruiner of lives. Her kids are a mess.'

How many more times was I going to hear that?

Lamorna was thoughtful. After a while, she murmured, 'Have you considered whether the letters your mum has received from Natasha are genuine? I mean are they the ramblings of somebody not of sound mind? She never was the same after her eldest son died, you know.'

'I'm not really fully clued up on what happened there,' I admitted. 'Mum said Natasha blamed Lance for his brother's death.'

'None of us know the full story to be honest but it was an accident. An adventure where two young kids bit off more than they could chew. They were ghost-hunting in the dead of night, apparently. Natasha treated Lance terribly after Kai's death. These things have a habit of self-perpetuating – her childhood was pretty dreadful too. Have you got the letters with you?'

'No, Mum has them. Tris thinks the handwriting is genuine so we assume the contents are as well,' I told her.

'But in order to accuse people of murder you have to have sound reasons. From what you've said Natasha died of natural causes.'

I recounted what BJ had said at the funeral, the information I'd had from Wenna, the supposed drugs that Natasha had been on and Izzie's strange behaviour.

'Sometimes, Mel, you have to take people at face value. Maybe Izzie was just taking a walk at midnight genuinely due to insomnia. It's not against the law. Maybe he is having an affair… that's not against the law either. You can't just look for danger and drama around every corner. That seems to be your mother's modus operandi and look where it's got her.'

I had to admit in the cold light of day I was seriously wondering whether we were all delusional and Lamorna was the voice of reason.

We grinned at one another.

'How's Bedouin?' I asked trying to hit a lighter note.

'Oh, he's much the same; he staying with my friend Will in Bodmin, at the moment. Probably, bounding across the local moors as we speak.'

I told her about Piskey and Iris's assertions that it was ritualistic voodoo killing.

'Oh, my goodness. That is worrying,' she said aghast. But I find it hard to believe that Vivienne would cross the Atlantic just to make a point. Anyway, let me look at the Malory and Tennyson passages; they may give us a clue as to what Natasha was thinking.'

I handed them over. She thumbed through.

'I didn't realise there'd be so much. You know Natasha was totally obsessed with Arthurian legend like your grandfather and convinced that her family was linked to the legend somehow. All perfect nonsense. Give me a few weeks and I'll let you know if I find anything sinister. I have to dash, but lunch is on me!'

I smiled gratefully and watched her disappear off into the square.

It was time to pay Ginny a visit.

I arrived at Crystal Palace shortly after four. I traipsed through the dinosaur park, wishing fervently that I was a child again, away from all the worries that assailed me. Ginny's house was a Victorian three-storey divided into flats. I searched for her name: Lawson-Morrison glared out at me and I pressed the buzzer. A faint voice answered. I trudged wearily up three flights of stairs. Ginny ushered me inside at once.

She was painfully thin and there were livid scratches over her wrist. She was clothed entirely in black and her face was devoid of make-up.

'Ginny, you look awful. What's the matter?'

'Apart from my mother dying, you mean?'

'I didn't mean to be insensitive Ginny but you were often at loggerheads.'

'That's true,' she admitted. 'But she was my mother and don't we all love our parents no matter what? I'll get you some coffee.' She smiled weakly.

We seemed to have lapsed back easily into our former friendship from when we were kids although I hadn't seen her for quite some time. Last year at Tris's party she had been with Rick, distant and preoccupied.

She pottered off into the kitchen.

I gazed around the flat. It was sparsely furnished, pristine, but surprisingly, a photo of Natasha and BJ their arms around each other adorned the mantelpiece. I wandered over and picked it up. Natasha stunning as always, was clothed entirely in green, an emerald scarf draped loosely around her neck; she looked happy and serene. BJ suave and sophisticated, was smiling smugly into the camera.

'Their marriage wasn't all bad, you know,' announced Ginny. She had two steaming mugs of coffee on a tray; a selection of chocolate biscuits was spread out on a small plate.

'Like my parents, they had their moments,' I confessed.

'Your parents were much happier and for longer.'

I wondered how much she knew. The silence was palpable.

Then she blurted, 'You know we are kind of related?'

'Tris?' I enquired.

'Yeah, he called me. 'It was a shock to me too, but hey, I think it was free love in those days, wasn't it? And we all have our little aberrations.'

'Ginny, I'm pretty mad at my dad and your mum right now so maybe we should leave that topic. Suffice to say, the letter to Tris was hand-delivered and we are trying to puzzle out who the mailman was, but it could have been my Dad.'

'So, were your mum and dad unaware of Tris's parentage? Why did they split?'

'I think my dad just decided to up and leave after his fleeting affair with your mum.'

Ginny was pensive for a while.

'I do have something I need to tell you, Mel,' she said after a while. 'Our lives as children were hell. Mum'd walk out, after a blazing row, just disappear and nobody knew where she was. On her return, there'd be a few weeks truce and then it'd start up again. No wonder we are all so fucked up. Strangely, I miss her terribly. And we'd been getting closer lately.'

'Ginny, I don't know what to say but I think you need psychiatric help. Look at your wrists!'

Globules of blood were soaking into her clothing.

'Family habit,' she replied.' Mum had self-harming issues and struggled with anorexia for years. It all kicked off after Kai died.'

'Ren and I thought the all-encompassing clothing was down to your dad, knocking her around,' I suggested tentatively.

'Occasionally, but sometimes self-inflicted. And it was a two-way street. She broke his jaw once!'

'Ginny, why did you want to see me? Not to pour your heart about your childhood?'

Ginny's was refusing to meet my gaze.

'On the day Mum died we were going to meet up at Tunman Woods. Rick and I had split up and I was all over the place emotionally. She told me she wanted me to meet somebody special and that was all she would say. Anyway, I had just left the LARA lot – I needed to speak to them about Rick... it's not relevant really.'

'The animal rights lot?'

She nodded.

'I got to the venue to meet Mum later than the appointed time – a lot later. Dad's car was there. There was absolutely no sign of Mum, nor of anybody else. It was getting dark; the fog was coming down thickly but as I was approaching, I saw Dad emerging from the woods. Although I couldn't see clearly, I felt distinctly uneasy, I can't explain, but I was scared. I knew he and Mum were on bad terms again. I reversed really slowly not wishing to have a confrontation with Dad and just parked out of sight. He was so absorbed in whatever was troubling him that he hadn't even noticed me. I heard his car start up and he screeched away. I remember thinking: "What, really, Dad in this fog?"'

'I stayed there a few minutes and then I just went off, found myself a place to stay in Lincoln and came home the following morning. There had been no word from Mum. Then of course I heard the news. I thought: "Oh shit – he's done her in!" Isn't that awful? I knew I couldn't go to the funeral. How could I accuse my father of murdering my mother? I also believed I'd be a prime suspect. Our family are no strangers to media scrutiny. I was devastated, Mel. But now it seems she met with an accident. Mike told me about the funeral, and of course it was all over the papers. How could she get pregnant at that age? Now I will never know if we could mend that rift or not. I have no idea who the someone special she wanted me to meet was – maybe the father of her child? And, I cannot face Dad.'

Ginny dissolved into tears. She was scratching furiously at her arms. I grabbed a handful of tissues from the coffee table and placed them on her wrists.

'Look Ginny, I'm sure your father would never do such a thing. I'm sure we will get to the bottom of it eventually.Shall I stay with you tonight?' I asked gently

She shook her head.

'No, I'll be fine, Mel, it's good to talk to you.'

'You know about Ivan?' I asked.

'Yeah. The man was a complete son-of-a-bitch – no sense of humour, no light of human kindness. No wonder Mum was as fucked up as we are! I shan't be at that funeral either!'

I got up to leave. On the way out I noticed some tiny blue glass bottles labelled Belladonna, Wolf's Bane and Digitalis. Had Natasha paid Ginny a visit and seen the bottles and suspected her daughter of a plot to murder her? Then sent an innocuous letter to her daughter wishing to confront her at Tunman Woods?

I plodded down the stairs. What had my visit achieved? Now there was the mystery of what on earth BJ had been doing in the woods? Tampering with evidence after murdering his wife?

The sky was now transformed into an intense violet as I emerged into Poplar Street. What to do now? Should I go and see Lance? Could I trust myself to remain on an even keel? Would he see me? I made a snap decision. It was to prove life-changing.

Like his half-sibling's, Lance's residence was disturbingly gothic. I lumbered up the driveway.

The lamps, one either side of the rickety gate, cast a supernatural glow; the path was almost submerged in overgrown shrubs. A machete might have been useful! I passed a couple of beaten-up old cars which were parked haphazardly under the ground floor windows. My footsteps, crunching up the gravel drive, sounded like drumbeats pounding out an enemy's approach. I glanced up at the windows and noticed a curtain twitching.

I made my way to the entrance which turned out to be at the side of the house. It was unlocked. The passageway was dimly lit but I could make out a door on the right and another on the left further down the corridor. I peered at the numbers on the doors. Lance lived in Flat 7. Suddenly a door opened and a most unprepossessing old woman glared out.

'Who are you? What do you want? Never seen you before and I know everyone around here.'

'Yes, I'm sure, you do, Mrs....?'

'Never you mind, what my name is.'

She repeated her previous words like some old crone from a Shakespeare play.

'I'm looking for number seven.'

I thought I'd try politeness, a quality in which she seemed to be singularly lacking.

'Top floor. He never gets any visitors, not since ...' she stopped mid-utterance and then continued. 'Does he know you're coming?'

'I don't think that's anything to do with you, but thank you kindly for your help. You should get back inside; you'll catch cold.'

She hurumphed loudly and turned on her heel. The door slammed shut. I climbed the three flights of stairs to number seven. Below I could hear scurrying as though of rats and the muffled sounds of voices from somewhere indeterminate.

In answer to the incongruous peal of the door-bell, Lance appeared.

'Blimey, Lance, where's Lurch?' I asked trying to mask my nervousness.

'Meaning? Not sure why you're here but now you are, you'd better come in.'

'I was visiting your sister. We had a little chat about a few things. She's not in a good place, Lance and I really want to speak to you.

'Right. Sit down. Coffee, wine, something stronger?'

I turned him down.

'It's all a bit Walpole-esque here,' I began trying to adopt a neutral tone. 'You know, in Putney it's all a bit, well, normal: lights that work, door-hinges well-oiled, shrubs that are cut back, that kind of thing.'

Lance muttered gruffly that the place was all perfectly normal as far as he was concerned. I thought of Ringmore Heights wondering what it was about the Lawson boys that they had to reside in dreary, dark environments where only the rats and foul-tempered old ladies felt at home. At least Tris's place was set in more beautiful surroundings.

The large sitting – room looked out over the treetops and down the hill a thousand street lights had erupted, giving the appearance of normality.

'By the way, who's the old bat downstairs?'

'Oh, that'd be Mrs Ramsbottom. She's harmless, just nosey. She has a rather delectable daughter, Janine – gorgeous, blonde, voluptuous, bit on the plump side but I can forgive her that, silky-voiced, bit of a vamp.'

'You really are a chip off the old block, aren't you?'

He bristled but didn't rise to the bait.

'Look Mel, shall we just try to bury the hatchet? After Mum's funeral, when things kicked off with Tris, I felt pretty bad, to be honest.'

He touched the barely visible scar above his left eyebrow.

'What was all that about, Lance?'

'I have no idea; did it escape your notice that HE attacked ME! Lucky for him I decided not to make too much fuss and just put it down to his besotted worship of our mother.'

'What was YOUR relationship like with your mother, Lance?' I asked. 'Ginny said that things were very difficult at home when you were growing up.'

'That's for sure. The arguments were relentless. Screaming, shouting, and sometimes physical, were the norm. After Kai's death, it all deteriorated. What's up with Ginny anyway?' he asked, as an afterthought.

'Apart from being emaciated, and staining the carpets with blood from self-inflicted wounds?' I couldn't conceal my sarcasm at his apparent indifference.

He gave no sign of having heard.

'We had a crap childhood,' he repeated, as if that explained everything.

'Tris has discovered BJ's not his father. Your mother wrote him a letter before she died.'

'Did she? Played away from home more than once then?'

He appeared to be caught off guard.

'Yep, with my father.'

'Oh Christ! So, we're sort of related! That explains the sudden attack at Mum's funeral, although it was hardly my fault.'

'But Tris didn't know that at Natasha's funeral, Lance.'

I related the details of my recent trip to Ringmore Heights.

'So how did he get the letter?'

I told him about the lack of postmark and our suspicions that my Dad had delivered it.

'Does Ginny know?' he asked.

'Tris called her.'

'He didn't think to let me know!' he said, peevishly.

'You're hardly on the best of terms.'

He put his head in his hands. I'm not sure what made me get up and put my arms around him but it spiralled from there. In an instant, he was sobbing in my arms. When he'd recovered some composure, he started to speak.

'Mum hated me after Kai. I've forgotten how to talk to Tris or Ginny for that matter. We all live in our own private hell.' His voice trailed off as I cradled him once more.

'Why don't you try?' I asked gently. 'Talking to Tris, I mean.'

'What about Vin? Are you still together?'

Lance's ability to cut to the chase, unnerved me.

'It's over.'

The words hung in the air for a few minutes and then he resumed, a little diffidently.

'Whisky?' he enquired.

I declined. I was already starting to feel more than a little the worse for wear. I decided to take the bull by the horns whilst I still had my faculties.

'Lance,' I began, 'do you think we can cast more light on your mother's death? She had so many enemies and there are many mysterious circumstances. Where were you, on the night she died?'

'Oh great, so I'm the culprit? I happened to be in bed with a rather delectable redhead, named ... now what was her name? But you imagine I took a trip up to the deep dark woods of Lincolnshire and did her in. Knew exactly where to find her and at exactly what time, caused her to fall over a tree trunk by whatever devious means I had at my disposal resulting, by the way, in an agonisingly slow death, knowing she was pregnant and might have a miscarriage. Come on, you know me, hopeless Casanova, what's the likelier scenario? I'm afraid you'll never be a Sherlock Holmes, Demelza.'

I changed tack, not wanting to admit defeat so easily.

'Your mum had many enemies. Even you and your sister were waxing and waning as far as loving feelings were concerned. Do you think it is possible that she was killed?'

'Not by any of us!'

'Ginny has a selection of vials of poison – at least that's what the labels say. I noticed them in her flat.'

'So, she poisoned our mother! Get real, Mel, you really are grasping at straws. Those vials of poison are imitation. They're mock-ups, they're absolutely NOT what it says on the bottle.'

I persisted.

'How do you know?'

'I know my sister.'

'There was no inquest, Lance.'

'The body was examined and the doctor established that she'd been pregnant and had bled to death because she'd stumbled over something in the dark – that's what Dad said and I believe him.'

'My mother has received letters from Natasha claiming she was in fear of her life.'

'My mother was totally paranoid of late. I thought she and Ruth hadn't spoken for years?'

'They hadn't, but she wrote notes to my mum immediately before her death, voicing her fears.'

'My mother was irrational,' he insisted.

'Your mum mentioned LARA in her letters. We kind of assumed at first it might be a person she knew... you know like in Dr Zhivago.'

'That romantic drivel!' He retorted.

'It's far more than that,' I assured him. 'Have you read it?'

'Nope, seen the film... with some bimbo I happened to be dating at the time. She was drooling over Omar Sharif and I was drooling over Julie Christie.' He grinned. 'Oh, come on Mel, lighten up. Lara is important, because?'

'Because Ginny's husband has an axe to grind and Natasha was part of LARA - Lincoln Animal Rights Association. Rick was into vivisection. LARA along with Natasha, exposed him and his practices.'

'Another suspect – the dastardly Richard Morrison who practices vivisection?'

There seemed little I could say to persuade Lance that his mother's death was suspicious. Should I bring up his grandfather and the supposed link to the KGB and see what he made of it? He was, after all, a journalist – maybe he would know much more about such matters than I. I refrained.

However, his tongue had loosened enough by then to tell me a little about his brother, Kai's death. Natasha had been away from home when the accident occurred and this had exacerbated her feelings of guilt. She had vented her feelings on her remaining son.

He stood up, managing a feeble smile. The level in the whiskey bottle was sinking by the minute. I marvelled at his capacity to remain lucid.

'I'm starving. How about take-away pizza? We could go for a little stroll? We're all fairly well-adjusted in these parts, despite my own dubious family background.'

I hadn't been warm, all the time I'd been here. Lance didn't seem to believe in heating and we'd been sitting in the gloom as the evening wore on. At one point he'd got up to light a few candles but they flickered alarmingly as though a sudden draft would extinguish them all.

As we wandered down the driveway, Mrs Ramsbottom kept herself to herself although the curtains most definitely twitched. We found a take-away at the parade of shops nearby and came back with one each and some garlic bread. That'll keep *Drac* away, I thought, grimly.

'I have a spare bed; you can stay,' he offered.

By the time we finally turned in for the night, having consumed a large amount of red wine, Lance was in riotously good humour and both he and I were slurring our words.

I went out like a light as soon as my head hit the pillow. It was well before dawn when Lance came into my room.

'I can't sleep, Mel. I need you. Please.'

Later that morning the place had been transformed. The sun was filtering through the curtains and I could hear birdsong. I was alone. I looked out of the window. A grey squirrel was scampering along one of the branches. Further up the tree I could see a clinically obese wood pigeon terrorising his smaller mate. His rose-grey feathers shone in the sun's rays. Below the tree was a surprisingly well-manicured lawn, on which there was a mini-trampoline and a child's swing. At the far end of the garden, there was a small grove. I realised in total panic what I had done – what we had done!

'Good morning and my head hurts,' murmured a voice as a face appeared round the door. 'Sorry about last night; verbosity and whiskey got the better of me. Not sure whether it's allowed us being sort of half siblings? We share Tris!'

'How can you be so matter-of fact?'

'Oh Christ – one night! We were drunk! But it was great fun anyway!'

'Get out, you bastard!' I screamed.

Minutes later I cluttered downstairs, tears sheeting down my face. With my coat-collar firmly clenched around my neck, I marched resolutely down the driveway. A couple of jays were squawking in mockery from the bare branches near Lance's bedroom window. Mrs Ramsbottom's words nagged at me, 'he doesn't get visitors, not since…' Not since who or what, I wondered? Ren's words echoed in my brain: 'you still got the hots for that pillock?' A torrent of fouler expletives came to mind as I broke into a run.

Although the day was bitterly cold, the air was crisp and invigorating. I slowed to walking pace, mechanically placing one foot in front of the other and entered the Jurassic age. Kids were gazing in awe at the colossal stone dinosaurs, firing questions at their parents. I turned and walked away. I wandered into the Concert Bowl where I had attended a memorable rendition of the 1812 overture, complete with cannons firing from the bushes. Ren and I had met up with Ginny. We'd sipped wine and nibbled olives. It was a lifetime ago.

Just as I was exiting the *Bowl* a figure, bundled in an old Parka jacket, fur-lined hood turned up against the cold, emerged from a clump of trees and raced off furiously into the distance. It was my sister-in-law. What would Joodee be doing here? Did she and Ginny know one another? My mind flew back to Morgana - Joodee's half-sister – could there be a link? Sure enough, she marched up to Ginny's place and buzzed at the door. The door swung open and she nipped inside. Ginny had been expecting her!

I waited what seemed like aeons. Nobody emerged. Admitting defeat and utterly bereft, I headed for home.

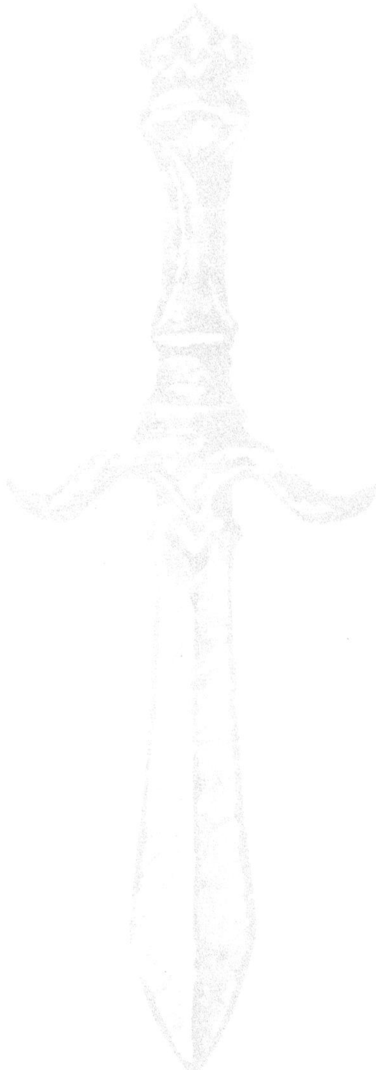

Kai

'Now assay, said Sir Ector unto Sir Kay. And anon he pulled at the sword with all his might; but it would not be. Now shall ye assay, said Sir Ector to Arthur. I will well, said Arthur, and pulled it out easily.'

Le Morte D'Arthur by Sir Thomas Malory

A mere twelve months separated Kai and his brother; of necessity, they were inseparable. Kai was curious by nature, always seeking adventure. He was full of bluster and bombast. Often, he would lead the timid Lance into danger and their mother would become angry. The boys would be locked up, confined to their rooms. Their mother meted out the punishments that had been meted out to her.

But then Kai would find a book, tales of knights of old, war heroes, demi-gods and assorted deities from classical myth, derring-do, bravery, the winning of fair maids, damsels in distress. On winter nights they would sit together besidea log fire because in the Fensthe winds blew in icy blasts form the Arctic and Russia. The wind would howl outside – a demented banshee wailing – and the boys would huddle together with their books propped between them. Their mother would peep in at them, regretting her harsh treatment and smile, remembering another time when she would sit at Arthur's knee, enrapt and cossetted by the magnificence of a court where laughter reigned and beautiful ladies were wooed by valiant knights.

One day when the boys had nothing much to do Kai decided they should visit the local graveyard in the dead of night. The day had been wet and drizzly and now a fog was beginning to descend. It crept up from the marshes beyond their home – a will-o-the-wisp, muffling the sounds of voices, or the hum of the occasional car which would inch its way precariously down the track that ran past their house.

'Let's make a plan,' he said to his brother.

As always, his brother was all ears.

'Shall we ask Ginny?'

'Don't be ridiculous! She'd ruin everything. This is a task for men, not stupid girls.'

Kai recounted a story. The locals said old Lucy Greenaway walked through the churchyard after midnight. As soon as the clock struck twelve, she would creep in a black cloak and pointy shoes.

'I didn't know she had a black cloak and pointy shoes,' said Lance.

'She's a witch. They all dress that way,' said Kai.

'Mum doesn't,' said Lance, doggedly standing his ground. He felt a little scared, if truth be told, but Kai said, 'I'm Sir Kai, you're Sir Lancelot; we are the Knights of the Round Table.'

Lance was uncertain that he could be as brave as Sir Lancelot. It seemed a tall order when you were only small.

All day long, Kai pottered back and forth to the kitchen, fetching food for their adventure. 'Vittles,' he called them. He'd coined the term from some book or another. Lance wondered how long they were going to be gone. The churchyard wasn't so very far away. But Kai was sure it was better to be on the safe side. He made Lance go and fetch a little rucksack from the attic. Lance hated going up there. It was at the top of some dark stairs and the door creaked eerily. Mum kept saying it needed oil on the hinges but somehow, she never seemed to get around to doing it. She didn't seem to get around to doing much these days. There used to be a light in the attic but the bulb needed replacing. Something else Mother never seemed to get around to doing.

'You're not much of a knight if you're scared of the dark,' scoffed Kai at Lance's disappearing back.

Lance returned with the rucksack. The attic had thoroughly unnerved him. He felt sure no good would come of this adventure. The evening seemed to drag.

'You are a couple of fidgets,' their father said as they munched their way through a totally unappetising supper.

'When's Mum coming home?' asked Lance, miserably.

'When she's good and ready, I suppose,' retorted their father angrily.

The boys had heard raised voices long before supper. It was nothing new but there was no mistaking the heavy slam of the front door late in the afternoon. They knew it was their mother who usually fed them. Tonight, Dad had summoned them to the table. The boys had looked in total dismay at the blackened edges of toast and sloppy mound of beans that threatened to spill over onto the kitchen table. Ginny burst into tears. Kai would have complained except that at midnight tonight their adventure would begin and they'd be having a little feast in the church after their mission was accomplished. For they were to seek out the bones of Lucy Greenaway, who had been laid to rest in the crypt. They knew it was dangerous but knights were used to danger. Lucy had met a grisly end at the hands of her jealous husband. And that's why she 'walked,' a tormented soul, adrift in limbo-land. Kai let his imagination run riot. What if Lucy 'walked' tonight? Through the graveyard, up from the crypt where she had been placed in 1765? Or was it 1665? Maybe even 1565? Did it matter? She was in the crypt, so they said.

At half past nine that night their mother had still not returned. Their father packed the boys off to bed. He was preoccupied so he didn't even question that the two complied at once, uncharacteristically.

Eventually, at about one o'clock, his father's bedroom door thudded closed. He'd given up on seeing his wife before daylight. Lance was sound asleep. Kai could hear gentle snores from the bed next to his. Kai slipped out of bed. The little rug felt chill to his feet. He tiptoed over to his brother and shook him gently awake.

'It's time to go,' he whispered.

'What time is it?' murmured Lance, drowsily.

'Dad took forever to go to bed. I'll bet Lucy's long gone. It's way past midnight.'

'Shall we go another night?' asked Lance, a little too eagerly.

'Not on your life. We've got a rucksack packed and ready In any case, it's just the sort of night Lucy's bound to be abroad.'

'Abroad?' queried Lance.

'Not really abroad, you idiot... it's a word they use in books. Don't you know anything? Ghosts are abroad in the dead of night; it just means they're walking around.'

They crept downstairs in their bare feet. They tiptoed across the hall and made their way cautiously to the front door. Not a sound could be heard. Kai gently eased the bolts and they inched their way outside. Both boys shivered. It was cold and damp. Lance buttoned up his coat and looked around anxiously. The fog was swirling all around.

'It's s-s-scary, Kai.' Lance stammered.

'Don't be such a sissy. Hold the torch; I'll take the rucksack.'

They edged their way along the path. Somewhere in the distance an owl hooted. There was an answering cry. Silently the two boys went in single file towards the church. The two o'clock chimes were muffled, distant.

'Can you see the dyke?' asked Lance.

'Of course, I can see it. It's on the left.' Kai was irritated.

He could dimly make out a large stone edifice. The streetlight just beyond the lych-gate cast a wispy, silver glow on the bare branches to the side. Was it his imagination or was the fog getting denser? He seemed to have lost sight of Lance.

'Where are you?' He tried not to shout too loudly, just in case.

'I'm here,' was the response, a few paces behind him.

'Can't you shine the torch properly? Come on in front.'

'I'm not going first.' Lance was insistent.

'Fat lot of good, you are. Give me the torch.'

'Don't leave me behind.'

'Give it here."

Reluctantly he handed it over.

They moved forward into the churchyard. The headstones were tilting as if listening to their footsteps. An owl swooped suddenly in the near distance.

Kai stepped slowly up the path with Lance right behind him. They got to the great wooden door. Kai gave it a gentle nudge. It wouldn't give an inch.

'You need to turn that ring, that one there,' said Lance, quietly.

Cursing himself for a fool, Kai grabbed the colossal, brass ring attached to the door and twisted it to the left. It remained obstinately static. He heaved again, grunting partly in frustration, partly with the sheer exertion of yanking the thing. Then he tugged it to the right – nothing! He stood stock-still wondering what to do now.

Tentatively, Lance ventured, 'Do you want me to try?'

'Bah!' growled Kai. 'As if you'd manage it.'

He tried again forcing his weight against the door. Resolutely, it refused to budge.

Angrily, he knocked past Lance.

'Go on, then.'

Lance gave the ring a gentle turn to the left. The two boys gasped as almost imperceptibly, the ancient door eased open, revealing the blackness within. Something flew perilously close to their heads.

'Bats,' hissed Kai, angrily.

'No, they don't ever fly into you. They've got radar,' said Lance knowledgeably.

Why did Lance have to be so superior?

'At least I'm not an old *cowardy-custard,*' said Kai venomously.

They entered the church side by side. Kai could see their breath in the cold night air.

'Where's the crypt?' he asked.

'Over there, on the right,' answered his brother.

They made their way down the central aisle. About half way down, Lance nudged Kai and pointed.

'Over there, look!'

Despite the façade of grim determination, Kai was beginning to feel apprehensive. The church was totally silent and he was numb with cold. He hefted off the rucksack.

'We'll have some food when we've found her,' he stated matter-of-factly.

Kai put his shoulder to the door. He tried again. Nothing! Kai gave his brother an angry poke in the ribs.

'You try.'

Lance prodded the door. It yielded at once. A steep flight of stone steps led down into a black hole. Kai was in no mood to be pleasant now. He felt thoroughly humiliated. This was HIS adventure and Lance was taking all the glory.

'Shine the torch,' he ordered, frostily.

The other boy aimed the feeble light down into the vault.

'Come on.' Kai's tone was brusque.

'I can't. It's creepy and it smells funny.'

'You're just a big sissy.'

In the glow of the torchlight, Kai saw the wounded look on his brother's face. Kai had found his lever to get back at the irritating little worm.

'Sissy! Sissy! Sissy!' It became a chant, rising to a crescendo echoing around the old church.

'Baby! Coward! Sissy! Where's your dummy? Where's mummy? Diddums want his mummy.'

A black tsunami of anger hit Lance. He stabbed at his tormentor with the torch head and pushed him with all his might in the stomach. Kai stumbled and then he was bumping, thud, thud, thud, down the stone steps and the torch was clattering after him, until there was a splash, and then a horrible gurgling sound as though some kraken from the deep was gobbling him up. Total silence. Lance was left alone in the gloom, a little boy, desolate, and very, very frightened.

At six o'clock that morning the Reverend Digby Jones made his customary check of the church of which he was incumbent. As he walked up the pathway from his rambling, ivy-bedecked vicarage he reflected on the remarkable change in the weather. Yesterday had been dull, with a miserable fog. He had promised an elderly parishioner, Peggy Rafferty, that he would pop by and see her but not in that 'pea-souper.' The Fens could be dangerous and Peggy lived in the middle of nowhere. He would make her his first port of call after breakfast.

The Reverend Jones was a tall man, several inches over six feet and he had to stoop to get under the lych-gate. The wind was getting up – a biting north-easterly coming in off the Wash. He hated this dull, flat landscape, the antithesis of the rolling hills of Derbyshire where he had grown up. And these locals were so superstitious, one of them even pleading with him to exorcise Lucy Greenaway from this very church. What fanciful hogwash. As he neared the church door, he frowned. Surely, he hadn't left the door ajar? How very remiss of him and in this weather. Recently, too, he'd been aware of local youths hanging around late at night. He supposed he would have to start locking it in case things got damaged or stolen.

Reverend Jones pushed the door gently open and flicked the light switch. He heard a scuffling which seemed to come from somewhere to the right of the nave. He hoped it wasn't rats. He'd seen some huge beasts in the dykes near the vicarage of late. The locals called them coypu. The scuffling came again. The vicar walked purposefully up the aisle. He almost jumped out of his skin – a small boy was struggling to his feet, bleary-eyed. He looked dishevelled, his jacket was torn and he appeared to have congealed blood around his nose. The boy stared in recognition and began to make a dash for it.

'Hey, not so fast,' said Reverend Jones, sternly, barring the boy's way at once.

The youngster began to struggle frantically, as the Reverend held him fast. Out of the corner of his eye the vicar caught sight of the door to the crypt. It was wide open. The boy ceased wriggling and suddenly burst into floods of tears. Reverend Jones led him gently to one of the pews and eased him down. He waited patiently for the sobs to subside. He knew the child. Lancelot Lawson. He had a brother, slightly older, if the vicar recalled correctly. The family lived in the big house on the edge of the Wash. The story was that the mother of the children belonged to a coven of witches somewhere down in Cornwall. Ridiculous nonsense! The woman seemed perfectly normal to him. It was true the family weren't church-goers but he supposed these artistic types were quite eccentric. The couple often walked up to the local shop – never together. Perhaps the villagers' accounts of a disharmonious relationship were true, but that was no reason to shun them, in his humble opinion. The child was quite still now. The vicar took off his overcoat and placed it around the boy's shoulders.

'Perhaps you'd better tell me what you're doing here? Do your parents know where you are?'

The boy shook his head and looked nervously over at the crypt.

'Were you trying to get into the crypt? It gets flooded down there.'

Huge blue eyes gazed up at him.

'We were looking for Lucy.'

A flash of recognition. 'Where's your brother?'

The boy looked at the older man with horror, his eyes wide and unblinking.

'I didn't mean to. We were fighting. He called me names. He fell.'

Tears welled up in the big blue eyes and the little voice broke.

The vicar's internal voice became urgent. He could feel the panic rising. He imagined law-suits, accusations of negligence; he could almost predict the headlines.

'I didn't want to come here anyway,' said the boy, bleakly. 'He called me sissy. He fell down the steps. There was a splash... will I be hanged?'

The vicar said nothing. Then he took the boy's hand and led him quickly from the church, dragging him up the nave, through the huge oak door, with its enormous brass ring, along the path between the headstones, under the lych-gate, to the house on the corner. Still holding the boy firmly by the hand, he rapped loudly on the door. It took a while for his sexton to open up. Paul Forrest was enjoying a seldom-realised luxury, sleeping in until seven thirty. This morning it wasn't to be, however.

'Paul, I think there may have been a very nasty accident. Dial 999, would you? We need the police and probably an ambulance.'

Lance was sobbing again by now, imagining dark dungeons, gallows poles. He heard the vicar talking urgently to the man who was still in his pyjamas. A woman came to the door and, taking one look at the little boy, she put her hand over her mouth and yelped, 'My God, whatever's wrong?'

'Take the boy and phone his parents, Miriam. I think he's been in the church all night.'

The next hour was a blur. When he tried to recall his life in the immediate aftermath and then later as an adult, Lance would vaguely remember Miriam Forrest wrapping him in blankets and talking to him gently, dabbing at his face, cleaning him up. His father arrived shortly after. He remembered sirens wailing, a flurry of activity... but the image he would take to his grave was his mother screaming hysterically – an ear-piercing, heart-rending wailing and keening that cut the little boy in two. He, Lance, was a murderer. The vicar, who had heard his story, said nothing and after his original confession to the holy man, Lance's lips were also sealed forever. Between his mother and father there was now something irreparable. His mother blamed his father and his father blamed his mother and life was as black as the hole into which his big brother had fallen to his death. As far as Fenland was concerned, Kai's death was due to that irresponsible mother leaving two little boys to fend for themselves. Oh yes, she was to blame.

A Taste of Russia

As soon as I got inside the door, I found a new resolve. Walking alongside the Thames at Putney, my sadness had morphed into anger. How could I have been so stupid? I felt humiliated and ashamed.

I began by looking at the small ads and circled possible jobs yet again. I didn't rate my chances at getting any sort of decent reference from Felicia so I turned my attention to the menial vacancies: cleaning, mothers' 'helps', postal delivery. I imagined my mother tut-tutting if her daughter landed a job in pizza delivery.

Oh God, Mother! Had Iris managed to extricate her from the police cell? As if through telepathy my sister called.

'Our mother is home. Neil's sister showed up at the police station and exonerated her totally. Her brother had spoken of suicide ever since he'd lost Inez. The police seemed to think that automatically let her off the hook as cat murderer too. So, how're you doing, Sis?'

I recounted my trip to Ginny, and told her I'd seen Joodee. 'Ren we most definitely need to investigate exactly what BJ was up to in the woods. And why he was being so furtive. He has to be the prime suspect now'.

'It certainly looks that way. Furthermore, why was our sister-in-law in that neck of the woods, miles from home? She and Ginny barely know each other.'

'Have they actually met?' I asked.

'Maybe we should ask Sam?'

'I'll get onto it.' I said.

'So, you resisted popping in on super-journo then?'

'Oh, cut it out Ren,' I yelled angrily.

'Oh touch-y! On another front, I have more good news to report, Dad sent over a stash of money – I called and sold him a sob-story about my out of work status! I'm sure he'd do the same for you!'

'There's no way I'm sponging off our father,' I retorted indignantly.

'Suit yourself.' The conversation had terminated.

Ren clearly had no clue about Tristan then!

I called Sam and asked if he knew where Joodee was. I told him I'd seen her going into Ginny's house.

There was a minute's silence, then he said, 'Joodee doesn't know Ginny.'

There was an awkward pause.

'I'll get back to you. Joodee has been behaving very oddly lately.'

I awoke the following morning and true to his word Sam called.

'Joodee was very guarded,' he admitted. 'Some cock and bull story about selling some of her jewellery to Ginny. I didn't buy it.

Look Mel, I'll have to go but things aren't great between my wife and I right now.'

I decided on a whim to call on Felicia and see if I could beg for my job back. Fifty-fifty chance, I reasoned. As I got off the Tube at Knightsbridge, the sun was blazing and it was quite spring-like. Oh, to be back in the West Country, where the tiny yellow aconites would be piercing the banks; their larger cousins, the primroses, wouldn't be far behind. After those first tentative explosions of snowdrops, their pearly, white heads camouflaged amidst the dew of the morning, the new season came with a sudden rapidity, exploding into a riot of colour. Here, all was concrete and high-rises.

To my huge surprise, Felicia accepted my offer. My replacement had not come up to scratch. For the next few days, I worked my socks off anxious to make up for my aberration. My boss was delighted and, albeit hesitantly, said I could take a day's paid leave to go to Ivan's funeral.

I arrived at the Russian Orthodox shortly before midday. Everyone was huddled outside, clad in black. Grandma, a veiled concoction on her head, seemed energised.

'These Russian Orthodontists are very impressive, cariad,' she muttered looking up at the enormous doors in admiration.

I spotted Iris. We had not seen one another since Natasha's funeral.

She smiled and gave me a peck on the cheek.

'You're looking well' I remarked.

'That'd be Leila! She moved in a month ago.'

Pleasantries over, we moved towards the church. The exterior was plainer than I'd imagined. There was a bell-tower to the right, and above the entrance a large, circular window. I glanced around. A handful of figures, all talking quietly together, were huddled in front of the huge, wooden entrance. One woman stood apart from the rest. She cut a forlorn figure and was dabbing at her eyes beneath a black hat with a drooping brim. Her shoes were scuffed at the toes striking a discordant note with her chic black trouser suit. There was no sign of the Lawson clan.

The doors swung apart. The air was laden with incense. The interior was supremely ornate, bathed in red and gold. We followed the priest along a scarlet carpet as he swung the censer from side to side. The place was awash with candles, all crammed into elaborate candelabra. Separating the nave from the altar was a construction with three distinct gates.

'The iconostasis,' whispered Iris in my ear. 'It's the door to the High Altar. Men only!' She raised her eyes to heaven.

'How do you know?' I asked.

'I came here with Natasha and Ivan just after your grandfather's funeral.'

'You forsook the paganism?'

'Just once. Ivan and Natasha had settled their differences and he wanted her to learn about her roots.'

Before long, the priest moved through the Royal Doors of the iconostasis and began to chant loudly in Russian. I studied his attire: a black robe was topped by a white mantle; it reminded me of pictures I'd seen of the Cornish bards all in blue at the Gorsedh.

We were being invited to approach Ivan's casket. Solemnly, we ambled around the coffin in an anti-clockwise direction. Ivan appeared just as in life. Iris threw flowers on the recumbent corpse, mimicked by others and finally came the Priest who threw in a handful of soil.

An hour later Ivan's remains had been committed to the earth, (accompanied by a tot of vodka) and a few of us trudged off for the wake. The woman in the scuffed shoes had disappeared. After about half an hour the other guests departed leaving our family alone with Leigh, Ivan's carer.

'Ruth,' began Leigh. His voice was strained. 'I have something to tell you.'

Mum looked at him anxiously.

'Ivan left something to you and your ex-husband.'

'Which one?' asked my mother, politely.

Ren tittered. There had been a ten-day period when our mother had become Mrs Rhys-Howell. Mr RH had run for the hills one day after a coven meeting. Leigh looked embarrassed.

'I meant Mackenzie.'

'Actually, we had a hand-fasting ceremony at Lanyon Quoit – so not married in the eyes of the law.'

Leigh looked perplexed.

'Mac is in the States right now,' she added.

Leigh resumed.

'There's a specific item that Ivan wanted you both to keep in lieu of Natasha. He altered his will when she died.'

Grandma suddenly erupted.

'It's not that strange casket he had, is it? Arthur often talked about it. We wondered for years what was in it.'

Leigh looked amazed.

'How on earth did you know about it?'

'It was on display in his house. In full view. It was quite a work of art. Very Russian.'

'It contained personal effects, papers and birth certificates,' continued Leigh.

'Birth certificates?' asked Mum, hesitantly.

'Possibly this is best done in private.'

Grandma let out an audible moan.

'I have to admit I hoped it would be left to lie after Ivan's death but I suppose....'

'What is it you know, Mrs Trelawney?' asked Leigh.

'Twins were born to Ivan and Vera, Ludmila and Natasha. Ludmila was put up for adoption with a friend of Ivan's, a fellow factory worker in Finchley. She was never mentioned again. A debut subject, as they say.'

'Taboo subject, Mother!' my mum hissed.

I glanced across at Iris who was impassive.

Leigh allowed us time before continuing, 'Ivan had many regrets over his treatment of Natasha.'

'He was downright cruel,' announced my mother.

'And you did nothing to intervene,' shouted Ren.

Leigh gazed at the floor.

'As I said, Ivan was deeply regretful. I think everyone is entitled to try to redeem themselves and Natasha wanted to mend fences...'

Iris intervened, 'She and I and Ivan came here once. The two of them were reconciled and Natasha seemed to be willing to forgive and forget. She wanted to learn about Ivan's Russian past and to make up for lost time.

Leigh continued.

'Before he died, Ivan informed me that Rachel Dennis his colleague at the factory in Finchley was, quite by coincidence, living near to Natasha's home. I have her address should you wish to contact her.'

He proffered a piece of paper. Ren seized it at once.

'Yep, it's that woman out on the Wash that Mike and I went to see,' she announced.

'You have already made contact?' asked Leigh.

Ren confessed we had not managed to do so.

My mind flashed back to the woman I'd seen outside the church.

I enquired of Leigh who she might be.

'I didn't get a chance to ask; I assumed she was one of Ivan's acquaintances.' he admitted. 'I wrote to Mrs Dennis informing her of Ivan's death but she did not reply.'

He handed over a small brass key which had a tiny censer hanging from it.

'The Russian casket is yours, to do with as you see fit.'

At about 5.30 we said goodbye to Leigh and in sober mood I accompanied Ren, Grandma, Iris and Mum to Paddington. No further mention had been made about the twins. My grandmother looked diminished and frail.

As they boarded the train, Mum turned to me.

'Why don't you come down to Pen-Towan for the weekend, you're looking peaky? I think we needed to talk when we have all calmed down.'

'I'll let you know.' I turned and walked away.

I need to try to get some answers from BJ. I called Plumtree Hall.

Ferguson answered and said BJ was away from home.

'Still? Do you know where he is Ferguson? I need to talk to him.'

'Shall I tell him you called when I see him next, Miss?'

I muttered that I'd be very grateful if he could do so.

To my utter astonishment, a few hours later BJ called me.

He was abrupt.

'What do you want, Demelza?'

I recounted what Ginny had told me about seeing him in Tunman Woods.

'Guinevere was mistaken or she is lying. I was nowhere near the woods when my wife died.'

I put the phone down. Who could I believe?

The Magician

I had returned to Cornwall for the weekend, taking a flight for once, courtesy of my mother. Mum, to my horror, stated that she had still not plucked up the courage to tell Ren about Tris and our dad. She felt that the latest news was enough to contend with for the time being.

'Mum for God's sake,' I blurted, 'she'll find out by other means if you don't tell her and then she'll be even more upset.'

'Perhaps we'd better wait until you get back from America,' she suggested. 'In any case, your grandmother has taken it very badly and Ren is spending a lot of time with her...'

My sister and I were now sitting mulling everything over with a huge pot of coffee in front of us. I had finally disclosed my short-lived 'relationship' with Lance. Ren had come up trumps and neither scoffed nor chastised; on the contrary, she had been extremely sympathetic.

'Mike and I have bitten the dust,' she admitted. 'Seems he wasn't happy about Jay.'

'Jay?' I asked.

'James, the pharmacist.'

'Like Jay Gatsby... James Gatz, without the wealth.'

Ren looked totally blank.

'Should we get back to the matter in hand – namely who murdered Natasha and was it in the library with the candelabra?'

I sighed. 'I suppose.'

Firstly, I contacted Ginny. I needed to satisfy myself that Lance's opinion on the Belladonna, etc was correct.

'Why the poison vials?' I asked. Not at all fazed, she informed me they were for an am-dram production locally. On further probing, she revealed that Joodee had been delivering a set of jewellery Ginny had ordered. This appeared to corroborate what Sam had been told. Could we discount Joodee simply on Ginny's good character reference?

Ivan's wooden chest, gloriously named *The Russian Casket*, had been transported to Cornwall in record time and had revealed documents as Leigh had told us. Lamorna would no doubt have contacts who could translate. The casket also contained a pile of yellowing christening robes presumably set aside for the deceased son. Most astonishing of all Gorsedh robes belonging to my grandfather. He had attended an annual celebration which took place wherein bards gathered together to recognise the Cornish language and customs. In an inner pocket was a faded photograph of two tiny babies, yellow with age.

Since Ivan's funeral Grandma had become incommunicado relying solely on Ren's daily visits. Mum said she wanted to be left alone to grieve.

This morning, Mother had gone out with Trelly, who, unusually, had an appointment at the dentist. She had finally succumbed, having tried to treat Trelly's persistent toothache with crystals and an assortment of potions from Morwenna. None had worked.

Suddenly there was a clattering from the letterbox which foretold the delivery of mail. Growler immediately set up a ferocious racket of yelping and we heard the frantic clumping of paws scurrying along the hallway. We both rushed to pre-empt him destroying any important household bills which might be in the offing.

'This looks suspicious.' said Ren.

'Not another missive etched out in blood?'

'Script is different so it's not Natasha,' she replied, slowly.

We stared at the address. The words were capitalised and in assorted fonts and colours.

Grabbing the envelope, I tore it open. Inside was a series of newspaper headlines, one of which was in French. They all announced the torture and killing of cats and appeared to come from a variety of different sources. On a separate piece of paper were inscribed the words: 'I know who killed your cat. It was a man with no hair wearing funny clothes. He looked like a magishun.'

I looked at the envelope, there was no postmark. It was local. Somebody had bothered to cut out and compile accusatory sentences which left us no nearer finding the culprit than we were before. Eventually Ren spoke up.

'The language is infantile. It's either somebody semi-literate or a child.'

'Seems sophisticated for a kid to paste together newspaper cuttings,' I remarked. 'What does a magician wear traditionally? Is it a hoax?'

'You don't think it's that bloke Lois Shaw was on about, do you? Mum was a bit put out about that!'

'Could be. I think this is something else we need to keep under our hats,' I said, wryly. 'It'd spook Mum even more. Why don't we give Iris a call and say we'd like to meet for coffee.'

We made it to the Bubbling Cauldron by 2.30pm.

Behind the counter was Leila, Iris's new partner. She was about the same age as Iris and had a ready smile and close-cropped hair. From one ear there dangled a long hoop in which was encased a purple feather. We introduced ourselves.

'Iris won't be long. I'll get you some drinks... on the house.'

A few minutes later Iris arrived. We showed her the letter. She was convinced it was a prank.

'Looks as if it's been painstakingly thought through,' she muttered. 'You'd be surprised how some people delight in playing games like this. I'm sure this killing is voodoo. The talisman is indicative. When we get to New Orleans, we have some searching questions to ask.'

I recounted Nathan's mother's visit and wondered again if the 'warlock' could be the culprit?

Iris was dismissive.

'A man dressed in such outlandish clothing would attract attention in Penzance High Street. Why don't you come to New Orleans, Mel? You need a break.'

'I'm only here for the weekend. Felicia already fired me once.'

As we made our way to the door, I caught sight of an unfamiliar face peering in through the window. His gaze fixed on me, like a gorgon. I was rooted to the spot.

The man was completely hairless. His eyes were penetrating, like freezing rain on an Arctic tundra, beneath brows that were dark and bushy. He was clothed in a black cape. A mustard-coloured woollen scarf was draped across it like a sash. A faintly lascivious, sneer played around the corners of his full lips. His left cheek was almost completely covered by a huge birthmark similar in hue to the elderberry bushes surrounding my grandma's house

in Zennor. His eyes remained glued to mine: I was powerless to look away.

In reality a few seconds may have elapsed. I was aware of Ren and Iris beside me and, distantly, coins jangling in the till. The enchantment broke as suddenly as it had started. I blinked. The man was entering the café. I remember nothing more.

I was lying on a couch; the room was in shade. I could feel a hand on my forehead. I opened my eyes, aware of a blinding pain in my left temple. Ren's voice filtered through the mists of my semi-conscious state. I detected a floral scent: a heady mix of lilies and hyacinth. I struggled to surface, to make sense of my surroundings.

'Where is he?'

The note of concern in my sister's voice was evident.

'You fainted in the café. It was unbearably stuffy and we've both been subjected to horrendous stuff lately. Iris is here; Mum's on her way.'

The room was coming into focus. I made out an enormous vase to my left with the offending lily-blossoms in. I vomited copiously. Dimly I recall someone placing a cold, rough stone in my hand.

'Obsidian,' my mother murmured.

I spent the next couple of days between waking and consciousness until the arrival of Grandma's friend Zeus.

I was vaguely aware of firm hands being laid on my head, then, my shoulders. I felt a calm acceptance swathe me. It was instantaneous. Zeus spoke in Portuguese and then in English.

'My name is Zeus, I help you. I think a bad person tried to harm but now you better.'

He appeared far older than I imagined with wisdom beyond time. His face was lined, and deeply tanned, his beard flecked with grey. He looked, with infinite kindness into my eyes.

'A Mesmer,' he said gently.

'I've been hypnotised?'

Almost at once Zeus became energised.

'Yes, parecido. I veel call your family into ze room. Mas no deve a Novo Orleans. Zis time I help but is bad things para – no posso fazer nada. Now descanso e good comida.'

His warning not to go to New Orleans puzzled me. What did he know?

My family filed solemnly back into the room. Zeus smiled kindly at my grandmother, who repeated,

'Good food ... good comida. I have learned some of his language. It's just like Welsh.'

The two of them left hand in hand.

It was now several days later. I cannot recall a time when I had felt so tired; I could have out-slept Rip Van Winkle.

Lois Shaw visited, dragging a tearful Nathan. She held him by the collar of his tee shirt. Nathan looked abashed.

'What have you got to say to Mrs Lowe, Nathan?' she barked. With eyes downcast, Nathan's voice was barely above a whisper. 'We wrote that note about your cat. We are very sorry.' Mum looked puzzled. Lois explained that her little boy, *acting totally out of character*, had compiled a note with his friend, Gervaise. This had been delivered to our door, purporting to know the identity of our cat's killer. 'Nathan will of course be grounded untill further notice.' Mum was horrified and, as Lois and her contrite son said their gooobyes, declared that it would be a while before she would allow Trelly to play with *that young man* again.

Poor Trelly, he had few friends as it was.

St Valentine's Day, had come and gone, not, of course, that such a commercial load of twaddle was taken seriously by my family! Iris had been a constant visitor.

'There is no obvious physical evidence for Mel's fit, except that this person, whoever he is, has worked some evil influence on her.'

I tried to recall the face at the window. All I could remember was total paralysis as he stared into my eyes.

My mother was speaking quietly to Iris.

'Maybe there's some substance in that awful prank of Nathan's. Lois saw a strange man that matched their description.'

She turned to me. 'Could that be him, Mel?'

I admitted that it was possible although he didn't have one side of his face painted white, as I remembered.

'Perhaps we ought to ask Lois to come with us to the police and corroborate Mel's description and let them deal with it?' Iris suggested.

Ren laughed.

'Well, you see, Officer, there was this strange man who was looking at Mel through the window. Zeus, who, by the way, is a faith healer, thinks he hypnotised her.'

Ren was right. It sounded totally implausible, particularly since nobody else had apparently seen the guy.

The next morning Iris arrived laden with oils and unguents. She also had a weighty tome on voodoo. She said she and Mum would be looking at it later.

'Beats Agatha Christie,' quipped Ren.

'Let's go somewhere quiet, Mel. I want to help you,' said Iris.

Perhaps the most striking aspect of Iris was the eruption of Titian locks that danced around her shoulders, moving like tutus on a stage of ballerinas. Her eyes, behind pink-framed glasses were the violet of the Aegean.

She sat beside me and took my hand. It was a cold day and Mum had made up a fire in the library. After a few moments, Iris reached into a bag and drew forth a ceramic pot, cream-coloured and emblazoned on it, in brilliant scarlet, was a pentagram. She placed the pot on the desk in front of us and poured a few drops from an ivy-leaf green bottle. I watched her in silence, wondering whether her next offering might be an umbrella with a parrot-head handle. She fumbled around again and located a tea-light which she inserted into the small drawer beneath the pot. We waited, concentrating on the flickering blue flame. An exotic scent pervaded the room. It conjured up images of bracken and rose hips mingled with musk and crisp, newly-laundered linen.

Iris patted my hand affectionately and said in a low voice, 'Let's make a start. Can you recall that incident? Let's see if we can get to the details.'

I recounted meeting up in the Bubbling Cauldron for coffee and walking towards the door. As I described the man I had seen, Iris's soft voice soothed me like snowflakes hitting a pebbled beach.

She remained motionless. In profile she looked exquisite. A slightly aquiline nose suggested Jewish ancestry. She was dark in complexion, despite the red hair.

'Mel, I think there is dark magic afoot. I have been considering whether there is some connection with your cat's death. Voodoo is still practised by some in New Orleans. Don't worry, I'm not, suggesting your father is connected with all this. I adore the man.'

'You too,' I muttered.

She looked at me sharply.

'I have Leila remember? But I do adore your dad nevertheless. Yes, he made a serious error of judgement over Natasha. It was a one-off. He's paid the price. Mackenzie's wife has recently been to Haiti which is steeped in voodoo.'

'Is Iris your real name?' I asked in attempt to steer her away from a disquieting topic.

'No, it's Jane, plain Jane. Actually, Roisin Esther Jane Rose but I was always Jane. My mother Siobhan O'Connor was from Donegal and my father Jewish, Elijah Rosenstein. He changed it to Rose.'

'There's nothing plain about you. You're beautiful.'

She smiled.

'Iris was my chosen name once I became initiated into the Wiccan faith. Do you know who the original Iris was?'

'An Egyptian deity? She had a son by her brother,' I replied.

'No, that is Isis. Iris was the daughter of Thaumus and the Oceanid, Electra. My sisters are Harpies. On the plus side, I'm goddess of rainbows, the sea and sky. I bring nectar to the gods on Mount Olympus.'

The name suited her so much more than Jane.

'Mel, please come to New Orleans with us.'

'Zeus said it would be ill-advised.'

'Natasha, like Zeus, was gifted with second sight. Did you know that?'

I admitted I didn't.

'If we can do anything to track down her killers, then we should do so.'

'You believe she was killed then?'

'Yes, Ruth has convinced me of that. Whether the killing of your cat is linked to that, I don't know. It's possible.'

Then she continued, 'Natasha had a gift. She, like Zeus, was a faith healer. She laid hands, like your grandmother's friend. She had charisma.'

'Like her husband,' I said bitterly.

'Not like him at all. There is a world of difference being a consummate actor like BJ. Natasha's ability to ensnare everyone who came within her orbit was hugely powerful.'

I wasn't sure, 'ensnare' was a word I would have chosen for Natasha. It was malevolent like the Black Widow Spider.

'Natasha's ability was subtle, insidious at times. I loved Natasha and accepted that as part of her, but it made her many enemies. Now I shall make enquiries in town about the man you have described. Leila is good at eliciting information.'

The next morning, the weather had changed again and with it, my mood. I got up slowly and carefully placed both feet on the floor. I stepped over to the window, drew aside the pale lilac curtains and peeked out. Mr Davy's head was just visible in the lower part of the garden. What was he doing here? His cap was slightly askew and Growler was amusing himself with a large stick. The world seemed to have regained its equilibrium.

There was a soft tap on the door and Mum stepped in carrying a beautifully presented tray on which she had placed a single daffodil bud in a cut-glass thin-stemmed, miniature vase. Ren, clad in scarlet bounded in like an overgrown pup.

'I've spoken to your father,' Mum began. 'Iris reckoned it would do you and Ren good to have a little holiday and, although you've missed Mardi Gras, New Orleans will be wonderful at this time of year.'

I started to protest. I still felt decidedly uneasy about meeting my father given what I now knew about him and if Ren knew the truth, I dreaded to think what the outcome might be.

'And before, you ask I've talked at some length to that Felicia Galsworthy woman who speaks like she has several very large dolmens in her mouth! We agreed you needed a break.'

'Felicia's from Roedean,' I remarked wryly.

'The prison?' gasped Ren.

'No, Kerensa, it's a school for posh people,' retorted my mother.

'What did Iris have to say about that weirdo you saw, anyway?' asked Ren.

'She's going to get Leila to ask around,' I replied.

'Maybe your coffee was laced?' she suggested.

'Leila made the coffee, so hardly!' I retorted.

'Yeah, but you were the only one to see that weirdo."

'Except, possibly Lois!' I said, angrily.

Ren muttered something under her breath and we said no more on the subject.

By way of vindication, Iris arrived later that day to inform us that a customer told Leila she had caught a glimpse of the retreating black cape of my mental tormentor. In his haste, he had knocked a small child on a scooter sideways into the wall. All of this had happened in the blink of an eye, but the observant customer had imparted it all. So, who was he and where had he gone? I wondered whether Penzance had been drugged comatose for the day if only one passer-by had noticed his presence!

I tried to look forward to New Orleans. The Mardi Gras had ended for another year, the jazz turned out to be not my scene and the voodoo experience had disastrous consequences. Such is life!

The City of Jazz

On the plane I am forced to reassess who Natasha really was and my feelings towards her. I stare morosely out of the window at the billowing, cotton-wool clouds below.

We landed in New Orleans at 9.45 in the evening, local time. It was like stepping into a sauna. It would be March tomorrow – Ostara (the Spring Equinox to non-pagans) was fast approaching. Prior to our departure our mother had been gathering the stone hares she kept in the temple in readiness. I hoped fervently we would be back in time for that. It was as near normality as we ever had during our childhood.

During the flight Ren had barely said a word. I asked her what was wrong but was told, 'Nothing!'

Mum informed us that Dad had seemed buoyant on the phone, especially at the news that Iris would be with us. Perhaps he hoped she would be peacemaker in the perennially frosty interchange between Dad's wife and Ren and I.

In the arrivals lounge I espied him frantically waving in our direction. He was sporting an outrageous sombrero and a bright orange kaftan.

'Oh God, he looks like an overgrown Mexican in drag,' I muttered.

Dad came bounding up grinning from ear to ear.

'Wow, it's so good to see you girls. Vivienne's at home. She's been making cakes in honour of your arrival. They're not a patch on your mother's – but don't let on!'

Home for Dad and Vivienne was on the banks of the Mississippi. It was plantation size, and commanded magnificent views over the river. I marvelled at the unadulterated opulence of the place. As the car ambled up the driveway, we were flanked by gigantic trees, sombre sentinels of a sojourn that would prove to be fraught with sadness and disaster.

Dad's money came from his lectures on and mendacious use of artefacts he claimed had been handed down to him by Aleister Crowley. Not only were his talks a sell-out in the state of Louisiana but the spin-offs, publications and DVDs were highly lucrative.

On our arrival Vivienne emerged from the house, immaculately turned out in a pastel-blue trouser suit. Heavy gold bangles jangled on her wrists and matching earrings fell to her shoulders. Her auburn-tinged curls tossed and swayed as she told us, in purring tones, how much she had been looking forward to meeting up with us all.

'I just know you and Iris'll get along famously,' boomed Dad.

The two women looked each other up and down. Twin, auburn curls vied for attention and four eyes looked daggers.

We entered the enormous vestibule feeling over-awed. The place had an air of decay despite the pristine surroundings. I imagined Rhett Butler emerging from the study, inhaling deeply on a large cigar. Vivienne ushered us into the kitchen.

'And how's your Ma?' asked my father.

Vivienne gave him a glacial stare and thumped five cups down on the counter top.

'Ruth sends her warmest regards and says she can't wait to see you again.'

Iris was in mischief-making mood.

She took one of the anaemic-looking buns that were scattered in haphazard fashion round a large dinner plate and sunk her teeth into it.

'I'm not much good at baking,' admitted Vivienne. 'I like to watch my figure and Mac certainly needs to keep an eye on his.'

Dad helped himself to an iced bun and slurped his coffee noisily.

At midnight, I was about to turn out the light when Ren padded softy into my room.

'I know about Natasha and Dad, Mel,' she said. 'I found her letter in Mum's coat pocket. I was so angry, and hurt, but you were ill, so I just sat on it.'

'Ren, I'm so sorry. We just thought...'

'...I couldn't be trusted?'

I nodded mutely.

'Well, I'm here if you feel able to trust me now.' Her voice was a whisper.

I put my arms around her neck. She grinned ruefully.

On her way out of my room Ren casually tossed a large crystal onto my bed.

'Courtesy of our mother: Clear quartz for clarity and inspiration. Weighed a fucking ton in my suitcase!'

The following day we were late up. Our beds were gorgeously soft and capacious and we all slept like logs. Breakfast was US-style ham and eggs, followed by waffles with maple syrup washed down with mugs of strong coffee. Dad suggested we take a stroll along the river since the day was warm.

Vivienne grabbed a voluminous, tan-coloured shoulder-bag from the chair, giving my father a cursory peck on the cheek, and strode from the room.

When she had disappeared, I enquired as to the whereabouts of the mysterious Marie-Ghislaine.

'She and her sister have had to go home to a family funeral. Their mother died suddenly,' said Dad.

Having cleared that little matter up, it was decided that after our stroll we'd see whether it was possible to book a trip on one of the paddle steamers.

The following day things started to go seriously wrong. Iris announced her intention to visit the Voodoo Museum. She then declared, 'Demelza had an unfortunate encounter with one of their number last month. Maybe Ruth neglected to tell you?'

My father blanched. Vivienne erupted.

'I presume you are having a dig at me? There is nothing wrong with voodoo.'

'I beg to differ,' said Iris quietly.

'What the hell do you know about voodoo – you moron,' fired my step-mother.

Ren's glance flipped from side to side as they volleyed it out like a couple of tennis players at a Grand Slam.

'Look ladies, let's cool it, huh? You're behaving like a couple of alley cats.'

Both women looked highly indignant. Iris looked at her lap. Vivienne stormed out, slamming the door behind her.

Iris seized her advantage.

'Right, Mackenzie, that's settled then. I'm taking the girls into town. I know my way around.'

Dad sighed but made no attempt to stop her.

Hence, we found ourselves wandering around the pretty streets of the French Quarter. The balustrades and balconies of the half-timbered houses were ornately impressive. Many were so finely wrought that they had the appearance of gossamer-thin lace. Hanging baskets resplendent with ferns and assorted evergreens festooned them and remnants of the recent Mardi Gras parade were much in evidence. Beads of every hue hung grandly from the trees like multi-coloured leaves seen through the eyes of someone on a vivid acid trip. Snow-white chimney stacks stood proud reaching into an azure heaven whilst lanterns, casting a wan light in the brilliant sunshine, suspended themselves luxuriously from every pole on every corner. We strolled down Bourbon Street, halting in front of an impressive hotel. Wrought-iron gates led to a path which terminated in a dozen steps. Two grand pillars stood astride them.

Catching my envious look, Iris said, 'Why don't we take a peek, before we hit the museum?'

Ren and I almost galloped through the gate to the front door. Iris went straight up to the receptionist at the desk who looked us up and down and asked if we were lost. The poor woman was flattened by the juggernaut-load of charm.

'Your hotel looks so pretty. We haven't anything like this in England. Can we take a look around?'

'Well, o' course, Sugar-pie. You go right ahead.'

Everywhere was sumptuously decorated. I gazed enraptured at velvety chaises-longues and elaborate mahogany tables into whose legs were carved assorted mythical beasts. Enormous gilt mirrors reflected the light, twinkling and glistening from gigantic chandeliers.

We emerged into the dazzling sunshine about half an hour later.

'I wouldn't want you to get a totally negative view of this beautiful city, but now it's time for business,' announced Iris.'

We found ourselves outside a tacky establishment, purporting to be, 'The Museum of Voodoo and Witchcraft.'

An outsize picture of a demonic goat was pasted on the wall.

'Baphomet,' said Iris knowledgeably. 'Seal of the wondrous Aleister Crowley and linked to the Knights Templar. The pentagram is from La Clef de la Magie Noire.'

Iris shoved at the door which yielded without a murmur. Behind the counter was an old dame flicking through a magazine. She was sporting a tee-shirt on which was emblazoned in gold, 'BROWN SUGAR.'

'Yes?' she barked.

'Three tickets for the next show, please,'

The lurid pink finger-nails riffled through a large box on the counter. 'Twelve thirty, sharp!'

'That'll be seventy-five dollars and fifty cents, Ma'am.'

Without a word Iris proffered the cash. Three ludicrously small tickets were thrust into her hand.

'Let's have a look around the delightful boutique, shall we?'

Ren and I had a quick look at the cheap tat on display. 'Gator heads and chicken's feet were displayed on large shelves draped in black cloth. There were books on Le Grand Zombi, whoever he might be. I enquired of Iris.

'A large, menacing snake that appears to enter the body of the voodoo deity, Damballa Wedo,' she declared matter-of-factly.

Ren had picked up a black and white postcard showing a prostrate doll with an arrow piercing her heart. Above it, in bold white type were the words, 'Keep in touch with your ex.' Ren suggested we buy it for Mum. I pictured Piskey with his legs splayed, the athame thrust into his belly and turned away.

Twelve thirty rolled around and by this time a queue of eight had built up.

'Like rush hour on the Tube, isn't it?' quipped Ren.

Suddenly a well-camouflaged door behind the counter, where 'Brown Sugar' was still reading her magazine, opened and from it there emerged a seriously eccentric man, dressed in safari shorts, a Hawaiian-style floral shirt, a yellow-blond wig and a name badge, *Raoul*. Horror of horrors, around his neck there was an enormous python. Was this Le Grand Zombi? The man grinned broadly, displaying brilliantly enamelled white teeth, one of which was a prominent, gold-capped incisor.

'I'd like to introduce you to Monty. He's just had his midday meal. He won't be fit for much again until Tuesday next.'

'Predictable name,' muttered Iris giving both snake and owner a withering look.

The man began his spiel. His hands were bedecked with rings and from one of his ears a brass-coloured earring gleamed malevolently through his golden locks. His eyes were hidden behind dark-lensed, glasses. His face was painted down the left-hand side. It was the white of alabaster and added to the air of malicious delight he exuded. I felt a mounting sense of déjà-vu. Iris took hold of my arm, her grip firm but comforting. I searched frantically through memories recent and distant. Surely that garb couldn't be his workaday choice of apparel? Did he go to the mall in that get-up? He was barely as tall as Iris, but broad as a barrel. He talked in a low, monotonous drawl. The accent was indistinct but it seemed to me that English was not his mother tongue.

Then he lifted the dark glasses and placed them above his forehead until they were nestling amongst the blonde curls. His gaze met mine and I knew he was the same man I had encountered in the Bubbling Cauldron. He was shorter than I remembered. Iris edged nearer. Her scent reminded me of warm summer meadows, home and safety.

As our eyes met, he recognised me too. He replaced the shades, abruptly. I felt strangely calm. He could no longer hurt me.

Iris's voice emerged into the room like a clarion – a mellow sound but imperious.

'Excuse me, young man, but my friend is feeling a little under the weather. We will have to make our excuses.'

He raised the sunglasses. There was a discernible flash of fear in his eyes. He nodded assent and we left the room.

I was steered towards a taxi that had appeared from nowhere and Iris herded us both into the back seat. The journey back to my father's was conducted in complete silence.

I was aware of the low, almost imperceptible hum of the engine and our driver making small talk, peppered with odd phrases uttered in pidgin French. His parting shot, issued from between gold capped teeth, which glittered in the afternoon sunshine was,

'Now, y'all take care, ladies, ya hear me? Laissez les bons temps rouler.'

'May the good times roll for you too, Sir.'

When we reached the front porch, we could hear raised voices inside. Ren held back and looked anxiously at Iris who knocked loudly. Dad arrived immediately. His tone was apologetic.

'I've just come off the phone to your ma. She's anxious to know how things are going and whether I'm taking good care of you.'

That would explain the heated argument from within.

'I need to talk to you, Mackenzie.'

Vivienne emerged from the kitchen.

'Any conversation that is conducted under my roof will be within my earshot too, Iris, if you don't mind.'

'Ok, suits me, since what I have to say pertains to your unfortunate choice of friends.'

Iris marched into the living room. We all followed: it was like the Pied Piper leading us to the Weser. She motioned us to sit down.

'We were in the Museum of Voodoo and Witchcraft.'

Vivienne rotated her gold wedding band and studied the floor.

'Before we left England...' Iris began, her voice strong and steady, 'I did some research. It seems your friend Raoul paid our little town a visit. C'est ton ami, oui?'

Vivienne was silent.

'I believe that Raoul practises grisly animal sacrifices. In fact, he relishes such grotesque pursuits. He was sent to England by you to intimidate Ruth, wasn't he?'

Iris's gaze held Vivienne's in an iron grip. Then she let rip. We were caught in a molten lava flow of abuse.

'I refuse to feel sorry for that bitch Natasha or her friends and family. If I'd had my chance, I would have done her in. As it happened someone else had the presence of mind to do so. She was a vampire who preyed on every male she came across, Mackenzie included. You needn't think I don't know the full extent of it all. Raoul would do anything for me, including taking a poke at your wife.'

Our father is a placid, kindly man. It takes an awful lot to rile him. 'Get outta here. NOW!'

It was then that Iris intervened. There was something unnerving about the two of them together. Next to my dad, she was diminutive.

'*Taking a poke,* as you so elegantly put it, is made even more despicable by the fact that you sent a henchman to do your dirty work. If it wasn't you who killed Natasha, was that your friend, Raoul, too?'

Vivienne regained her composure enough to wax indignant.

'Of course not,' she countered. 'I had no idea that Mackenzie had had an affair with that harlot until recently. Of course, I had my suspicions. I called one of her kids and he spilled the beans.'

'Tris?' I asked.

'The other boy, Lancelot, is it? He seemed more than willing to dish the dirt.'

Iris was contemptuous. 'Ok, Mackenzie. Do what you want with her.'

As swiftly as it had come, Dad's ire subsided.

'Vivienne, I suggest you take a walk upstairs and pack your things.'

We could hear the clicking of her heels fading away into the distance. It felt like we'd just reached an all-time nadir.

'Dad,' I began, 'do you believe her?' My voice sounded distant not my own.

'Are you asking whether I think they killed Natasha?

I nodded.

'I think they killed your cat, honey, but no, I am pretty sure if she had been guilty of murder, she would have admitted to it.'

Iris broke the silence.

'We need to get out of these four walls and do something totally innocuous.'

My mother's panacea for all ills was tea and crystals: Iris believed in action.

'Sound advice, Iris.' said Dad. 'I booked a paddle steamer for this evening. How about it?'

'Do you have nothing to say about our half-brother down in Devon, then Dad?' Ren enquired. 'No apology, no explanation?'

'No Ren I do not. I have paid my penance and if your mother can forgive I kinda hoped you would too and by the way, I have never stopped loving your mother. She is and will always be my soul mate. Natasha was one night of complete insanity which we both regretted. I was in complete ignorance of the pregnancy being due to me. What are the odds, after all? As it was, that evening wrecked my peace of mind; I was consumed with guilt. In the end I felt unable stay with your mother. Now subject closed.'

'Dad,' I ventured, 'it was you who delivered the letter to Tristan after Natasha's death, right?'

'It was. She begged me to do so if anything were to happen to her. So, when she died, I did as she asked. I cut myself on those goddam stone dogs. I couldn't see in the dark an' all.'

'Blood Type A?' asked Ren.

'That's me,' he admitted.

A couple of hours later we found ourselves embarking on the Creole Queen bound downstream, surrounded by an eclectic mix of tourists, local 'Southern Sultries,' and a group of raucous guys in military uniform. The 'Sultries' were regaling one another with tales of previous boat trips.

'Now, Ethel, when ma dear Wilbur was alive, we wen' on this cruise to Memphis, Egypt. Do y'all remember? The Cap'n was an absolute rascal, flirtin' outrageously I do declare...

'But, Hon...'

At this point there was an excited screech from Ethel who pointed a chubby finger at our dad.

'My oh my! Can it really be you? Ya ARE Mackenzie Lowe, right? Y'all wait till I tell Gracie. She will be SO jealous!'

My Dad favoured them all with a gracious smile and said, 'I will agree to sign my autograph on whatever part of your anatomy you deem fit. But you gotta leave me alone after that. Agreed?'

A queue of eager old biddies bore down on us, amidst a frenzy of flabby arms and orgasmic screeches of delight.

Iris corralled Ren and I into the saloon. I stared out onto the green-grey waters. The banks of the river were fringed with lush willows. Overhead enormous herons, their wings flecked with grey-blue feathers, were circling. The breadth of the Mississippi was awe-inspiring, its grandeur unquestionable. I turned my gaze to the opulence within. Above us, the ceiling was bedecked with stars glinting on a midnight-blue background. The musicians were tuning their instruments. All were attired in maroon jackets and straw boaters, the colour of Cornish, clotted cream. A grand piano stood to the side. A solitary female sat on a barstool in a figure-hugging, emerald green lamé.

After a few drinks, Ren's face had taken on a beatific glow and Iris was beginning to waft in and out of my vision, whilst my father sat with tendrils of grey hair escaping in haphazard fashion from his pony-tail, perspiration glistening on his upper lip.

A gibbous moon could be discerned through the porthole and fronds of mist hung from a few wispy clouds. It lent the whole vicinity a ghostly feel, as though the dead might arise from their super-terranean tombs.

Dad informed us that the boat would be returning to port soon after midnight. My sister had become silent and morose.

'Are you ok?' I asked.

'I feel weird,' she replied quietly. 'Something's not right... I can feel it.'

My sister was not given to superstition. I looked at her anxiously.

'We need to get Ren home Dad. She's feeling out of sorts.'

Beads of perspiration were breaking out on her forehead and she was clutching her stomach.

The taxi was waiting at the dockside as we disembarked. As we drew up at the colonnades either side of the entrance to Dad's home, I could see dark stains of something indeterminate pooling on the steps.

Instinctively, I grabbed Ren's hand. I was aware of Mackenzie barking at our chauffeur to swing back down the drive again. The guy needed no second bidding. We careered up the oak-lined avenue, as though in flight from Dante's infernal demons.

'Where to, man?'

'Just stop right here,' commanded Dad grimly.

Dad produced a wad of notes and we all piled out.

The night sky was inky black as our only link with human civilisation disappeared.

I realised that we were about to confront carnage of a calibre that would make Piskey's death seem anodyne. The steps were mired in thick blood and entrails.

Dad's grip on my arm was vice-like. He pushed the front door; it swung open. Inside, the hallway was strewn with feathers of shades of tan and cream. The stench was unbearable; we clasped our hands over our noses in a vain attempt to block it out. A gelatinous, congealed gore beckoned us upstairs. We followed the grisly trail up to the door of the room which Ren had been using since our arrival a few days ago. Dad turned the handle and we tiptoed in, as if entering a morgue. The floor was awash with bright green and yellow feathers, clearly from a different source than those outside. On the bed, propped against the crimson cushions was a stuffed doll. There was no mistaking that this was meant to be a carbon copy of Ren. Strands of white blond wool erupted from its head. It was clothed in a bad imitation of the jogging suits worn habitually by my sister. Most horrifying of all, the doll's forehead was streaked with excrement and congealed blood. Tiny darts had been thrust into the torso. From the crown of her head, semi-hidden amongst the viscous matter smeared there, a Victorian hat-pin lent a macabre touch to the grotesque tableau.

Dad ushered us out without a word.

'I'll call the cops. Iris, take these two downstairs.'

Since we had entered the house, Ren had uttered not a single word. She appeared to be catatonic. Iris led her gently to the kitchen, where everything remained precisely as it had been before we left. She proffered a chair. Ren's face was expressionless.

I put my arm around her shoulders and blurted out, 'Ren, this is just superstitious nonsense. We are all unharmed. It's just scare tactics. The police will deal with it in no time.'

'Mel, we need to get a doctor fast.' Iris's tone was urgent.

I went to find Dad. I met him in the hallway.

'How's Ren?'

'She's in bad shape, Dad. Iris says to get a doctor.'

Back in the kitchen, Ren's glassy stare was worrying. She was fixated on an object in the distance. I felt a rising sense of panic.

'Is this normal, Iris?'

'I'm afraid so. Voodoo can have serious, instantaneous effects on those who are susceptible.'

'What do you mean?'

'Where people become convinced that they are going to die, they do so. Women are often more susceptible than men, particularly young women.'

She surveyed me with a profound sadness.

'We have to trust to medical science, I'm afraid.'

We heard the sirens wailing in the distance. Within minutes Dad had reappeared with two uniformed guys in tow, who had their hands hovering over their holsters. The younger of the pair seemed scared witless.

'Have you any idea who coulda done this, Mr Lowe?' enquired the elder cop.

'I'm afraid I do,' retorted my father.

The policeman stood waiting apprehensively for Dad to utter the accusation. Before he could do so, Ren clutched her stomach and let out a torrent of abuse in a curious mixture of Cajun, French and American

English. Her eyes glazed over and she sank to the floor, still gripping her stomach with both hands.

'Get an ambulance, Joe.'

Iris and I simultaneously dropped to our knees beside Ren, who was foaming at the mouth and writhing in agony. My father let out an expletive and looked helplessly at the two cops. Within seconds two paramedics appeared. A white-coated young woman frantically sought in her bag for a hypodermic. My sister was eased onto a stretcher and they disappeared out of the door.

Tulane

How can I adequately express what we all endured during that terrible time? We went back and forth to the Tulane Medical Centre. Parcels arrived from across the Atlantic, containing crystals and potions. Mother called every day. Wenna suggested herbs and tisanes but Ren was in a deep coma. I felt as though I had been sucked into a dark vortex from which I would never emerge. Our father spent his days and nights pacing the floor, cussing himself for an almighty fool for ever marrying that woman. Iris stayed on for moral support poring over articles pertaining to voodoo.

Marie-Ghislaine and her sister returned to the mansion and took over the daily running of it. Evangeline, known as Evie, would enter the dining room every day, bearing copious amounts of Cajun dishes which we picked at unenthusiastically. Marie-Ghislaine, known as Emmie, apologised profusely for not relaying my messages to Mackenzie but declared that, not only had she had the death of their mother to contend with but Vivienne had threatened her with all kinds of bad juju if she had breathed a word.

According to the best Dad could find, experts in their field, we simply had to trust that Ren would pull through eventually having youth and fitness on her side. We were appalled to find out that as yet, medical science could do little. There appeared to be no tangible symptoms. It was all psychosomatic and therefore impossible to medicate for.

Meanwhile Dad had been visited by two distraught neighbours. Doc Donahue Junior banged on the door early one morning just before we were about to set off for Tulane His rheumy eyes looked me up and down.

'Where's Mac? I wanna see him right now, gal!'

On hearing the ruckus, my father emerged.

'Doc, I'm real sorry, buddy; we're just about to go see my daughter.'

Donahue was unimpressed.

'Right now, I don't give a goddamn. What I wanna know is how you intend to compensate me for ma hens.'

Dad looked exasperated.

'Them hens was ma livelihood. Rhode Island Reds, imported from up country... prize specimens, they was.'

It began to dawn on us that the old man was talking about the massacre we'd witnessed two nights ago.

'I knowed that stoopit floozie you was married to was no good. Allus givin' herself airs. Flauntin' hersel' 'bout town like she owned the place. I jes' knowed her and that weirdo wid dat python was real bad gris-gris.'

My father cut him off mid-ramble.

'Doc, I sure am sorry about your chickens and let me reassure you that the police are on the case. But I got a kid in Tulane who's fighting for her life right now and if you'll excuse us, we gotta get down there.'

Donahue looked sheepish.

'Well, I guess, I'll be goin' along but I jes' want some kinda reckernishun for ma finanshal loss. I reckon'd you'd unnerstan' dat, huh, Mac? We bin friends, right?'

Doc Donahue sauntered down the path, his battered old hat in his hands, still muttering about 'dat darn' floozie.'

In the evening, as we drew up in the drive, after another harrowing session with my sister, we caught sight of a smart, powder-blue Lancia parked under the old chestnut tree. Climbing wearily out of Dad's station-wagon, we were accosted at once by a hysterical, white-haired woman and a younger version of her who screeched at my father like a herring gull on the sea-walls.

'Mackenzie Lowe, my mother was widowed last year. Her parakeets were her only comfort. She talked to them, fed them, had them flying all around the house and now there's only silence. Can you imagine what this has done to her?'

'Yes, I can,' responded my father soberly. 'I can also understand that you all want compensation because that's all you people care about, isn't it? Well, you'll get it just as soon as I can get my kid nursed back to health. Right now, Wanda, I couldn't give a tinker's cuss whether the entire wildlife of this here state has been exterminated. I want my daughter back.'

Two days later, the police called. Vivienne St Martin-Lowe and Raoul Lebusier had been apprehended and were now in the county jail where they would remain pending further questioning. Doc Donahue Junior, had relatives who owned a diner near Salinas who recognised the pair when they showed up at their cafe. Josephine and Maurice Donahue alerted the local cops that those Voodooists from down south were presently tucking into a plateful of boudin and grits and perhaps someone might like to drop by and take hold of them before they murdered any more innocent critters.

It was Beltane, Mayday, when Zeus arrived. Grandma had begged repeatedly that he come to New Orleans and he had finally relented. He came up the front steps looking grave. Dad ushered him inside.

'Zeus, it's good to see you,' I said genuinely touched that he had made this journey for a family he barely knew.

He smiled weakly. 'And like the Greek god I will try to make ze magic.'

We talked him through Ren's current situation. He was silent for several minutes and then he asked if we still had the Voodoo doll.

We told him we had destroyed it. He frowned.

'It will be difícil mas I vill try,' he said in his broken English and Portuguese. 'I need de total paz e calma para twenty-quatro horas.'

Nobody questioned him. Marie-Ghislaine prepared a room and meals were carried upstairs and left on a tray outside the door.

The following day at about four in the afternoon he emerged. Most of the food had remained untouched.

My father drove Zeus to Tulane immediately. They arrived home five hours later. There had been no change in Ren's condition. Zeus looked worn out and despondent. My father thrust a wad of bills into his hand. Deeply offended, he shook his head.

'Zees is ver'dark magie noire,' he said. 'I vant nothing.'

The following morning, he boarded a plane back to Rio.

Zeus had been gone two hours when we received a call from Tulane. We were to go at once.

On arrival we were ushered into a small room where a doctor informed us that Ren was much worse. There was little hope. Did we need a priest? We declined. The three of us filed silently into Ren's room. She lay there immobile and barely recognisable. A maze of wires ran from a contraption emitting alarming hums and flashing red and blue lights.

Suddenly Ren's eyelids flickered and she began to rock from side to side as on a distant ocean.

Frantically, I pressed the nearest buzzer. Three doctors rushed into the room.

Ren's eyes were now wide open.

'Have I missed Ostara?' she asked.

One of the doctors sprang into life.

'Hey, Kerensa... you seem to be better,' he announced. 'Who's Ostara?' he enquired.

'Cornish festival,' I murmurred. I didn't feel like going into an explanation of Pagan celebrations.

'Your Brazilian friend seemed to make her worse with all that mumbo jumbo. But maybe he's done the trick after all...'

Back at the mansion, Evie and Emmie wept when we told them the good news. Dad opened a bottle and then another and we drank way into the night.

The following day, Iris got straight on a plane back to the UK.

I spoke to Mum. She took full credit for my sister's recovery.

'I tied violet and grey ribbons around the Maypole, and the temple is awash with turquoise and tiger's eye.'

Meanwhile we had become nationwide celebrities and voodoo had catapulted into the country's psyche as the topic most denigrated. Following Ren's recovery, the hospital personnel were becoming increasingly frustrated at the media presence.

She was discharged after five days. Dad insisted she should have complete recuperation before travelling home. Thus, it happened that I found myself helping nurse my sister alongside those amiable twins, Evie and Emmie. Ren and I decamped to their house in the French Quarter.

As soon as we set foot inside their beautiful home, we felt we belonged. They were of mixed parentage, their mother being Creole/French, their father Caribbean.

Evie was rotund with an engaging smile which was never far from her ample scarlet lips. She loved to cook and Ren and I were treated to all kinds of delicacies: not only the Jambalaya for which the region was famous but Crepes Suzette, American blueberry muffins, New York bagels, clam chowder and soul food recipes.

Whilst Evie saw to it that we were nourished, Emmie took us places far and wide within the state of Louisiana. She was quieter and slimmer than her twin but had the same cheery smile and the same huge, ebony eyes. Sometimes we'd swim in the azure waters of the Gulf of Mexico or Emmie would take us outside the city limits in her pink Mustang. We'd coast along tree-lined boulevards and avenues smelling the sweet fragrance of bougainvillea and cottonwood. Or we floated down the dreamy bayous, Spanish moss hanging like drapes from the bald cypress trees. Egrets stood inspecting us from the banks on their long spindly, legs. Alligators opened an occasional eye to consider whether they were hungry enough to launch themselves into action. We discovered a raft of Louisianans: Marie Lavaux, Toussaint Louverture, Jean Lafitte. We hit the nightclubs and contemplated the wall-bedecked posters of Satchmo, Mahalia Jackson and Fats Domino. I renewed my acquaintance with Tennessee Williams and Emmie gifted me a cute cuddly toy with the moniker, 'Streetcat named Desire.'

On 13th June Ren and I boarded a plane back to Heathrow. The horror of the last few weeks faded in an instant as we drunk in the fluffy white clouds, the golden orb of the early, summer sun and the levees receding beneath us.

At the airport neither of us was quite prepared for the vision that was our mother. Gone was the dowdy, frazzled woman we had left behind three months ago. Her hair had been cut, shaped and tinted a flattering, honey-coloured blonde. She had a light dusting of pale lilac on her eyelids, a few delicate sweeps of mascara and a dusky pink lip gloss. From her ears dangled long, silver dragons (inevitably!) and around her neck she'd loosely wrapped a vibrant, turquoise scarf. Figure hugging black leggings topped by a beautiful cashmere sweater of powder blue completed the ensemble. Ren was the first to recover.

'You look wonderful, Mum.'

Mum beamed. There were further surprises awaiting us.

'Where's Loulou?'

Mum flashed a key fob at a swish, black Merc, which emitted a long, loud wail.

'Oh God, these technological nightmares. Why do I need an alarm, in any case? Nobody could steal the car when I've got the keys!'

We were in the kitchen at Pen-Towan tucking into chocolate cake when Rick Morrison called from a pay phone in Switzerland; he had important information. Two days later, I was on a flight to Zurich.

A Trip to Switzerland

I made a feeble attempt to smile as I caught sight of the lanky form of Morrison, standing near the door of the arrivals lounge. We shook hands. I made a concerted effort not to recoil.

'Let's try to make this as painless as possible.' he cajoled, softly.

His tone did nothing to reassure me; on the contrary, it resembled a serpentine hiss of threat. My voice took on a business-like timbre, which was at odds with my feelings.

'I have no idea why you deem it necessary to meet like this. Why couldn't you fly back to England?' I enquired.

'I hold down an important and lucrative job here in Zurich: you have time on your hands. I have information for you. Do you want it or not? My darling wife has informed me that you became embroiled in nefarious deeds in the US so I think you'd better take heed of what you're getting yourself into. Because this makes a bunch of voodooists look amateurish.'

Meekly, I nodded. Without a word, he headed off in the direction of a plush-looking coffee lounge. He strode purposefully in front as though I were an inferior encumbrance in a harem. I noticed the frayed trouser bottoms and faded jacket suggesting a poverty I knew he did not possess. He ordered two large cappuccinos.

'Ginny went to meet her mother shortly before she died,' he announced. I remained silent.

He handed me an envelope. It was streaked with mud and on the front was scrawled in the now familiar blood red ink, 'Guinevere'. I fingered it dubiously and let my eyes meet his gaze with more equanimity than I felt.

I opened it as carefully as possible, to disguise the panic I felt and began to read:

> I have never understood our mutual dislike. I loved you as a baby; my only daughter... such a lovely little girl, eager to please, ready with your smiles. When did it all change, Ginny? I am scared for my life. Which one of you wants me dead? You? Your brother? Your husband and his abhorrent organisation? I suspect everyone. Who can I trust? I am mentally ill. This is the lie my family have decided on to mask my murder which I know is inevitable. Then you can pretend it's suicide. Why don't we reconcile, Ginny? It's not too late. I have so much to tell you...

The letter ended as abruptly as it had begun.

'How does this prove that Ginny met Natasha before her death?

His eyes betrayed nothing.

Ignoring my question, he smirked.

'Ah, but the plot thickens, my dear.'

'Where did you get this?'

'I got it in a roundabout way from that old queer who lives with your friend Tristan. I thought I'd sit on it for a while until the time was ripe.'

'You're despicable!'

He shrugged. 'Do you want to know more or what?'

'Do you have some axe to grind? You and Ginny don't exactly seem to have a relationship made in heaven, do you? Apparently, you spend more time apart than...'

His eyes flashed. 'My relationship with Ginny is none of your concern. You and your sister have got yourselves into some very hairy situations of late. I was attempting to protect you from any more harm.'

'And why, precisely, would you want to do that? So far, you've never shown any consideration towards our family.'

How did he know about Ren? My mother would never have divulged our whereabouts to Natasha's children. Did he know about Piskey's death?

'I found this little gem at Ringmore Heights,' he said.

'What were you doing there?'

'It was in October – probably your lot were prancing around the bonfire stark naked at the time.'

He leered at me.

'That little pervert, Tristan, was becoming worried about Natasha. It was a family conference and I happened to be in the UK at that time.'

'So, you, Ginny, Lance, Izzie and Tris were all at Ringmore Heights discussing what to do about Natasha's supposed mental decline?'

'That's about the size of it, yes. I wanted to be anywhere other than in that room with those two degenerates and a wife who was just as much of a slut as her mother. I went to the study, the domain of old limp wrists, Isaacs. I happened to glance down at the floor, and underneath the table was an envelope addressed to Ginny. On closer inspection, I noticed that rather unusual script. I pocketed it and kept it for future reference.'

'Does Ginny know you've got it?'

'I showed it to her recently and she said she had never seen the letter. Begs the question why did Isaacs have it? Ginny was really cut up about her mother suspecting her. They didn't get on but Ginny's no murderer. Neither am I, although I admit I couldn't stand the woman.'

'So why are you disclosing this to me?'

'We need to establish who killed Natasha because they're out to get me too. I'm not the altruistic kind it may surprise you to learn. I have been doing some investigating. This is not your exclusive domain, Demelza. I suspect Natasha's father may have engaged in some shady dealings in the past.'

My mind flew back to Ivan's funeral.

'If Ginny was in ignorance of the letter, why was it on the floor of Izzie's study?'

'I surmise that those two old poofters are in cahoots with whomsoever from Ivan's past.'

'Could you refrain from the offensive language?' I yelled.

He loved it: a malicious smile played around his mouth.

'But it's against nature, my dear. I thought you'd be grateful...putting you on the correct trail after all the red herrings and all that your poor sister has gone through recently.'

I refused to believe that Tris could be implicated in this; he adored his mother. Izzie – well, I had my suspicions about him and his creepy friend Mark, not to mention Dora.

Morrison cast a look around him and stood up abruptly. A man with greying hair, dressed in a dark suit was standing by a newspaper stand. As I caught his gaze, he looked away. Rick sprang into action. He grabbed my forearm and dragged me towards the exit. Outside, he hailed a cab and pushed me inside. I stumbled into the seat with Rick pressed up against me. He barked an address and we sped off.

'What the hell is going on?' My voice shook with anger and fear.

'In my job, I make all sorts of enemies. That was Nils Ekenberg... let's just say there's no love lost between us. I owe him money.'

'Is he dangerous?'

'Very.'

'Russian?'

'Scandinavian, as it happens.'

The taxi ride was interminable. We zipped past office blocks and car dealerships. From time to time, we'd come across parkland but it was sparse. Switzerland seemed to be in denial of its picture-postcard image.

'Where are we going?' I enquired.

'I have a friend with a place should I need a bolt-hole.'

Eventually, the cab pulled up outside a modern apartment block. Morrison handed over a fistful of notes and told the driver to keep the change in precisely enunciated German. We were in front of a glass-panelled door leading into a lobby. To the right was a desk, behind which sat an indifferent individual who could have been anywhere between forty and sixty. He was wearing a navy, peaked cap and a jacket of similar shade with gleaming brass buttons and scarlet trimmings around the lapels.

'Guten Morgen, Herr Morrison.'

Rick addressed the guy as Heinrich and fired some rapid German at him, to which the man nodded a response. We emerged from the lift on the fourteenth floor. The kitchen, into which Rick ushered me, was sparsely provided with an expensive coffee machine, a juicer, alongside which was a ceramic dish laden with a mountain of large oranges and alongside that a garish lime-green toaster.

I needed to ask questions and fast in case this all turned very sour.

'Recently your relationship with Ginny ended abruptly due to Ginny taking her mother's side against you, because of your work, correct?'

'I make no apologies for what I do. It's lucrative and Ginny enjoys the life-style. I could masquerade as a financial whizz-kid in Zurich. Unfortunately, Natasha was too astute. There was no love lost between us, but out of a warped sense of loyalty to Ginny, she kept stumm until latterly. But I did not kill her. I keep my murderous instincts for furry little creatures only.'

I turned away.

'Sometimes I think I'm pretty disgusting and immoral too. But you could argue it saves human lives. I tell myself it won't be forever. I'll probably be bumped off before long.'

We heard a key turning in the lock. Rick showed no sign of surprise. Footsteps approached; the door behind me swung open. It was the grey-suited man from the airport coffee shop.

Rick looked petrified. He had clearly been expecting somebody else.

Ekelberg's eyes gleamed maliciously. I sat down wearily in the proffered chair, wondering how or even if I would be able to make an escape. The man began to speak. His voice was low and guttural, his English impeccable.

'Demelza, I believe ... you are investigating matters that are quite beyond your remit. Natasha Lawson also meddled in matters that did not concern her and she came to the "sticky end." I cannot stress strongly enough that you and your family would do well to leave things alone from now on, if you value your lives and those of the people around you. Mrs Lawson was, so zu sagen, barking up the wrong tree. She suspected entirely the wrong people of meaning to do her harm. You seem to be cleverer. I believe, many times you have met the red herrings, but there... this adds to the adventure, nicht wahr? Quite the little detective. Your tenacity does you credit.'

I shifted uncomfortably in my seat, trying to quell the rising panic.

'Look, you're not going to get away with this. My family will not let things rest, if anything happens to me.'

'But, my dear Demelza, don't be a child. Nothing is going to happen to you. We are simply advising you for your own good and then you can go on your way again, back to the bosom of your family. Mrs Lawson-Rodomski and her murderer is none of our concern either. It is this gentleman, Herr Morrison, with whom I have the issues. Unfortunately, he has not been entirely honest with us? It is now the pay-back time.'

Morrison's eyes did not move from Ekelberg's face.

'Let me out of here.'

I doggedly refused to be beaten by these two thugs.

'You can go. But let me ask you: is the woman for whom you all seem to have the hero worship worth all of this?'

He stepped aside, giving a low bow.

When I reached the ground floor, Heinrich was no longer at his station. Outside a steady rain had started to fall. I turned up the collar of my coat and turned in the direction the taxi had brought us. The street was deserted apart from an old lady encased in black who was hobbling along with a small, dishevelled dog. In my poor excuse for German, I walked up to her.

'Entschuldigung, können Sie mir helfen? 'Ich muß die Flughafen finden. Gibt es ein Autobus?'

She rattled off a load of rapid instructions. I gleaned from the direction in which she was waving her arms that I needed to proceed along this road and turn right at some point. I was to look for traffic lights and a large supermarket on the left.

I thanked her profusely, bent to give the mutt a brief stroke and went on my way. Her smile broadened, furrowing her weathered face with a thousand lines. I could hear her gabbling excitedly to Rover about what a 'guter Hund' he'd been.

Fifteen minutes of trudging past towering blocks of flats and smart looking Mercedes got me to the supermarket, where there were bus-stops galore. Once more my abysmal GCSE German was put to the test! An hour later I was outside the terminal building. I hurried thankfully inside.

I wasted no time in calling Mum. I kept it brief. She barely listened to what I had to say.

'I have exciting news,' she confided conspiratorially and then she hung up.

I touched down the following morning at ten, having had a sleepless night on a bitterly cold and uncomfortable airport lounge bench. Apparently, Zurich had experienced its coldest summer night on record and I was a lucky participant.

On the way back to Gulval, I recounted the past twenty-four hours.

'Well, whatever is to be Rick's fate is none of our concern. Lamorna's Russian translator is hard at work.'

And with that she moved on to more pressing matters.

'Your sister is going to be initiated into the coven.'

'What!' I was completely flabbergasted.

'It will be at Litha. At midnight we will gather at Lanyon Quoit. The moon is nearing its zenith. I think Kerensa has inherited my close communication skills with the Earth Mother. We decided on Artemis as her initiate name; since we are hunting out the truth for Natasha's killer and Kerensa is the prime mover and shaker. She is much changed since New Orleans. Morwenna has started to instruct her in herbs and potions.'

'Sounds like something out of Harry Potter,' I muttered.

Kerensa cast in the role of, 'prime mover and shaker' was a bit of a slug in the guts. I had been lost and alone in Zurich, whilst Ren had been contemplating prancing around a stone circle and having a jolly nice time, thank you very much. Had the New Orleans trauma completely addled her brain?

At Pen-Towan, Ren had adopted a golden glow which was unfathomable. She was no longer my sister but a superior being to whom I was to pay homage. She had taken to wearing a braid of green, silk, ivy leaves in a coronet around her forehead which looked both bizarre and pretentious and jarred with the ubiquitous jogging suit.

Litha was fast approaching and preparations were being made. To the rest of the universe who content themselves with either ignoring it or amassing at Stonehenge to watch the sunrise, it was another day in the yearly grind.

Amber, garnet and moonstone were being placed all around the house and Ren had gone into overdrive collecting honeysuckle and roses.

The house seemed unbearably quiet and my mood was desolate. Whilst we had been in New Orleans, Janis had gone to join her brother.

When I quizzed my sister about her sudden desire to join the coven, she would only say she had been feeling the call for a long while. I felt an increasing draw to Aunt Lamorna.

On 19th June I left to spend a few days in Exeter. Scarcely had I arrived, when Ginny called me. Rick's body had been dragged from Lake Zurich. His car had careered off an icy road at speed last night.

Murder in Zurich

Ginny pre-empted my unvoiced thoughts.

'He was dealing with underworld criminals But, you know what... I don't care. The Swiss authorities say it was a fatal accident. I think not.'

'I saw Rick, Ginny, and possibly the guy responsible. Ekelberg - a Scandinavian to whom Rick owed money. He followed us to a flat outside the city.'

'You saw Rick? What in Zurich?'

'Yes, he summoned me out there. He showed me your mother's letter – the one he discovered on the floor of Izzie's study.'

'I'd intended to ask mum about that letter when we met up in the woods...'

'Maybe one day we'll discover the truth, Ginny. Rick seemed to think Ivan's past held a clue to Natasha's murder.'

'I only hope I'm not next on the list, Mel. My mother was messed up in something way beyond our ken.'

'Stay in touch, Ginny,' I begged.

Little did I know when I put down the phone that was to be the last I would hear of her, in a very long time.

Lamorna was peering anxiously at me over her glasses. Bedouin had launched himself at me – all one hundred and forty pounds of him. Great globs of slather were dropping on my sandaled feet.

I patted him absent-mindedly.

'Want to talk about it?' Lamorna asked.

I updated her. Her face took on an extremely concerned air: since this was Lamorna, not given to melodrama, I was worried.

'I have looked at the highlighted Arthurian passages and can find nothing of relevance. They are just random tracts concerning Arthurian characters who have connections with Natasha's family: Guinevere going to a nunnery; Sir Lancelot and the Lady of Shalott; Tristan's love for Iseut; Arthur passing to Avalon; Merlin and Vivienne. I cannot connect it to foul play. These are legends made up about a man who was a war lord in the fifth century AD!'

'Well clearly Natasha felt it had relevance,' I reasoned.

'Evidently, since there are references to her belief that her fate was tied up with it all! Nevertheless, this latest incident with Guinevere's husband is quite another matter. I understand your sister has been drawn to the dark side.' Lamorna grinned broadly.

I burst into tears. Lamorna stood up and walked to the cabinet.

'Get that down you. It's a single malt, from Islay.'

I gulped it down in one.

'You can always come and stay with me. I love your mother dearly but we have nothing in common. Maybe that will now be the case with you and Ren.'

I asked her if she'd had a chance to get the documents from Ivan's wooden chest deciphered yet but she replied in the negative.

'My Russian translator is a busy woman; she won't let me down.'

'If any of you had any sense, you'd have got the police involved by now but your mother was never was in favour of law and order.'

It was 10.30pm on the following day. Lamorna and I had spent a wonderful day walking Bedouin along the red sands at Teignmouth just down the road from where Tristan lived. I was about to turn in, knowing that Ren would be preparing herself for the initiation tomorrow when my mobile buzzed.

It was my sister.

'Well, you'll never guess what...'

'Nope, I wouldn't.'

'Joodee's gone off to live with Ginny. Left the kids. And Rick has been discovered at the bottom of a lake somewhere in Switzerland.'

'Lake Zurich, to be precise. Ginny called me yesterday. How's Sam?' I asked.

'Not good. Obviously, we have enough on our plates here but we wondered whether you'd come back and help.'

'Fuck you, Ren!'

I turned the light out and tried to sleep.

The following day dawned. The rain was pelting down and it felt unseasonably cold. I mused smugly on the bedraggled *Artemis* cavorting around Lanyon Quoit at midnight.

When I got downstairs Lamorna had prepared some warm croissants and coffee. Bedouin was galumphing around the garden like a possessed heavyweight boxer. He appeared to be kicking a large pumpkin along the lawn.

Over coffee, Lamorna and I hit upon a plan. She would come with me to Boston and we would search for Ludmila's adoptive mother. We might also pay a visit to Plumtree Hall. LARA was also on my list.

We arrived in Boston just before 6.00pm and settled ourselves into a guest house a mere stone's throw from where we had attended Natasha's funeral a few months earlier.

The next morning, we strolled into town. Lamorna was impressed with *The Stump* and wanted to explore.

'What a beautiful sky!' she exclaimed. 'It would make a gorgeous painting if I was of an artistic bent.'

I gazed up at an azure heaven dotted with tiny cirro-cumulus and sighed. Boston still wasn't for me, unhappy memories notwithstanding.

I sat on a bench and stared glumly at the muddy waters of the River Witham.

About an hour later, Lamorna emerged. It was time to seek out Rachel. We parked a respectable distance from Freiston Shore and tramped along a muddy path towards the sea. On the mudflats to the right of us a dead porpoise was attracting a swarm of flies. A brisk breeze was blowing in off the sea far in the distance so we judged we could make it safely to Rachel's and back before the tide turned.

We spotted a small stone building, wreaths of smoke emerging from the chimney. An enormous dog barking fit to burst hove into view. A woman stood holding him at bay. I recognised her as the forlorn mourner at Ivan's funeral. She looked warily at us.

Lamorna called out cheerily, 'Are you Rachel? Mrs Dennis?'

'Yes.'

'We would like to ask you a few questions, Mrs Dennis. It's about Rebecca.'

There was an audible gasp.

'Is she alive?' The woman's voice was faltering. Her hand went to her forehead whilst she maintained a steady grip on the Mastiff.

'Could we come in?' asked my aunt.

Rachel tied the dog to a post. Within minutes we were inside.

It was tiny. A meagre lunch was laid out on the table: a small apple, a morsel of cheese and two crackers thinly spread with butter.

She motioned us to sit down. The chairs were threadbare and smelled strongly of wet dog.

'Mrs Dennis,' began my aunt. 'My name is Lamorna Trelawney and this is my niece Demelza Lowe. Did you know Natasha Lawson?'

Rachel nodded glumly. Lamorna handed her a tissue from her bag and the woman dabbed at her eyes.

'I cannot believe she's gone,' she said. 'I loved her like my own daughter.'

'Where is Rebecca?' I asked quietly.

'She and I parted company. There was a huge misunderstanding she and Godfrey, my husband, clashed badly. She left over twenty years ago. Natasha tried to find her – it became an all-consuming passion. Ivan wanted to see her again before he died. He was such a strange man, but he had a kinder side that few people saw.'

'So, you have no idea what happened to your daughter?' Lamorna asked.

'We had no contact number, no address, nothing. A light went out in our lives after she went.'

'What can you tell us about Ivan?' I asked

'He came to live in England in the fifties. We worked together in Finchley. We struck up a friendship. Then he met Vera and they married. Godfrey and I discovered we couldn't have kids of our own and he gave Ludmila to me. Said he and Vera couldn't cope with twins. Ivan and his friend Arthur sent money, regular as clockwork. When Rebecca was a teenager, Godfrey and I told her she had a twin. She brooded on it for a few days, then she left. Walked out, without saying goodbye.'

Rachel was sobbing now.

When she had calmed down, I said, 'Rachel I know this is hard for you but can you tell us anything else about Ivan that might be of use? We have reason to believe that Natasha may have been murdered.'

'Good God! I had no idea. There was no mention in the papers that her death was suspicious.'

Lamorna interjected.

'Well, it's only surmise but Natasha wrote to Demelza's mother implying that there may have been people who meant her harm.'

'Natasha came here on several occasions. She was desperate to find Rebecca. But she had also discovered that Ivan was not her father.'

Lamorna and I both gasped in horror at this revelation.

'Do you know who the father was?' I asked dreading the answer. I remembered my grandfather's deathbed summons to Natasha. My heart was pounding furiously.

'I have no idea. Natasha didn't tell me. Ivan accused Vera of adultery. I believe there were problems sexually and Vera found comfort elsewhere but she was a very private person. I didn't know her well. Ivan vented his anger and frustration in physical abuse – both to Natasha and to Vera. I often thought it a blessing that my Rebecca was spared that. Godfrey and I never laid a finger on her ever. We treated her well.'

Another bout of sobbing overwhelmed Rachel. We realised we could get no further so we thanked her and left.

I wondered whether Rebecca had had friends. Nobody disappears without trace, surely?

'Did you know about Arthur's confession to Natasha, Aunt?' I asked.

'What confession?'

'Grandma told me that he summoned Natasha to his side when he knew he was dying and told her something that upset her terribly.'

'And you believe my father could be Natasha's father also?'

'I don't know, Aunt, but something upset Natasha and it was something he only wanted her to know. Grandma has no clue and I'm not about to suggest it to her now!'

'God, no, it would kill her,' agreed Lamorna. 'I must get those Russian documents and diaries translated quickly. Maybe they hold a clue. I wonder if Ivan suspected?'

'Oh Aunt – this is all so awful my dad being Tristan's dad and now this. I feel completely incapacitated by the enormity of it all.'

'Look let's go and get a warm drink somewhere and calm down and think what is practical to do next,' she suggested.

I tried to compose myself.

'I want to see BJ. Let's go to Plumtree Hall.'

'I can't see what that'll achieve other than upsetting you further.'

'I'll take the risk, Aunt.'

About twenty minutes later I found myself outside the gates of Plumtree Hall. I pressed the buzzer firmly. Eventually a voice said, 'Who is it?'

'Ferguson,' I replied, 'It's Demelza Lowe. Can I speak to you?'

He hesitated. 'I will meet you outside, Miss Lowe.'

The gates slid open soundlessly. I walked into the forecourt. As they closed behind me, I felt a sense of panic. Did the butler have evil intentions? Was he a secret KGB agent sent to infiltrate the Lawson family? The unmistakable form of the obsequious Ferguson emerged from the mansion.

'What is it I can help you with? Mr Lawson is away from home.'

'Do you know where I can reach him?' I enquired sweetly.

'I'm afraid I do not, Miss.'

There was a sound of smashing glass from inside the house. Ferguson had left the front door wide open. Seizing my chance, I made a dash for it. As I scampered past him, up the stairs and into the hall, I could hear him lumbering after me. Voices were coming from the next floor, female and male. I tore up the stairs two at a time, my heart racing. Ferguson was yelling at me to stop. Barely a second later, a door opened and out stepped Natasha.

I stood stock still.

Her beautiful chestnut hair, now flecked with white had been cropped short; it looked jagged and uneven. Her clothing was hanging off her. At her shoulder, stood the master of the house, fenland artist BJ Lawson, himself. She looked changed, diminished.

It was Natasha who regained her equilibrium first.

'It's alright, Ferguson. Let us take it from here.'

Natasha's voice was deeper than I remembered.

'So, you have discovered our lair,' BJ said with a wry smile.

Natasha looked at me and smiled. Behind the smile, I sensed malice.

'We are both very grateful to you and Ruth. You have both gone above and ....'

I cut in.

'You've been here since 21st December I presume?'

She nodded, without batting an eyelid.

'How have you deduced this, Demelza?' BJ looked at me curiously. He was still a slime-ball.

'I could sense somebody was looking at me on the day of the so-called funeral. Perhaps you'd have the grace to tell me exactly who is in the coffin?

Natasha sighed.

I tried to remain focussed; then I let rip.

'Just to sum up, Natasha: Ren nearly died having been struck down by some voodoo weirdo in New Orleans. I was similarly affected by the same individual. Our cat was murdered. Your son-in-law is dead; your private detective bit the dust. We have expended money and time trying to find your would-be killer. Your darling son, my half-brother is being two-timed by his charming partner Izzie. Your father, died a few weeks ago. Your elder son sweet-talked his way into my bed, then chucked me out like a stained floor-cloth the following morning. So, ain't life a peach?'

There was a flicker of an emotion that was hard to place on Natasha's face. Somewhere to the side of me, I sensed the butler's gaze.

'Ferguson, be a dear and get us some tea, would you?'

'I don't want bloody tea, Natasha. My mother agreed to help you because she still loves you. Your friendship means that much despite all the shit you have put her through. I adored you... once. Now I find you utterly despicable.'

'I understand your anger, Mel. You and I always had a special bond. I love your mother. I also love BJ. Without his support and considerable influence, this might have turned out very differently. Ferguson has been our rock.'

The butler bowed his head.

'How did you persuade the world and his wife that it was Natasha in the coffin?'

He shrugged as if his major deception was an insignificant peccadillo.

'Friends in high places. I have some standing in the community, Demelza.'

Natasha began again.

'If those pursuing me have any notion that the body in the coffin is not mine, they will redouble their efforts to kill me. The people involved are ruthless and leave no trace; we are in far deeper waters than we thought.'

'I and my family are! You are cocooned here with not a care in the world.'

'You think I am impervious to your distress and the losses you have suffered. But surely you can see we need to get these people incarcerated and we cannot go through the normal channels in order to do so.'

'No, I don't see, Natasha. We could involve the police, for example... now wouldn't that be radical?'

She shook her head vehemently.

'We need concrete evidence, Mel. We are practising pagans, outcasts from society. Surely you of all people should know that?'

I was struggling to cope with her soothing tones, her platitudes and utter disregard for what she had done. I had a deep desire to hurt her.

'Let me guess, is it your twin in the coffin. Identical and easily passed off as you?'

She nodded.

'Have you no moral compass? Your father is dead. We went to his funeral along with Rachel who apparently felt something for him.'

'I cannot mourn the death of a man who was never a father to me in act or deed.'

'Indeed. I have just had a very interesting chat with Rachel and I discovered that Ivan is not your father. But... my own grandfather, Arthur, might be your father and Ludmila's. Have I hit the nail on the head?'

A flash of something resembling puzzlement appeared on Natasha's face but it vanished as quickly as it had come. I was perplexed. Was I wrong about my grandfather's confession after all?

Natasha was watching me closely.

'Was Rebecca actually pregnant or was that fabricated too?' I blurted suddenly.

'She was no longer Rebecca. She had reverted to Mila. She was looking forward to becoming a mother despite the risks. Na... well... I was about to introduce Mila to Ginny ...'

She turned away. I stood in silence, my thoughts racing. BJ was regarding her curiously.

She whirled round. 'Ludmila visited Morwenna. I needed to know about poisons.'

That explained Wenna's feeling that 'Natasha' had a pregnant 'aura.' Had Ludmila deceived Wenna entirely? Something here was not ringing true.

'I thought you were an expert in healing herbs, Natasha? Iris said you had a gift.'

I enunciated the words very slowly to give maximum impact. It worked.

Natasha changed tack, immediately.

'Mel, tell me about what happened in New Orleans. I know Ren ended up in hospital. Lance contacted BJ.'

'How did he know?' I enquired feebly.

'I'm afraid I didn't ask.'

I recounted Vivienne's part in the voodoo. I told her that Lamorna was getting Ivan's documents translated into English adding that we now hoped to cast light on who her father was. I felt this gave her ample opportunity to come clean on what my grandfather had told her. Instead, she sat in deep reflection.

'Maybe Izzie has become embroiled in this. It is written in Arthurian legend that Isolde was unfaithful to Tristan. Morgan le Fey was evil.

Faye is Joodee's mother, Morgana her daughter. Are they and Izzie connected?'

'This is not some fairy story from times of yore, Natasha,' I said bitterly. 'This is real life. People are dying and you wax lyrical about some legendary being and your fates being intertwined – it's all claptrap!'

'Nevertheless, as it says in the legends, so it must be.'

'Oh, please, Natasha, cut the crap.'

Her eyes flashed angrily.

'Presumably since you have stolen two very important, treasured tomes connected to Arthurian legend you are well aware of all the *claptrap*!'

I studied her face closely. It was a mask. I was convinced that she was hiding something. Was she truly crazy as her offspring believed?

Her eyes bored through me.

'What happened at Tunman Wood, Natasha?'

I wanted to wind this up. How long could I leave Lamorna without her trying to gain access?

'As I told you, I wanted to reconcile with Guinevere and introduce her to Ludmila, so I chose Tunman – no big deal about it,' she barked. 'I was unavoidably delayed. I arrived. There was no sign of Ginny. Luckily, I know the woods well. I went in and eventually I found the body – blood everywhere. I had the presence of mind to touch nothing. I took a gamble. I called BJ. To my relief he came to my aid. Nobody was around. We agreed a plan. He told me to drive back to Plumtree Hall and he would deal with everything. I left at once, forgetting Ginny, in my anguish; I suspect she chickened out.'

'No, she didn't; she saw her father emerging from the wood,' I told her. 'BJ neglected to inform you that I called him and asked a few searching questions?'

BJ walked over to the window turning his back on his wife.

'Tell me more, Demelza,' murmured Natasha looking in puzzlement at her husband's back.

'Ginny thought her father looked furtive. When she heard you were dead, she suspected him at once.'

'Poor Ginny. What she must have gone through.'

Again, I was left with the quandary of who to believe. Was she really in ignorance of my call? Which one of them was lying? Or were they both lying?

'Mel, I hope you and Lance can reconcile. You would be good for him. How is Mackenzie?'

'Oh, yes, Natasha, don't let's forget your one-night stand?' I retorted.

She ignored the barb.

'I spoke to him before Yule and asked him to give a letter to Tris confessing it all.'

I no longer felt like making small talk. Picking up my bag, I muttered, 'I'm going.'

Natasha grabbed my arm.

'Not one word to a living soul if you value your life,' she hissed. 'Nobody is to know I am here and still alive. Got it?'

Shaking like a leaf, I nodded and made my escape.

Ferguson was nowhere in sight but the gate creaked open as I approached and I sidled out.

I could see Lamorna's car still parked where I had left her. She had fallen asleep.

'Well, what did you find out?' she asked, immediately alert.

'That Ferguson can talk the hind legs off a donkey. We need to get working on Ivan's Russian link.'

'Do you still want to go to those woods?' she asked.

I shook my head.

The next day we drove back to Exeter.

Not for the first time, I was questioning what on earth I was doing.

My family were more interested in upholding the Wicca festivities than supporting me.

That night, Lance called. He had received a frantic message from his sister. Ginny had been abducted. Could I go to Crystal Palace and give him a hand?

He had one hell of a nerve! I felt on the brink of a precipice into which I would inevitably plunge.

Guinevere

'So it befell in the month of May, Queen Guinevere called unto her knights of the Table Round and she gave them warning that upon the morrow she would ride a-Maying…'

Then the queen stole away… she went to Almesbury; and there she let make herself nun, and ware white clothes and black…'

Le Morte D'Arthur by Sir Thomas Malory

'Guinevere had golden hair, Mum. Why am I called Guinevere? My hair is dark.' It was the first serious question her daughter had asked her. Natasha's laugh tinkled around the room. 'King Arthur must have had a queen. How she may have looked or what colour her hair was is a mystery. It's probably a mis-translation because the word, *fair* meant beautiful, and not a colour at all. Guinevere means *fair one*. You should ask Demelza's grandfather about it. He's the expert.'

Arthur was unhelpful. All he could say was that Guinevere must have been quite a woman to have married so noble a king. And with that, Ginny had to be content.

Her father said 'their Guinevere' was special because she had been made at a very special time – a time when Mummy and Daddy really loved one another. Evidently Ginny was to interpret this as meaning that now they had fallen out of love. So, she asked her brother. Lance muttered angrily that they were always arguing. It got worse after Kai's death, he told her.

'Tell me about Kai,' pleaded Ginny.

'It's too long ago. I can't remember.'

It was a lie: the truth was too painful.

Tristan was no use. Mother spoiled Tristan.

During her teens the arguing between her mother and father got much worse. Lance left for university, and didn't come back. Ginny ran wild. She was the talk of the village with her outrageous behaviour. She painted her toenails and fingernails black and then sought out some black lipstick, for good measure. She stayed out all hours hanging around seedy pubs and clubs, smoking, drinking, having partners of both sexes just to be difficult. Then she met Rick. At thirty, he was a sophisticated man-of-the-world with an ostentatiously sporty car and a lot of money. She was sixteen.

'We're getting married,' she announced.

'That's great, darling,' said her father, absent-mindedly.

'What?' shrieked her mother.

Another battle ensued.

BJ turned up at the Register Office to give his consent. Natasha had sent hers by proxy. The ceremony was short. The couple sped off to Monaco and her father placed an announcement in The Times. Rick had a brilliant job, earned shed-loads of money – or so Ginny told her friends. One day her mother called in unexpectedly. Rick was away somewhere – he could be very vague at times - Ginny had just come to accept it. Natasha stormed in, her face like thunder.

'Do you know the provenance of your husband's ill-gotten gains, young lady?' she screeched.

'He's in finance – not sure exactly what he does. Money's so boring. He's in Zurich right now, I think.'

'A harmless little gnome.' Her mother's voice was laden with sarcasm.

'Gnome?' queried Ginny.

'Oh, Christ, forget it!' Her mother was exasperated. 'He's into animal experimentation – vivisection, to be precise.'

'Don't be silly, Mum.'

Ginny refused to believe it, although it was true her husband did seem to have an aversion to animals, especially cats, now that she came to think about it.

'Vivisection – the cutting up of innocent creatures whilst they are still alive,' her mother spat.

'I know what it means, Mum.' Ginny sighed. 'Where's your evidence?'

'I refuse to betray a confidence but he is guilty as charged. How can you live with this monster?'

'Can't be worse than living with you,' Ginny exploded.

Natasha slammed the door behind her. Ginny didn't see her mother again for eighteen months.

Ginny met Mike Mills one evening in London. He and Rick worked together.

'Your choice, Sis,' said Lance, 'but it's a dangerous game you're playing. Remember our parents?'

'Pot and black springs to mind, Bro!' Ginny replied, indignantly.

'What'll happen should you get preggers?' he asked.

'More than I'll ever do from Rick's endeavours,' she responded, bitterly.

Lance raised his eyebrows.

But of course, Lance was right – partially. Rick was tipped off.

'He went ballistic,' said Ginny, when she called her best friend, the day after the event. 'Mike's been sacked.'

But it appeared that Mike's affection for her wasn't that deep, after all. He found a replacement for Ginny and then he found another job.

Ginny drowned her sorrows in red wine and promiscuity. Unable to cope, she took some pills but not enough. Rick returned. She was a danger to herself. They put her in a locked ward.

Six months later, she joined an amateur dramatics group. She was good and 'starred' in local productions. After RADA, she strutted her stuff on the stages of the West End.

One day in May, when the trees were awash with pink blossom and a pale, watery sun was bravely attempting to pierce the paper-thin clouds overhead, they came for her. She had barely emerged from the shower, when she heard a loud rat-a-tat-tat on the door. Clad only in a dressing gown, her hair swept up in a towel, she slipped downstairs to answer. Two men stood before her. The taller had red hair; his face was covered in freckles. The other was a journalist, he said. He wanted to ask some questions about her current production. Ginny widened the door and told them to go on up. Once in the lounge, the two of them sat down.

'I'll just get dressed. Make yourselves a drink,' she added, pointing in the direction of the kitchen.

When she returned, the man's tone was different.

'I'm afraid we have to be a little forceful. We need to know about your husband. You can supply us with all the information we require.'

With that, his accomplice sprang to his feet and produced a length of rope. Ginny began to protest.

'Look I have no idea what all this is about but...'

'Your friend Mills had a very unfortunate knack of opening his mouth to the wrong people. Have you heard from him recently?'

Did she detect a trace of Texan drawl? Ginny was well-attuned to nuances of accent.

Before she could scream, they had pre-empted her. A scarf was wound tightly round her mouth; she could barely breathe.

At that precise moment, the doorbell rang.

'One word and you're dead,' hissed the man.

The doorbell pealed again.

'Answer it. Come straight back.'

The 'Texan' nodded to his accomplice. The red-haired man removed the rope and scarf at once.

Thoughts flashed through her mind. Rick had tried to contact her and warn her – of what? She had intended to return his call. Then Rick was dead.

A familiar voice called through the door, 'Ginny, I need to speak to you.'

Her brother stood there, encased in a sopping raincoat. Thinking fast, she took his arm, closed the door quietly behind them and pulled him frantically down the path. The rain was sheeting down.

'What the hell is going on?' he asked. 'Shh! Run.'

They reached the safety of the park.

'Call the police!'

He obeyed at once. She snatched the phone.

'Two men are in my flat. They have tried to abduct me.'

When they arrived, the police forced entry into Ginny's flat but found no trace.

'I have to warn you, Madam that hoax calls are taken very seriously.'

'This wasn't a hoax,' she replied.

'Did you recognise these men?'

Ginny admitted that she did not. The description she offered gave them little to go on.

'If you see these gentlemen again, inform us and we will take necessary action.'

Lance insisted she come and stay with him for a few days. Ginny contacted Mel. When there was no answer, she contacted Ruth. Was Ren still involved with Mike Mills? In terse tones Ruth informed her that currently Ren and her sister were in New Orleans and Ren was fighting for her life.

It was two and a half months later when they came for Ginny again. She was getting ready for bed. This time there were no niceties, no warning. She was picked up bodily and bundled into a waiting BMW. They drove off at speed.

Ginny was terrified. Her mobile was in the pocket of her jeans. Neither man had thought to divest her of it as yet. Could she send a text to Lance?

Her opportunity came when the car stopped abruptly at a service station. The man with the red hair got out of the car. The other stayed behind the wheel. He seemed to be gone a while; the man in the front was immobile. Had he fallen asleep? Gradually, she pulled her phone from her pocket. Painstakingly, she tapped out a brief text: 'Help. In car at services.'

She saw 'red-hair' approaching the car. Hastily she shoved her phone back in her pocket. The engine started up once more.

Summons

I arrived at Lance's house shortly before midday. He opened the door at once and ushered me inside.

He showed me his phone. I digested the contents of the text and slumped onto the nearest chair.

'Do you know who these people are?' I asked.

'I have a good idea it's the same guys who tried to abduct her before. You were in New Orleans at the time. We called the police but... Ginny was unable to give any concrete details and they were long gone by the time police arrived.'

'Perhaps we need to contact them again?' I suggested.

'I fear that would only add fuel to the flames. Reckon we are dealing with very dangerous individuals.'

'I consider that good enough reason to get professional help.'

'Do you want my sister to die?'

'There have been more than enough deaths already, Lance. Let's look at this logically. We have no idea which road she's on and where the services are. The police have means of locating people in these situations. It makes sense.'

He began pacing the floor. My mobile rang. It was Lamorna.

'I have news on the documents,' she announced. 'Ivan's father had links to an underground network in the Soviet Union. His father Leopold was involved in the murder of a Russian woman named Mishka working for the Americans. Mishka was the wife of Alexander Levitov. who was given safe passage to the US. Unlike his father Leopold, Ivan was not a political animal. He became disenchanted with the regime in Russia. When Ivan's wife and child died in mysterious circumstances, the authorities refused all help. At that point Ivan came to England.'

'Interesting. Grandma told us that Ivan's first wife died in childbirth.'

'Not according to the diaries. Anyway, it would appear that these people have long memories.'

'Fifty years ago, maybe more, Lamorna?'

'Nevertheless Mel. It's my belief that we are meddling in very dangerous matters.'

'But surely Levitov would be extremely elderly by now and incapable of carrying out spurious vendettas?'

'Even so I think it is highly likely that Natasha's murder is connected. Why else would Ivan hide the documents so closely? Mel, you must go to the police now; this has gone far enough.'

'Aunt, did you find anything else out about the past?'

I tried to keep my words succinct. I didn't want Lance to know his mother might well have the same grandfather as Ren and I.

She twigged immediately and murmured quietly, 'No, Ivan voiced his fears regarding Vera but no names were mentioned.'

'What was all that about?' asked Lance when the call had ended.

I told him what I knew about Ivan's father's connections.

'It adds up, Lance. These men are going to extraordinary lengths to get the information they need and the deaths of three people connected to Natasha cannot be coincidental. Lamorna is insistent we go to the police.'

'We need to find Ginny. We have no clue where they are taking her. She could be on a plane to Russia by now!'

'Let's go to the police, Lance,' I pleaded.

'No – not until I've tried to find Ginny myself. If the police are too heavy-handed, she might be in even more danger.

Reluctantly, I conceded and tried to focus.

'What did Ginny tell you about the two men who abducted her?'

'One had red hair and freckles and was quite tall. The other did all the talking and had a Texan accent.'

Mark, Izzie's slimy friend had red hair and freckles. I recalled his stammer and declared, 'I think I may have met one of them.'

'Would you care to divulge more?' Lance hissed.

'Do you want me to go?'

'Sorry.'

'There was a guy working for Izzie as a gardener. He meets the description and has a pronounced stutter. He wouldn't want to talk, would he?'

'Would a gardener be involved in something as dangerous as this? Does he seem like a Russian spy?'

'I've had little experience of Russian spies!'

I told Lance of my midnight encounter with Izzie.

'Shall we pay Tristan a visit? Lance asked.

'If you can keep your tempers with one another,' I replied.

'If Ginny is there, God knows what they will be doing to her. She may be at the bottom of some lake by now.'

'If Ginny is at Ringmore Heights, Lance, which I somehow doubt, then Tris will be involved.'

Lance drove without stopping. When we arrived the Baskerville pups were there to greet us. Lance hammered at the door.

Izzie appeared at once.

'Where's my sister?' Lance demanded peremptorily.

'How the hell should I know? Maybe I should ask you where Tristan is?'

'Don't you know where he is?' I asked.

He shook his head. 'He left hours ago. We had a disagreement.'

'Care to tell us what that was about?' Lance had dispensed with any attempt at politeness.

Izzie looked abashed. 'I have been having a bit of a thing with Dora.'

'A bit of a thing? 'Lance echoed. 'And who the fuck is Dora?'

I remembered the three of them on Shaldon Bridge: Izzie, Mark and Dora.

'Where are Dora and Mark?' I rapped out.

'I have no idea.'

'We suspect they have abducted Ginny,' I replied.

I could hear the distant wail of a siren. It was getting nearer. We all stood stock still as a police car swerved into the driveway. Two uniformed officers emerged, looking grave.

'Mr Isaacs?' asked one of them. 'Could we go inside? Are these people friends or casual callers, Sir?'

'We are related to Izzie's partner,' I explained.

'Izzie, being...'

'Sorry, I mean Mr Isaacs,' I muttered.

'I see.'

The five of us trooped into the hallway, our footsteps echoing eerily on the flagstones.

'I'm afraid we have extremely bad news concerning Mr Lawson. A body has been found in Dozmary Pool. We believe it to be Mr Tristan Lawson. We need you to identify him.'

Izzie broke down completely. I looked across at Lance. His face was expressionless. I reached for his hand. He took it away at once.

I wrestled with my tears wondering if I should tell these officers that Ginny was also missing. Had she met the same fate? Lance gave me no clue as to how I should proceed. The silence seemed interminable.

After a while the officer in charge stood up.

'Are you ready to come with us, Mr Isaacs?'

Izzie nodded mutely.

'Do you want us to come? I asked tentatively.

He shook his head. Lance and I stood up and made our way back to the car. There seemed nothing we could do.

We sat in the front seats saying not a word.

Would the police be making their way to Plumtree Hall to tell BJ of the death of his *son*? What would happen if the police discovered Natasha there? Would we be arrested as accomplices to a crime? Did I need to alert my mother? What about my dad? Tristan was his child. Perhaps most pertinent of all: had Tristan taken his own life, having discovered his partner's infidelity or was it more sinister?

I broke the silence first.

'Lance, I'm going to take a train to Cornwall. I need to see my mother.'

'Did you hear me? I repeated.

'Loud and clear. Go! I'm sure there'll be a station a few miles down the road.'

He stopped the car, leaned across me and opened the door.

Without a word, I slung my bag over my shoulder and trudged down the road. The callous words of the man I had believed myself to be in love with echoed in my ears. I thought of my mother: 'That man is without emotion; he is capable of anything.'

I could see a sign ahead. TAUNTON. On an impulse I phoned for a cab.

'I need to go to the local police station,' I said.

Ten minutes later I was pouring out the entire scenario: Natasha Lawson was not dead but her twin probably was. She was 'holed up' in the family home near Boston, Lincolnshire with her husband BJ. Rick Morrison's death had most likely been suspicious and they needed to contact the Swiss authorities. Tristan's death was more than likely not suicide but foul play. His lover was in league with a guy who might be a Russian spy who was on a mission to wipe out our family and the Lawsons. I added that Tristan's sister Ginny had just been abducted by two men who I suspected were close friends of Tom Isaacs.

The two officers looked incredulous. The elder of the two who had announced herself as Sergeant Clarke began to repeat what I had just recounted. After each utterance she asked: 'Correct?'

I answered in the affirmative to every query. She turned to her colleague: 'Get on the blower to Boston will you, Ted?'

Before they let me leave, I had to give assurances that I would not leave the country (as if!) and that, wasting police time was a serious offence, and covering up information about a supposed death equally so.

I felt deflated rather than reassured and wondered at the wisdom of my impulsive outpouring, given Natasha's hissed threat as I left Plumtree Hall. Had it come about as a result of my anger at Lance's complete indifference – feeling like a pawn in his game? Would there be dire consequences? I decided I no longer cared. I'd hit rock bottom.

Back at Pen-Towan, Ren, was draped all in green. My words as I entered the house had the desired effect.

'Tristan's killed himself.'

'Jesus Christ!' she screeched,

'Most un-goddess-like,' I muttered angrily.

My mother appeared with Iris close behind.

'I've just left the cop shop in Taunton and told them everything. Could someone get me a coffee? I haven't eaten all day. Whilst you have been prancing around a bunch of fucking standing stones, I have been to hell and back in a hopeless attempt to solve the mystery of Natasha's murder which wasn't her murder at all but the murder of her innocent twin.'

'WHAT?' screamed my mother.

'Oh yes, Mother dear, she and BJ are holed up in Plumtree Hall as right as ninepence! Currently, we have a total of five dead bodies and possibly two more not to mention a dead cat, and several caged birds and prize chickens – all because of whatever the hell went on several decades ago with Ivan Rodomski and his gutless daughter. Why isn't she trying to solve this? To save her own skin, that's why, while the rest of us pile up the corpses.'

My sister was doing a quick count on her fingers.

'Morrison, Adam, Tristan, Neil, Ivan, and the corpse in the Boston Cemetery...that's six; who else?' she asked.

'Your ex possibly, and possibly Ginny by now.'

'James is very much alive. I saw him with some bimbo in town yesterday.'

'Mike Mills,' I retorted.

'He's dead?' asked Mum.

'More than likely. The men who abducted Ginny said Mills had poked his nose in where it wasn't wanted and would get what he deserved.'

In an attempt to lessen the statistics, Ren said, 'that stuff in New Orleans wasn't linked to Natasha's death, Neil's was suicide and Tristan too. Morrison's death was because he owed money to some bloke.'

'You really are a complete moron,' I screamed. 'It IS linked to Natasha: Hated by all and we are in the firing line. As Mum's darling friend knows too well. She actually threatened me! Told me not to say a word or else!'

'Natasha is not the woman I once knew,' said my mother quietly.

'You don't say, Mother!' I retorted. 'Ekelberg, Morrison's probable killer, knew about Natasha, Neil hated her, so did Vivienne and Izzie who is mixed up with this bunch of crooks. AND YOU ARE TRYING TO EXONERATE THAT BITCH FROM THE WHOLE FUCKING MESS.'

My mother stared at the ceiling for a few seconds.

'I'm going to call your father.'

I was left alone with *Artemis*, whose coronet of yellow rose buds was beginning to droop alarmingly. I sipped my coffee and ignored her.

When Mum came back into the room, I could tell she had been crying.

'Your father is getting the first plane over.'

'Lovely, we can all play at happy families,' I said.

'Mel, there is no point in behaving like this. I shall bring some crystals back from the shop; they will re-energise us.'

'More crystals, that'll do the trick – especially when the full force of the law descends upon us.'

BJ called my mobile at nine o'clock. There was no mention of a police visit. Had they decided to ignore me? Or was BJ checking up on me?

'Natasha is hysterical. She says it is written in the stars. Tristan kills himself for love of the fair Isolde.'

'Looks like Ginny's doomed then,' I replied, 'she'll be joining a nunnery next.'

'Lancelot fathers a child and abandons the damsel, who kills herself in despair, I believe,' came the rejoinder.

The next morning, I awoke to birdsong and for a moment I imagined that life had returned to the run-of the-mill existence I had known once a life-time ago.

Just as Mother had set off for the airport to collect Dad, the phone rang. I reached mechanically to answer.

It was Lance.

'It's Ginny.'

'Is she dead?' I asked, sure the response would be in the affirmative.

'She's been severely burned - an acid attack.'

'What?' I screeched. 'Who did it?'

'Red hair, freckles... ring a bell?'

I groaned.

'Where's his accomplice?' I enquired.

'Accomplice?'

'Dora? Isadora or whatever he calls himself.'

'Mel, I know I have behaved appallingly badly, can you be with me?'

'No chance.'

I hung up.

I couldn't believe it. Two of Natasha's children either dead or nearing death, in the space of two days. Surely the woman would come clean now? And surely the police would take me seriously and be in touch?

My sister sat down heavily in the chair. Then suddenly there seemed to be an epiphany. Solemnly, she removed the withered coronet and said soberly,

'Mel, what is wrong with me? That voodoo business unhinged me.'

She tore off the green silken garment and reached into the cupboard behind her. She dragged out the fluorescent jogging bottoms and a top, donned a pair of trainers from the floor next to the dog's bowl and announced, 'I'm going running.'

The next day Sam called. Joodee had returned full of remorse. I enquired if she knew that her former friend was in hospital with little hope of survival. He confessed that she did but had made no comment.

'Zennor is swarming with journos trying to get the dirt on the family. Gotta go!'

When Ren returned, she was glowing and breathless.

In the interim, Lamorna had offered us both a summer job at the University.

The frantic barking of Growler announced the arrival of my parents.

Dad burst into the room like an Icelandic geyser. He greeted us both in his booming baritone and beamed down at my mother who was looking up at him adoringly.

'Your mother and I have decided to take a little break away together. We are through with Natasha.'

'He knows?' I mouthed to my mother.

'I do indeed, honey, and the whole thing stinks.'

'We've got a job working with Lamorna,' announced my twin. 'We'll leave you two lovebirds alone.'

'Well don't leave on our account,' he replied.

When the doorbell sounded Ren went to answer it, along with Growler, yapping ferociously.

'Can I help you?' we heard her ask.

We heard a voice reply, 'Can I come in for a few minutes?'

'Are you from the Press?' I heard her ask tentatively.

'Ren, it's me,' came the response.

'Mike?' Ren stuttered.

I marched to the door.

There stood a man I didn't recognise. His head was shaved; a straggly beard adorned his face. He was wearing dark glasses and the collar of his coat was pulled up around his ears despite it being nearly the end of July. If I hadn't been so depressed, I would have laughed out loud.

Ren ushered him in without a word.

He refused all offers of coffee but plonked down wearily in the chair. Purple bruises were visible beneath one eye. Ren's hand flew to her mouth.

'What happened to you?' she asked.

'Seems I offended a couple of blokes. I haven't much time so I will be brief,' he announced. 'Ginny and I had an affair when I was working for Rick Morrison.'

'You told us you barely knew the man,' I shouted.

'I lied' he stated, matter-of-factly.

'Who doesn't?' I retorted bitterly.

Mills continued.

'I was fired when he found out. It was I who tipped Natasha off about Rick and what he was involved in. I discovered from my cousin Adam that he was working for Natasha as a private detective.'

'Ah, kept quiet about that one too.' I muttered.

He ignored me.

'I took it upon myself to try to find out more. I knew Rachel and Natasha were in touch and I knew why. I tried to help you Ren by taking you to her but sadly Rachel wasn't playing ball. I knew she'd have information about Ivan's past.'

'She did,' I said.

Mills took a moment to digest this, let it pass and then continued.

'I called you when I heard of Adam's death. It had to be murder but how could I go to the police without putting myself and others in even more danger? Ginny has been horrifically injured. The death toll is mounting: We need to pool our resources. Ivan was involved in some dodgy business in the former USSR. Those people are intent on revenge. Rick was working with ricin, a favoured murder weapon of the former KGB. He was supplying it to a man named Nikolai Levitov. The latter is in the UK living under an alias. I believe he has a woman with him.'

My father looked dumbstruck

'What your connection is to my daughter I do not know but I will tell you one thing right now. There is no way my girls, or my family, are going to get messed up in some Russian spook saga. I'm sorry but I have to ask you to leave right now and do not ever contact this family again.'

Mills stood up and walked to the door. we all stood in absolute silence. My mother's voice broke through.

'I have been blind where Natasha is concerned. Take me away for a few days, Mac. When we come back, we will go to the police and corroborate what Demelza told the Devon branch. Then maybe we can all rest in our beds at night.'

Things were starting to fall into place. The noxious plant being cultivated at Ringmore Heights was clearly a feeble attempt to mimic the ricin being produced by Morrison. It was incredible that somebody as seemingly low key as Ivan could be mixed up with Russian spies. Even more incredible, that after all these years people were still seeking revenge on a man now dead in an attempt to exterminate his entire family as well as anyone connected with it. To what end?

I made a snap decision.

'Ren, we have not investigated LARA. I have a sneaky suspicion that they might have information that might prove useful. I also want to go to Tunman Woods. Are you up for it? We can go straight to Lamorna's when we've done.'

The following day we checked into a cheap hotel a stone's throw from Lincoln station and set about hiring a car.

The LARA office was seedy and located in a side street where down-and-outs accosted us left, right and centre. I rang the bell and stated our names giving a half-baked comment about being interested in joining the group.

Behind the desk sat a bearded older man wrapped in a voluminous tartan poncho.

'I'm a friend of Natasha Lawson. We wondered if you had any information. When was the last time you saw her?'

'Striking woman... so tragic that she died. You need to speak to Clem and Nancy. They knew her well. I can give you a contact number. I know they won't mind. They were really cut up about it all.'

Nancy turned out to be really friendly and told us she and Clem would meet us in an hour. She gave the name of a vegetarian restaurant and café near the River Witham. I told her I would be there with my twin.

As soon as we walked in, she and Clem spotted us and they both stood and beckoned us over.

She extended a hand.

'Fairly obvious you two are twins,' she remarked.

We got to the point at once.

Nancy brushed a wisp of mousy-brown hair from her eyes.

'Yeah, Natahsa was absolutely adorable. So charismatic. Played down the cosmetics empire… just wanted to help the cause. Donated, helped fundraise, came on demos with us, the lot.'

'Yes, I think you met her daughter and husband Rick Morrison,' I ventured.

'Slimy bastard! Hated him on sight. Homophobic, misogynistic, vile.' Clem tossed a green braid of hair over his shoulder and snorted in disgust.

'That's him,' agreed Ren.

'Ginny was ok though,' said Clem. 'And that bloke Mike, he seemed ok, too. Very enamoured of Natasha, clearly.'

'What!' screeched my sister.

Clem looked dismayed.

'Sorry, do you know him?'

We admitted we did and Ren gave a brief description.

'Yep, that's the man,' said Nancy.

I was unsure how to proceed and Ren was silent and thoughtful.

'Did you know Natasha's twin?' I asked.

'Absolutely! Mila! They were carbon copies. I could never tell them apart. The only clue was that Mila was withdrawn. Can't put my finger on it, but Clem and I didn't feel we could trust her. There often seemed to be tension between them.'

There was moment's silence.

'Yeah, then there was that peculiar woman with the purple hair,' Clem added. 'She seemed to have a fascination with Natasha and Mila… as if she couldn't quite work out why they looked the same. We wondered if there was something wrong with her.'

'Morgana?' I asked.

'We never knew her name but she hung around outside the office a lot. She never spoke. Rod tried to engage with her, just a harmless comment, but she just fled like a bat out of hell. Most bizarre.'

'Have you seen Mila recently,' I enquired.

'No, but then that's nothing new. She often disappeared for weeks on end. We never knew where she'd gone. Natasha could shed no light on it either.'

'Have you any idea where she lived?' asked Ren who had suddenly shaken herself out of her reverie.

'Somewhere on Pond Street up the hill, I think.'

'Was she a member of LARA?' I asked.

'No, I think Natasha tried to encourage her to join but she wouldn't. Just before she died, Natasha had been really excited about Ginny meeting Mila. She thought it'd be the start of Mila coming out of her shell... but sadly I don't think it ever happened.'

'Was this at Tunman Woods?' asked Ren.

'I really don't know the ins and outs. Anyway, if you want, I could direct you to Pond Steet?' Nancy offered.

'That'd be great.'

Half an hour later, having exhausted ourselves climbing a one-in- four, Ren and I were in Pond Street.

Ren marched up to the nearest passerby and asked whether she knew a woman called Mila and if so where she might live.

Several passersby later we were still out of luck and about to give up when a man emerged from a shop.

'Excuse me – you're asking about Mila? She lives at number 37a. Haven't seen her in a while.'

Number 37a was further up the hill. We knocked at the door.

'Yes?'

'We're looking for Mila.'

'She cleared out months ago. No forwarding address. Some bloke in a van came and picked up all her stuff, settled the rent and that's the last we heard of her.'

'Do you have description of this man?' I asked.

'Fat, red-faced, dressed in a boiler suit. Foreign.'

'What did the van look like? Company logo?' asked Ren

'Nope, just a bog-standard white van. Not very big. Mila didn't have much.'

We gave up and made our way to Tunman Woods. Why had Mila decided to up-sticks and disappear? Was it because her twin had died? Or was she too linked to the possible murder? Didn't Nancy say there had been tension between them?

We parked up and entered the woods. They seemed unremarkable although pretty, with made-up paths, crowded with walkers, dogs and kids on bikes. If we hoped to glean anything more about Natasha's mysterious end, we were sadly frustrated. As we had been told, there were labyrinthine paths leading in all directions. It had been many months since the body had been found.

We made our way back to Exeter, deflated and miserable.

Bedouin licked us furiously – having nearly felled us both by leaping up with his not inconsiderable weight and shoving us backwards with his not inconsiderable sized paws!

'When do we start the job?' Ren demanded to know at once.

Lamorna smiled. 'I think, in 'witchy' parlance, it will be Lammas.'

'She's hung up her bow and arrow, Aunt,' I replied.

'What bow and arrow?' enquired Ren.

'Weren't you Artemis?'

'Oh yeah.' Ren snatched a biscuit from a plate on the table and bit into it hungrily. An enormous, hairy face looked at her, pleadingly.

On Saturday morning Lance arrived. I had no idea how he discovered my whereabouts and was exasperated.

'Mel, I am not going to give you up this easily. I am totally in love with you. After Elaine... well, enough said.'

'I have no idea who Elaine is. You're the last thing I need right now.'

I made to slam the door on him.'

He wedged his foot inside.

'Yeah, we share a half-brother, now deceased.'

And you're blissfully unaware of the other little connection we might have I thought to myself.

'Let's go for a drive,' he said, 'I'll explain.'

Lancelot

'"Sir," she said, I am Elaine, the daughter of King Pelles"... and therewith he took her up in his arms and kissed her, for she was fair a lady... as any was that time living.'

'And there the king told him tidings that his fair daughter was dead.... Then Sir Launcelot was right heavy of it.'

Le Morte D'Arthur by Sir Thomas Malory

Elaine Aston was an accomplished seamstress. She worked for a Jewish tailor in the heart of London's East End. Abe Fischer was a kindly man. He recognised a hard worker when he saw one and he gave Elaine many of his orders knowing that she would complete them in record time and faultlessly.

One day a young man with forget-me-not blue eyes entered his shop. The man announced himself as Lancelot Lawson and declared that he was a journalist and he wanted two top-of-the-range bespoke suits made in readiness for his new position at a well-known daily broadsheet. His mother, Natasha had heard good reports about Fischer's establishment and only the best was good enough for her son.

Fischer looked Lawson up and down, hating the man on sight but nevertheless showed him swatches of material in grey, navy and black. It was his pomposity and grandiose gestures that irked Abe. However, business was business, after all and the family was clearly well-heeled. Lawson opted for a single-breasted style in Italian linen; he pointed to a bolt of dark blue and another of tan. A price was arranged along with time and date for pick up.

Three weeks later, Lawson arrived. Fischer was out. He always lunched with his wife on Wednesdays. Elaine was temporarily running the shop.

The girl swept a stray wisp of hair from her face as she showed the completed article to her client. Lance looked appreciatively at the rounded contours of the girl's body. Strawberry blonde ringlets fell around her shoulders and a quite disarming fringe threatened to cover her chocolate brown eyes. Her face was littered with freckles. Her full lips were parted as she rather breathlessly showed him the finer details of the completed garments. Her front teeth were a little large but that apart she'd pass muster. Lawson reflected momentarily.

'Can I buy you dinner?' he asked.

Elaine hesitated. He wasn't unattractive. The eyes were particularly striking. She told him she would consider it.

'Ok, I'll be back next week.' Lawson shrugged his shoulders and offered a wad of cash. 'Keep the change,' he said magisterially and swept out of the building.

All week the girl couldn't keep her mind on her work. Fischer enquired whether she was well.

The girl's eyes filled with tears. Fischer was all concern.

'Are there problems in your life?' he asked.

She shook her head unable to admit that she had not been able to sleep or eat properly since the advent of a certain young man into Fischer's shop. Fischer strolled off. He'd have to keep an eye on her.

Wednesday came around once more and Lawson appeared wearing the dark blue linen suit.

Elaine arrived at the desk at once.

'What do you think? Am I up to scratch?' he asked, winking broadly.

The girl blushed to the roots of her hair.

'I'm glad you like it,' she murmured her eyes downcast.

'So, Miss Aston, what is the response, or should I call you the fair Elaine? Am I to be cast aside or will you take a gamble on this poor lovelorn knight? I know a very discreet little Italian place at the back of the theatre where my sister works. I have booked a table for two at eight o'clock tonight. I'll pick you up after work.'

'You're very persuasive,' she said shyly.

So I have been told,' replied the young man.

A whirlwind romance began. Elaine could refuse him nothing. One morning in early June she awoke feeling light-headed; she could barely raise her head from the pillow. She staggered to the bathroom.

This was the beginning of many such mornings.

On hearing her news Lance was thoughtful. When he left for work, he did not kiss her goodbye. That night she received a call. He would not be coming home tonight. He had to work late.

Elaine was distraught. What had she done? Each day became harder. She stumbled to the shop as if in a trance. The father of her child had vanished without trace. Fischer was alarmed. Between sobs she relayed her predicament.

Esther and I will help you. You're not the first young lady to be let down in this way.' He looked at her kindly.

On Friday morning Fischer discovered that Elaine was not behind her usual sewing machine. He asked a couple of the girls if they knew where she was. Nobody had heard anything. He rang her home phone. There was no reply.

Three days later a body was discovered half hidden under a willow on the banks of the Thames. The girl had taken herself to a place just outside Runnymede, clambered into *The Lady Fair* moored nearby and plunged a knife into her heart. A note was found clasped in her hand.

Fischer was inconsolable. Lancelot Lawson, hearing the news, hung his head in shame as his distraught mother hurled a torrent of abuse over the loss of her unborn grandchild.

Driving With Lance

Lance drove us silently through the environs of Exeter, picture postcard villages and sleepy hamlets, until eventually parking in a small layby.

I sat mutely in the passenger seat looking neither to right nor left. I could feel the man next to me regarding me quietly. I turned to face him.

'You owe me one hell of an explanation. I am not your plaything. I will give you ten minutes to explain yourself. If I remain unconvinced by your explanation and apologies, I'm out of here and I politely request that you get the hell out of my life.'

I think we were equally stunned by my outburst; the events of the last few months had hardened me considerably.

'I deserved that. I think you are an amazing woman. You are courageous and stalwart, honest and forthright and believe it or not these are qualities I admire. You are also beautiful.'

'Cut the crap, Lance. My mother says you'll never change; Ren has all sorts of names for you. I should have listened to my family.'

'I've changed Mel.'

By the time ten minutes were up, Lance had confessed he, like me, had had time to ruminate on his past and given all the agonies and tragedies of the last few months, he had begun to look at life differently.

'So, you want me to believe that after using me abominably in the space of a mere few months, you have now decided you wanted to test my gullibility yet again hoping that I'll fall back into your arms without a whimper? Evidently you believe I was born yesterday.'

He let go of my hand. His face took on an altogether altered aspect. He looked dismal, scared and actually quite pitiful.

Gazing at the windscreen in front of us as a slow pitter-patter of rain beat down, he said in a voice barely above a whisper, 'Please let me make it up to you Mel. I truly am so sorry and quite unable to face the future without you.'

I recalled Leigh at Ivan's funeral: he believed people deserve a second chance.

I hesitated then I took his hand. Cursing myself for all kinds of an idiot, my fate was sealed. Furthermore, he needed to know about our possibly shared grandfather. Would it change things? I was so besotted it seemed I'd stop at nothing to be with him.

I don't remember much of the next few hours. I only recall being blissfully contented and the misery and trauma of the last few months fading briefly from my mind. We walked along the beach at Budleigh Salterton, arms wrapped around each other. We kicked pebbles nonchalantly, giggling like school kids as we ran in and out of the waves that nipped and pecked at our feet, neither of us caring how wet we got. Neither of us talked about the momentous events that had occurred recently. With hindsight, it was like a Mills and Boon. Would I ever learn?

'Let's pop down to Dawlish; I love it there,' said Lance on a whim. 'The swans are quite remarkable.' We sat beside the stream running through the centre of the town. Before us, two swans glided past, jet-black feathers, necks stretched majestically, surveying us suspiciously.

'They pair for life, you know,' Lance mused.

'Like us? I asked.

'Of course!'

It was night when we arrived back at Lamorna's town house.

She came to the door looking flustered and anxious.

'Thank goodness you're ok. We were on the point of calling the police.'

Lance responded at once.

'I'm afraid we've been totally self-indulgent, Lamorna. I apologise to you both for worrying you. I'm going to drive home and leave this wonderful woman in your capable hands.'

At that point my sister appeared, eyes red-rimmed and flung her arms around me. She extricated herself after a few minutes and threw a malicious look in Lance's direction.

'Ouch!' he said. 'I'm off.' Giving me a brief peck on the cheek, he left.

'Maybe we should have a chat over a glass of something?' I suggested.

Lamorna disappeared immediately to fetch a bottle from the heaving wine rack.

We finally hit the sack around one in the morning but I knew I had not convinced either my aunt or my sister that this would be a new beginning.

The following morning Ren and Lamorna were already up when I sauntered down to breakfast still on cloud nine. They stopped their conversation in mid-flow.

I picked up an apple from the bowl.

'Talking about me?' I enquired.

With her usual penchant for honesty, Ren blurted. 'Are you really that effing stupid? Getting back into the f.... sack with that f...... excuse for a human being. The man is totally f.... untrustworthy. He's a f.... louse – always was and always will be. When are you going to wake up and smell the f.... coffee? Not to mention what we now know about our f.... grandfather.'

'Shall I find a thesaurus? You seem to have fixated on just the one adjective,' I remarked, sweetly.

'You are completely insane. The man cannot be trusted. Lamorna agrees with me.' She glanced across at our aunt who was staring mutely at the wall.

'You two are so like Ruth. You, Mel for your gullibility, and Ren, you for flying off the handle,' she said sadly.

I was still incensed with Ren.

'Oh, right and you're such an expert on all things pertaining to the heart.' I volleyed back. 'James, Mike...Mike, James. I really should bow to your better judgement – right?'

Lamorna intervened at once.

'Stop it, both of you! I think this is a very unwise decision, Mel. And as Ren has pointed out you are related. But it's your life, Mel.'

'Yeah, right... so butt out.'

Ren stormed towards the door but Lamorna grabbed her arm.

'You two have a contract to adhere to. You start at nine.'

It was more than half way through September when our work was finally over. I paid numerous weekend visits to Lance, in London, unhindered by Mrs Ramsbottom's shuffling curtains. It was time for Ren and me to return to Gulval and discuss our next move. The media frenzy surrounding the Lawson family had died down. Lance had battled through the throng of paparazzi to sit by his sister's bedside for hours on end. BJ had put in an appearance twice and then given up. Ginny was disfigured beyond all recognition and according to the doctors, it would take many years of restorative surgery before she would be capable of functioning in any meaningful way; she had suffered severe damage to her face, upper body, her arms and hands; it was a miracle she had survived.

The police had still not had any success in tracking down the perpetrators. Interpol was now involved but with no result.

Back at my family home, our parents had yet again baulked at approaching the police regarding Natasha's faked death. My mother had convinced my father to keep it all under our hats for the time being. She reasoned my own attempt at levelling with them had proved fruitless. Would she be taken any more seriously?

We had long since ceased to consider Natasha, her welfare or her feelings. We dissected it all endlessly. But we lacked nothing if not tenacity and finally we agreed we wanted answers.

Gran had been a constant presence since the latest tragedy with Ginny. Her frailty was increasing by the day. We could do little to improve her state of mind. Zeus had become a permanent fixture but seemed helpless in the face of so much adversity.

As she sat sipping a cup of hot tea in the conservatory. Ren and I went in to join her. We looked out over Mount's Bay. I put my arm around her shoulders. 'Is there any more news on the Russian KFC organisation that you all think Ivan was involved in?' she asked?

'No Gran,' I said gently. 'I'm sure we'll get the answers we need soon.'

Later that evening when she'd gone home again Mum said, 'I wonder if we should all go to Plumtree Hall en masse and talk to Natasha?'

We could see little point. After my last encounter, I had no desire to see the woman ever again.

'I wonder if LARA might hold the key?' said Ren. 'Should we take a trip there again?'

'I'm done with Lincolnshire,' I muttered.

'Do you think Ivan's diaries are reliable?' asked Dad suddenly.

The question hovered in the air like a bad smell.

Ren remarked, 'From the little I know about Kentucky Fried Chicken, it's quite capable of doing you in. Jay ate it all the time.'

At midnight, I spoke to Lance who told me Ginny was out of her coma. The police were at her bedside trying to elicit as many facts as they could.

After my parents had retired for the night, Ren and I stayed up another hour chewing the fat. It was inevitable that Natasha could not remain holed up at Plumtree Hall indefinitely and then what would happen? Would Levitov, wherever and whoever he was, keep doggedly to his task of wiping out the entire Lawson clan? My heart skipped a beat as I realised the true ramifications of this and any future life I hoped to have with Lance.

The newspapers had not been idle during this time and the fact that one Lawson child had taken his own life had been picked apart by the vultures in an assortment of tabloids, whilst the brush with death and disfigurement of a renowned West End actress had been speculated upon ad nauseam. Since Ginny had regained consciousness, Plumtree Hall had been besieged once again on a daily basis. Hypotheses about the possible identity of her abductors abounded. I imagined Ferguson feebly trying to fend them all off at the gate and wondered if BJ had appeared at any point to appease them.

Ren took my hand suddenly.

'I've had time to think. Mum said when I was asking about her ties to Natasha that she couldn't ever regret their friendship. Because of her she'd met our dad. Natasha, Lamorna and Mum first met him in the States. Natasha encouraged her relationship with him. Mum said she'd never turn back the clock. Don't you think that's sweet?'

'You do have a romantic soul, after all,' I joked. 'Who would have thought?'

'Yes, I do, and I hope it works out for you and Lance. I hope you have the relationship our parents clearly have, despite all the ups and downs.'

'Amen to that!' I said.

It was September. In two days, it would be the Mabon festival, and our mother had begun the preparations. I could see her in the conservatory gathering sheaves of corn and apples which would be placed on the altar in the temple at the end of the garden.

Ren appeared attired in a lime green tee shirt and scarlet, figure-hugging, jogging bottoms. Mr Davy arrived at 9.15am to announce sadly the death of his mother and to beg leave of absence to which, Mum agreed immediately, expressing her deepest condolences.

'Blimey everyone's dropping like flies,' announced my sister, with her usual diplomacy.

Tristan's funeral was scheduled for the end of the week. We learned that he had waded Woolf-like into Dozmary Pool with stones weighing down his pockets.

'All for the love of that creep, Isaacs,' said my sister.

I mused on this for a few seconds.

'Ren, how about a trip to Ringmore before the funeral? We could condole with the newly bereaved.'

I was hoping there might be a sign of his mates and we could finally solve the murder of Ludmila. Put an end to all this.

'Isn't that highly dangerous?' she asked, eyebrows raised.

'Come on, Ren, where's your sense of adventure?' I remonstrated jokily in a tone that belied my sense of impending doom.

She stood up without further ado, leaving the pyramid of apple cake slices my mother had plonked in front of us untouched.

'Better get packed up then.'

Before we left, we informed Mum of our plans.

'Just be careful, you two. I can't possibly come with you at Mabon – too much to do. Better go before your father gets wind of it – he won't approve.'

'Of course, Mabon must take priority, even if we are about to enter the lion's den," grinned Ren.

'Kerensa! If you are implying that you two are in mortal danger, it's not funny.' She turned her attention to the corn sheaves once more.

Five minutes later we were heading off in the direction of the A30. Kurt Kobain was blaring from the CD player with Ren screeching along. Conversation above several hundred decibels being impossible, I stared gloomily out of the window. Even though the morning was beautiful, sunny and warm nothing could lift my spirits not even Nirvana-land. Should I tell Lance? Then at least he could come to our rescue if necessary. But could he? Given the number of fatalities, unless he came armed with a Kalashnikov, Lance alone was more than likely powerless. I wondered idly about Arthurian legend and Natasha's insistence that the Lawson family's destiny was inextricably linked to it. What had been Sir Lancelot's fate? In the legend he and Guinevere had been lovers and Arthur cuckolded... you got that one wrong then, Tash!

Lancelot had been the bravest knight of them all, I seemed to recall and had tried to atone for the sin of betraying his king by becoming a monk – was that it? I definitely couldn't picture Lance in that role!

We finally drew up outside the Gothic pile that was Ringmore Heights. Ren swept into the driveway and the car came to an abrupt halt. The Baskerville brothers were still there in solitary splendour but what was this? It appeared that Izzie or someone had vacated the place in a bit of a hurry and left the door wide open. Leading to the entrance way was a trail of what looked like debris from stonemason's offcuts. Ren and I exchanged a brief look and then we both got out of the car and cautiously made our way towards the house. That was our first big mistake! We abandoned, with the car, all hope of contact with the outside world in the immediate future. In our bags, displayed for all to see on the back seat, were our mobile phones, cash and credit cards.

As we approached the front door, I stooped to pick up the first piece of discarded stone. It was about the size of a duck egg and jagged around the edges. I surveyed it closely hunting for clues. Ren picked up another larger piece. This was smoother and rectangular in shape. Puzzled, we edged forward, like Hansel and Gretel in the forest.

I poked my head inside the door and called Izzie's name. Determinedly Ren marched past me and called out loudly again: 'IZZIE!'

She strode purposefully into the kitchen to the right of the hallway.

Suddenly the front door slammed shut behind me and I felt the sharp edge of something cold and metallic against my neck. I heard Ren scream. I was frozen to the spot. Not a word was spoken for what seemed like several minutes and then Izzie emerged from the kitchen dragging my sister by the collar. We could only pray that Ren's former levity back at Pen-Towan was not about to become a reality.

'Move!' hissed a voice in my ear.

We were frogmarched into a small cloakroom behind the kitchen from which Ren had just emerged. There, we were forced into two chairs which had been placed side by side.

What had we been thinking? I had ignored the dread which had been steadily increasing as we had left the haven of Pen-Towan and travelled ever nearer to Ringmore Towers. Now we would be another statistic in the ever-growing number of fatalities.

Izzie was speaking.

'So, now we have another problem. What to do with you? I fear Dozmary Pool is too much of a coincidence. I have to say, your expertise at sleuthing is admirable. I understand there are rumours that Natasha still lives. Maybe therefore your arrival was fortuitous.'

'Natasha's dead.' My sister was now braced for the fight. 'There was a funeral, remember?'

'There is a twin of whom I know you are aware.' he retorted.

My voice sounded feeble, pathetic. 'You'll never get away with this.'

A figure emerged from behind my chair.

'Demelza, how could you have so little confidence in our ability to fool the world when we have been so clever for so long? Were it not for the idiocy of my daughter, things would have been done and dusted before now and I would be back in Ohio enjoying the good life. As it is we have a couple of small tasks to perform and then we can depart – mission accomplished, as they say.'

I stared at the face before me. Round his neck was a long, multi-coloured scarf – his trademark. But this was far from being some silly sci-fi kids' programme. It was the man on the bridge I had seen standing with Izzie and Mark masquerading under the alias *Dora*.

'Who are you?' I croaked.

'I have many names Nikolai Levitov being one. What we need to establish with your help, which we will elicit one way or another, is the exact whereabouts of Natasha Rodomski-Lawson – where is she hiding her pretty little self? She is not with that imbecile Rachel out on the marsh – that much we have discovered, even if we had to terminate the mastiff to get to the truth. Amazing what a little gentle persuasion can do though. We discovered far more than we could have hoped.'

Ren let fly a stream of expletives. She fell to the floor as *Dora* knocked her senseless.

We were totally powerless. Only my parents knew where we were and I suspected my mother would be too engrossed in Mabon to even notice how long we had been absent.

'Isaacs, get the knife,' he barked.

Levitov pulled my sister up into a semi-reclining position and held the knife to her throat. I could feel my head reeling and my mouth felt as if it were full of sand.

'Now talk! Where is she?'

'Plumtree Hall,' I murmured.

Now was not the time for heroics.

'Sit down,' he barked gesturing towards two flimsy chairs in the centre of the room. Ren staggered to her feet. Levitov shoved her into the chair. Blood was pouring from her nose and her eye was already half closed and swelling.

'Tie them up,' he nodded at Izzie who obeyed at once. 'Gag them, you stupid son-of-a-bitch.'

'Let's go.'

The two men walked briskly towards the door. We heard it slam shut once again. There was nothing but silence. I turned my head – Ren's face was turning blueish-purple.

We were completely trapped with little hope of getting out of here any time soon.

Ren appeared to be wriggling frantically in her chair. I gazed at her in disbelief.

Within minutes she was on her feet and ripping the gag from her mouth.

'He didn't spend time in the boy scouts then! Knot-tying def not his forte.' She grinned lopsidedly.

She half staggered, half limped over to my chair and untied me.

'You look dreadful,' I said.

'Thanks a bunch!'

We tried to decide what to do next.

Clearly Izzie and *Dora* were long gone probably speeding their way toward the fens. I got to my feet, a little woozily.

'You stay there. I'll go and get our things from the car and we can call Mum.'

Whatever made me think our possessions would still be there safely on the back seat of the car? Naturally enough, car keys and both our handbags were nowhere in sight.

I returned to the house and called to Ren. Resourceful as ever, she had found the house phone – I could see her frantically jabbing the numbers out. For a split-second, Ren looked puzzled and then I followed her gaze. The wires had been wrenched from the wall.

'Looks like we'll be walking into town to get help,' she hissed.

'No way! You're in no fit state to walk two miles. I'll go.'

'What, and miss out on all that fun... watching you explaining our plight to some country bumpkin and then downing several pints at the local. In any case, what if they come back?'

'Don't be daft; they're on a mission now to get to Natasha asap.'

The walk to the nearest house seemed interminable. The wind seemed to have whipped up into a force nine gale. The Teign was granite grey; waves were dashing ferociously against the rocky shoreline.

The first door we knocked at was fruitless. It was beyond frustrating to have to walk a further quarter mile to the next cottage. The roads were deserted. I hammered at the next door. We could hear furious yapping from somewhere inside. Eventually the door creaked open and a woman about our age opened the door, a young toddler at her heels.

She took one look at Ren's face and her hand flew to her mouth.

'My sister has been attacked; we need to use your phone,' I spluttered.

Soundlessly, she opened the door wide and pointed to the phone on the small oak table to her left. She gathered the toddler to her, who started to wail loudly.

While we were waiting for the law to arrive, the woman introduced herself as Lisa and offered us a cup of hot tea which we politely declined.

When the police arrived, things started to move forward at a speed we had hitherto not experienced. At the police station, a female officer bathed Ren's face, took detailed statements and allowed us to phone Pen-Towan.

Neither of us felt like repeating the entire story of Natasha's faked death, since my first attempt had not been taken seriously. We told them that the two men who had attacked us and held us prisoner were at this moment making their way to Lincolnshire and the home of BJ Lawson. We remained mute on the subject of any suspicions we might have as to why the two men should be targeting Lawson. No further questions were asked. There was a frenzied rush to put calls through to their colleagues in Boston in the hope that they could head the pair off.

Like two naughty children, we sat and awaited the arrival of our parents, who had assured us, horrified, that they would be there as soon as they could. Even Mabon had been discarded, to our amazement.

Morgan-le-Fey

'"Now, sir," said Accolon, I will tell you... Morgan Le Fey, King Urien's wife, sent it me yesterday by a dwarf, to this intent, that I should slay King Arthur, her brother. For ye shall understand King Arthur is the man in the world that she most hateth."'

Le Morte D'Arthur by Sir Thomas Mallory

When Faye Williams joined the Penzance and Marazion Coven in the late 1970s, she was in her twenties. It seemed like a good idea, a sorority, if you ignored the one non-female member. It reminded her of school days in Des Moines. Her coven-name was Morgan in deference to Morgan-le-Fey.

'Wasn't she the wicked woman in the legends of King Arthur?' asked Faye, with a dangerous glint in her eye.

'She was,' averred Ruth, 'so you'll have to work extra hard to dispel the myth.'

Ruth laughed; Faye laughed too, but somewhere inside her there sprouted a bud of displeasure.

Her sojourn here in Cornwall would be brief – a mere stop-gap – a means of meeting folk as, 'alternative' as she was, because Faye considered herself, *different*. At school the girls had smirked at her funny expressions, her strange dress; she didn't fit into small-town Iowa.

Born Faye-Louise Levitov-Steinhart, Faye had spent the first three months of her life in a State Penitentiary just thirty miles south-west of Danvers, formerly Salem, Massachusetts. The maternal side of her family claimed descent from Abigail Williams, implicated in the seventeenth century Salem Witch Trials. Faye's mother, Regina, had been given life without parole whilst Faye's father Alexander, was on death row for fifteen years before pneumonia finally put him out of his misery. The couple was the driving force behind the notorious Levitov-Steinhart gang who had a catalogue of bank raids and murders to their credit during the 1950s. America viewed them with a mixture of fascination and disgust.

Alexander Levitov was a Russian émigré. Back in his native country Vladimir Rodomski had turned informer and Alexander's hapless lover, Mishka, had been summarily executed as a traitor linked to the CIA. A flurry of activity ensued; Mishka's protectors in the Soviet Union ensured safe passage for Alexander who had arrived in New York with his tiny son, Nikolai in tow. Levitov was now bent on revenge. He became embroiled in criminality. Regina Steinhart, née Williams, happened along and the two embarked on a series of highly successful bank heists. One day their luck ran out.

Faye, as progeny of Alexander and Regina, had been sent to live with Faye's grandparents, Joshua and Sarah Williams, who moved to the Mid-West in order to escape their daughter's infamous past. Nikolai her half-brother came too. Puritanical, ardent church-goers, the couple kept a tight rein on their charges. Faye was isolated and alone; her half-sibling became taciturn and reclusive. For comfort, the two would sleep cuddled up together. Sarah and Joshua turned a blind eye even when the pair was well into their teens.

Eventually, Faye and Nikolai moved to Berkeley, California, altogether more exciting. Nikolai tried to make a living, selling cleaning products. He lasted two weeks. When he disappeared without trace, Faye was left alone and six months pregnant. She would sleep away the daylight hours and emerge at night to steal from garbage bins before completing a couple of hours waitressing at an all-night diner, where she would furtively stash cutlery and the odd bit of cash from the till into her pockets. Faye's daughter, Morgana, was born at six o'clock one morning in early May. Faye delivered her child, alone in a one-bedroom apartment. She kept the child for twenty-four hours, then, she trudged downtown to the diner and left her wrapped in a pink blanket, frayed at the edges, with a note attached. Morgana was another statistic in the ever-increasing number of unwanted and illegitimate.

Three years later, Faye got a job lap dancing. She saved enough money to buy a ticket for Europe. She took on casual employment, a chamber maid in Rome, grape-picking in the south of France, and then set off across the Channel to sample what the little country had to offer.

Having made a speciality of the history of the Salem Witch Trials during her brief period at college, she decided to give, 'real' witches a go. Within a month of her joining the Cornwall coven it was no longer a sorority. Mackenzie Lowe, charismatic partner of Ruth Trelawney had become warlock in chief by popular demand and everything changed. The women were in Mackenzie's thrall. He seduced them all with his charm, his knowledge and his wit. Ruth was the envy of the coven. Mackenzie only had eyes for Ruth and her best friend, Natasha. It seemed that whenever Faye was alone with Mackenzie, that snake in the grass would appear, make some provocative remark, tilt her head in that infuriating way she had and Mac would be all ears.

Faye began to plot how to get Natasha away from the object of her desire; she tried to befriend the woman but then it seemed impossible to release the stranglehold of Ruth. Natasha seemed to intuit Faye's ulterior motives so that her every advance was repelled.

Faye's jealousy festered bubbling over into an all-consuming torrent of hatred for Natasha. Faye felt sure that Natasha and Mackenzie had been lovers but would Ruth believe her? She kept her counsel waiting for an opportunity to strike.

It was the Summer Solstice. A gentle breeze blew in from the sea as they gathered on a hilltop amid the Seven Sisters standing stones. Natasha was dressed all in green which competed with her eyes and their long-fringed lushness. The sun was sinking slowly leaving a burnt-orange glow just above the horizon. The mood was joyous. Mackenzie, in his element, wore a flowing, white cloak, embroidered with silver pentagrams. He was laughing, his arms around Natasha, on his left, and Ruth, on his right. From beneath the folds of her billowing dress Faye could feel the cold blade, ostensibly to cut the locks of the newest initiate into the coven.

The voice of the coven leader rang out; Faye edged nearer, slipping the knife into her hand, feeling her fingers touch the cold shaft; she could see Natasha's dark hair two feet away, and Iris, with her keen eyes and tiny Morwenna, with those strange prophesies that had an uncanny knack of coming true.

Now! She raised her arm and the setting sunrays caught the silver of the blade and Iris was upon her and tiny Morwenna pushed her down. Mackenzie Lowe was taking the knife and Ruth shouted a warning to her friend. Faye fell, prostrate, on the ground sobbing in anger and frustration.

Faye disappeared back to California, nursing her grudges and biding her time. There came another daughter; Faye named her Joodee.

Faye sought out Morgana, the child she had abandoned years ago. Faye was never cut out for motherhood. Morgana was strange, hard to comprehend. She stuttered and tugged incessantly at her hair and was dull and unlovable. The girl became sullen and morose. Baby Joodee grew prettier and chubbier. Nikolai was back on the scene. He had a morbid fascination with poisons, having spent the intervening years in Europe founding an organisation which trialled and tested a variety of toxins. Faye told her half-brother about England and Natasha Rodomski-Lawson and within Levitov's brain there echoed a distant memory; hadn't his father, Alexander, made a vow to kill the man Rodomski?

A plan was hatched. They made a trip to Cornwall where they discovered Natasha to be very much alive. Faye secured a job, put down a deposit on a flat in Lincoln and made a life in the Fens. She and Levitov decamped for the summer to Paris. What to do next? They needed an ally. That ally came fortuitously in the form of Mark Banks.

It was December and bitterly cold; a woman with purple hair stood outside the Lincolnshire Animal Rights Association. She had learnt her lines. Her mother had gone over them repeatedly until her daughter had articulated them slowly, parrot-like, verbatim. She was waiting for Natasha to emerge. As she fidgeted, looking from side to side, nervously pulling at her hair, city life went on around her. In her hand, Morgana held a small gift wrapped in Christmas paper, tied up very prettily with red ribbon. She caught sight of her mother standing waiting opposite, clad all in black, her fur-lined hood pulled up around her face. A woman was emerging from the doorway, a bright red scarf wrapped around the lower part of her face, long dark hair visible below it. She pulled the scarf tightly up and over her nose. As instructed, Morgana approached her, smiling broadly.

'It is Christmas. I have a present to give you,' she said.

Rebecca Dennis looked at her. The woman's purple hair stood in spikes around her head like a bizarre sputnik.

'That's very kind of you, but I don't know you, do I? Are you mistaking me for someone else?'

'I want to give you a present. It's Christmas,' insisted Morgana.

What harm could there be in accepting? She took the present graciously, thanking the woman again.

Morgana gave a curtsey and walked away.

Rebecca walked on.

About forty minutes later she was sitting in the kitchen of her cottage in front of a roaring log burner. She was beginning to thaw out and wondering what to do next. In a few hours she would be seeing her sister, Natasha and would meet Natasha's daughter for the first time. She had plans of her own after that. Her twin had been trying to talk her into reconnecting with Rebecca's mother, Rachel. Then, she remembered the strange gift she had been given. She opened it tentatively – a very small box of chocolates, just four inside, but they smelled divine. Save them for later she thought

When Rebecca next looked at her watch it was nearly two. She needed to move fast if she were to make it in time.

The End of the Line

The next day the media was buzzing and there was nowhere to hide. The police had arrived at Plumtree Hall and found BJ and Ferguson with no sign of Natasha or any evidence that she had been there recently. Lawson was denying all charges. His wife was definitely dead. She had been identified and had been buried. We were charged with wasting police time and besmirching the name of a well-respected citizen. Detective Sergeant Newman informed us all gravely that we had committed a serious offence and, on this occasion, BJ Lawson would not be pressing charges but we needed to keep our noses out of his business in future. Newman proffered the opinion that we had better just keep to dancing around standing stones – a far healthier pastime.

The press was demanding to know how we had dared to make such outrageous accusations. How much did we know about Natasha's death? If not Natasha's body in the coffin – then whose? We parried their questions whilst trying to maintain a semblance of dignity. Our reputation as practising pagans wasn't helping in the media frenzy.

We hunkered down. Mother spent an inordinate amount of time in the *temple*, My father set about making marmalade. Two days after Newman's visit, I got a call from Natasha. Could I meet her? I was to go alone immediately to Truro Cathedral. Foolishly, I dropped everything, slipped out of the house and sped off, leaving a brief note.

Having parked, I walked swiftly towards the Gothic spires, hands thrust deep into the pockets of my coat and fingering my mobile phone in a vain attempt to reassure myself it would be ok. A chill wind whistled around my ears and I turned my collar up shivering. Then I saw her. A woollen hat was pulled down low over her forehead and she was buttoned up against the cold. She walked purposefully towards me. Without warning I was grabbed from behind and forcefully marched down a side-street. A familiar voice was hissing in my ear: 'I told you not to breathe a word. Do not make a sound. GO!'

I was bundled into a black BMW and we sped away, Natasha, BJ and I. At the wheel was Ferguson, the obsequious butler.

It was dusk when we arrived at a small farmhouse. There was a salty tang in the air and the distant sound of waves crashing against rocks somewhere below.

I was pushed inside. The place was bitterly cold and smelled strongly of mildew. BJ shoved me down roughly into a chair. Natasha pulled up another and sat regarding me in total silence.

'What do you want, Natasha?' My voice sounded far-away, not my own.

'I am flattered that my deception has duped you. My name is Rebecca, formerly Ludmila and I have to hand it you, you have behaved admirably on behalf of your deceased friend, keeping her secrets, trying to discover her murderer. I think we owe you something now: the truth. You must have many questions?'

My mind was racing. How could she have fooled me so utterly? There had been many warning signs: the slightly guttural voice, certain alien mannerisms, flashes of anger, uncharacteristic of Natasha; the fumbling over the supposed pregnancy. How did this woman know intimate details of Natasha's life?

'You're surprisingly quiet; aren't you curious?'

I said nothing.

'The bitch is dead. Obviously! Her body resides in a coffin six feet under in a Boston cemetery. She believed I'd be forever grateful at her wanting to meet up and forge a sisterly bond after all these years of complete ignorance of my birth, not knowing who my real father was, living with that cow Rachel and her bastard husband, a hand-to-mouth existence while she lived in the lap of luxury, charming everyone, frolicking around the country mixing with a bunch of oddballs, building her cosmetics empire, having four delightful babies. Did she really imagine she could work her magic on me and we could all play happy families?'

I found my voice.

'Why, Ludmila? You could have had a different life, a happy one, a proper family. Natasha appears to have wanted that for you.'

'But I have had many happy months with BJ - that has been ample compensation.'

She glanced across at Natasha's husband; his face was expressionless.

'And how does Joodee fit into all this?'

'I'm afraid your sister-in-law has not been quite so compliant as we would have hoped, although she aided us in ensuring young Guinevere would never strut the boards again!'

'But my finest hours have been those where I have learnt of how your family unravelled, how all Natasha's dreams of reconciling with her family and friends, those friends she once wronged and who forgave her despite it all, have come to nothing. That has given me great satisfaction. Ivan going to his grave, unable to make peace with his daughter; Ruth unable to put all this to bed and her daughters almost at death's door, Rachel, broken in mind and spirit; Guinevere, scarred for life, Tristan at the bottom of a deep, dark pool; my only regret is not to have finished off the blue-eyed wonder you are so infatuated with. And my partners in crime have been so co-operative. So many who had such a grudge against one beautiful woman – it's quite incredible!'

The woman was quite insane. I felt sick and exhausted and thoroughly disgusted with myself for being led up the garden path for so long. I no longer knew how to articulate how I was feeling. BJ stood a little to the side staring at me pensively.

'So, what are you going to do with me now? You have got everything off your chest but where has it got you? You can't possibly hope to get away with this. My family will be contacting the police when I don't return. I can't imagine how you got away with this for so long. As for you, BJ....'

He leered at me.

'Put it down to the incompetence of the police and my immense wealth which can be very persuasive. We have planned everything meticulously, all t's crossed and i's dotted. I have been more than happy to witness the demise of my erstwhile wife and aid in duping you all. The most fun I've had in years.'

Ludmila began again.

'In answer to your question, my dear, we cannot of course let you go back into the big wide world again; you know far too much but it must be gratifying to know that we admire you greatly for your fortitude, your dedication to my former sister and your sheer tenacity and expertise at sleuthing... which is why we felt we owed you an explanation.'

I obliged with a barrage of questions.

'How did you pull this off, Ludmila? Where is Dora/Levitov or whatever alias he's adopted. What part have Mark and Izzie played?'

'Nikolai is long gone and I shall be joining him in the very near future. I think you have heard the story of the long-standing and frankly, quite ridiculous, grudge between the Levitov and Rodomski families. I'm afraid Nikolai is quite unhinged, but nevertheless, willing to fall in with my plans. He too has enjoyed his bit of sport with you. M.M.M.Mark was expendable – but then most people are – and of course he was pitifully enamoured of Isaacs so became butter in anybody's hands. Nikolai and Faye had no trouble persuading him to join their exclusive club. And Isaacs would have done anything to get rid of Natasha – she had come between him and Tristan many times and that fuelled his rancour. Latterly, Isaacs's conscience was starting to get the better of him, sadly, so he too is no more. It seems he had a vestige of feeling for poor Tristan.'

I found my voice. 'And Joodee?'

'Joodee had no time for Natasha so was happy to play her part. Faye had a particular grudge against Natasha. Faye's sisterly devotion to Nikolai merely augmented her dislike.'

'What happened at Tunman Woods?' I enquired feebly.

'Ah yes, that was tricky. Natasha had arranged to meet me there. The timing was a problem because she wanted to meet that daughter of hers. That could have ruined all my plans. I was nearly thwarted because of that idiot in Lincoln who stopped me to gift me some chocolates. I stuffed them in my pocket - a nice little pre-Christmas gift for Natasha before I killed her; I rearranged the rendez-vous, telling her to come early because I wanted time alone with her. I parked some distance from the meeting-place in order to avoid suspicion and Nikolai was there with Faye and her daughter who recognised me. Nikolai twigged what had happened to the chocolates; incidentally they were laced with poison and given to me, the wrong woman. He asked me if I'd eaten them. I said I was there to meet my sister Natasha. I thought honesty would be the best policy as he looked dangerous. A wise move as it turned out. He pulled a gun. I would have been an unfortunate pawn in his game, had I not played it differently. He was there to kill Natasha. I confessed all. Showed him the knife in my pocket. It didn't take long to convince him. He gave me a vial and a hypodermic. Told me what to do. It was all comparatively easy from there on. She didn't feel a thing. It looked like a nasty accident as if she'd stumbled over a tree trunk lying in her way. Somehow the chocolates were mislaid but I gather an unfortunate little pooch located them! I took Natasha's phone and called BJ who arrived in record time. He didn't need much persuading as to our next course of action. Nikolai has kept me abreast of everything. It was relatively straightforward to persuade everyone that Natasha was delusional and paranoid, even though in reality she had been amazingly perspicacious. Many people were indeed out to kill her. So, we all worked as one cohesive team but unfortunately, we had to bump off a few people on the way.'

'But if you knew Natasha was dead why all the other unnecessary killing?' I asked.

'Much of that of that was pure circumstance, and connected to others with different axes to grind. Mackenzie's and Ruth's unfortunate choices of partners and of course Guinevere's, for example. The others were our bit of fun. Arthurian legend has to have its way. When one has allegiances with psychopaths, anything is possible.'

'So, Natasha was expecting a baby?' I asked.

'That too turned out to be fortuitous. She was apprehensive for sure and who wouldn't be at her age but it certainly was grist to the mill as far my plans were concerned. An elderly pregnant woman – vulnerable – and of course the child wasn't BJ's. She'd become involved with somebody called Mills, many years her junior. I believe you know him?'

'He was the father of Natasha's child?'

'Yes, your poor sister. But luckily she will never know.'

The feline eyes gleamed maliciously. She was pointing a small revolver at me; I closed my eyes and waited a millisecond.

From behind there came an ear-splitting explosion. The door shattered and there was a sudden flurry of activity in the room. Voices thundered from all directions and a shot rent the air. Two piercing green eyes gazed at me in shock and the body of Ludmila Rodomski fell to the floor. BJ's hands were in the air, a small handgun thrown against the wall in surrender.

My parents, noting my prolonged absence, had called the police who had wasted no time in obtaining camera footage from Truro and tracking down my captors. For once there had been many witnesses; a BMW travelling at speed down country roads had been a rarity for the locals; tyre marks down rutted, muddy tracks led them to Roman Farm, just outside Mevagissey.

A few weeks later we learned that the body in the coffin, having been exhumed and an autopsy performed, had been identified once more and pregnancy verified. The police had finally uncovered the extent of the deception. On closer examination, a puncture wound was discovered but no poison could be detected. Nearly a year had passed so perhaps this was unsurprising. Natasha had miscarried, of that there was no doubt. DCI Gerry Lambert informed us that it was likely that ricin had been administered, given what they had discovered about Levitov's connection to Rick Morrison. BJ corroborated Ludmila's confession in the farmhouse; they had planned the entire hoax, using the Russian connections to their advantage. BJ, having met Ludmila at Tunman Woods had instructed her to lie low for a while and they would use Plumtree Hall as a safe haven. Nobody would think to search there and of course the house was enormous and had several bolt holes in which to hide. Ferguson, was 'persuaded' that it was in his best interests to do as he was told. As BJ left the scene of the murder, Ginny saw him, having arrived a little too late to witness Ludmila. The wintry weather and darkness had been on the murderer's side – who would be walking in the woods in such conditions and just before Christmas?

It was assumed Izzie's cultivation of the euphorbia had been his own feeble attempt to find a means of poisoning Natasha without aid from Levitov.

A car had been found abandoned in the environs of Leicester, the body of Tom Isaacs bound and shot through the head in the boot. Levitov, Faye, their daughter, Morgana and our sister-in-law Joodee had boarded a plane bound for Canada.

Levitov was eventually picked up outside Glasgow, Montana, a remote community near the Canadian border where they had been holed up in a shack. It was Joodee who had finally crumbled and turned herself in to the police at Glendive. Things moved swiftly: extradition was organised and once more we were all over the papers.

BJ, the head of the local constabulary and the Boston coroner, had all been charged with falsifying evidence. As my mother had suspected, they were members of the masonic lodge. Our own family was given a stern warning about the part we had played in the deception, although admittedly there had been many mitigating circumstances. Rachel Dennis took her own life, completely broken by the turn of events. The whole case became world-wide news.

Back in Cornwall, life continued: Sam was resigned to bringing up his two daughters alone; our grandma set up home with Zeus; our parents tied the knot, officially this time.

Ginny was now in a Buddhist retreat in Nepal where she intended to live out her days in seclusion, unable to face the world with the horrific scarring she had suffered to her face and body.

We tried to rebuild our lives.

I emerged from Doctor Sawalhi's office not knowing if I was on my head or my heels. I was expecting twins.

I knew my family would be supportive. My dad had cajoled Mum into accepting Natasha's eldest son into the family, against her better judgement. In her company, Lance said very little and Mum would extend a lukewarm hospitality whenever we went to Pen-Towan.

On the morning of 1st July, I began to feel the first pangs of labour. Lance was away, it was just Biggles, the cat, and me in the house. We had moved three weeks ago from the flat in the treetops where we had first shared a pizza and a bed all those months ago.

I called the midwife, my mother and then Lance.

I turned on the TV determined to sit out the pains. Then a sharp sensation in my lower belly made me cry out.

I can remember little of the ensuing hours. I recall Lance arriving cooing over our babies.

'Maybe you should call them Natasha and Kai?' suggests my mother.'

'Definitely not,' says Lance. 'I think Jennifer – Guinevere in English.'

'Arthur?' I ask in deference to Natasha and her adoration of my grandfather rather than any real conviction on my part.

It is decided.

Twenty-four hours later I am home and Lance has gone back to finish his assignment. As I kiss him goodbye, he looks tired but happy. My mother and I discuss her friendship with Natasha and what her former best friend might have made of the situation.

'Thank goodness she wasn't around to see the death of Tristan and Ginny's terrible burns. She was never a bad person, Mel. I shall regret to my dying day never having properly mended the rift. Friends are like broomsticks – they fly away and you can never restore them to you.'

The friendship between them had been so special, and yet broken by one senseless act committed by two fallible human beings. What is more difficult for me to put to bed is the major part I played whilst most of my family seemingly carried on with their lives unfazed. It would be something I would need to address.

It is now early afternoon. I have had a steady stream of visitors: to my utter amazement, my former boss, Felicia arrives with two huge cuddly pandas and an enormous bouquet of roses. Iris and Leila breeze in laden to the gunwales with garments featuring witches and broomsticks and cauldrons. Dad arrives with Ren.

Kena Gwella

Obituary

Boston Journal, 7th July, 2005

'It is with deep sadness that we report the death of Lancelot Lawson, the son of the celebrated but now disgraced painter, Barry John Lawson and his deceased wife, Natasha, formerly head of Oh-Nat-urel, the beauty products and cosmetics company. Mr Lawson was travelling from St Thomas's Hospital where his wife, Demelza, had recently given birth to twins. The car, a top-of-the-range, steel-grey Porsche is said to have rounded a bend at speed and burst into flames on impact with another vehicle travelling in the opposite direction. Despite Mr Lawson's repeated attempts to pull the occupant of the car from the wreckage he was unable to do so. Tragically, doctors were unable to save Mr Lawson who sustained horrific injuries. It is understood that his wife is being comforted by her family. A close friend of the family confided: 'The entire Lawson family appear to have been jinxed.' Also travelling in Mr Lawson's car was Belinda Fairfax, a colleague and close friend, who died at the scene.

Mel is standing screaming down the corridor of the hospital. My mother and I grab her, both trying to hold her, mutter some words – but there are none! 'We will get through this; we are strong,' our mother does her best to placate my sister. Images of a car wreck are on screens everywhere; words come from afar, jumbled in a fog of disbelief; babies crying; Mel is on her knees... my shirt is saturated with her tears. Her howls are like a tortured animal.

My sister became a complete basket-case. She was placed in care, considered a danger to herself and to her babies.

Two weeks after Mel's incarceration, BJ Lawson died at the age of 75, apparently from a heart attack, presumably brought on by a surfeit of remorse. But that would be giving him too much credit.

Luckily perhaps, we Trelawney-Lowes are made of stern stuff. We all clung to one another in our horror and grief. Eventually my sister was restored to us, somewhat diminished, but once more in the bosom of her family where we hope she will make a full recovery. I will leave it to her to put this sorry tale to bed.

Kerensa Lowe

Four years later:

We are on the cliffs at Zennor. Our grandmother's ashes have been consigned to the deep as Arthur's were all those years ago. A gentle breeze is blowing inland from the sea and we have a sumptuous picnic spread out before us.

Jennifer and Arthur watch as Ren makes a daisy chain. I gaze out to sea, reflecting on the events that changed all our lives. There is a loud mewing by my elbow and a sleek grey cat appears – could it be Greymalkin or his progeny? The cat approaches and nuzzles me with his nose. I gently stroke his fur, wondering idly if Wenna's spirit is within him, trying to give me comfort. Time was when I would have laughed at such foolishness.

But now I dismiss nothing. Natasha has gone and her evil twin. A young woman, named Morgana, sent on a mission by those too cowardly to do the deed themselves, languishes in a secure mental health facility, deemed unfit to stand trial. Her father sees out his days in Belmarsh. Faye, has served her sentence, a sentence all too brief, along with my former sister-in-law, Joodee.

The intervening years I remember as a blur. I know only that I lost the only man I will ever truly love.

My years in the sanatorium, my mother refers to as *the asylum*, I recall in cameo – a palimpsest of faces and voices who helped me to heal. But my healing is only partial – how can it be otherwise? In time, I shall get to know my two children and learn to care for them but until I am able to do so, Ren does a brilliant job.

My mother no longer looks back on what could have been but what once was. The friendship she and Natasha once shared was precious and much water has flowed under the bridge since then. She reiterates constantly that without Natasha, Ren and I and our brothers would never exist for it was Natasha who steered her towards Dad all those decades ago.

We supported Natasha through the worst years of her life and continued to do so after her death. She died, having never met her grandchildren. We remain secure in the knowledge that our two families were reunited, in one way or another, which is something Mum says Natasha fervently wished for.

So many questions remain unanswered. I think of the letters. Who wrote them? Natasha must have been responsible for some of them but the one Morrison had discovered... how did that fit into the plot? How did Ludmila have such intimate knowledge of Natasha and her life? Had Natasha herself divulged these details? Or BJ? It was a mystery and would remain so forever. Not least of all the strange coincidences of Natasha's life seemingly connected to Arthurian legend. Had they been coincidences or engineered by others for their own amusement?

The cat wanders away and my mother is at my shoulder.

I say, 'I'm trying to evaluate the essence of Natasha and what she has been to this family.'

'Impossible to quantify,' she answers. 'Natasha affected us all, sometimes for good, sometimes for bad. Friends are jewels, Mel. Treasure them and love them, warts and all, and there's a witchy thing to say!'

She laughs gaily, as she fingers the ever-present Citrine on a silver chain around her neck. The golden gem sparkles a reflection onto her face, giving her, as Ren whispers, 'an air of jaundice.' I assume the stone has significance and I realise, with a pang, that my mother is the most content she has ever been.

As we wander over to join the others, I admit that I wish to get a feel for Mallory's Arthurian legend and Natasha's insistence on its importance.

'Natasha was a remarkable woman,' Mum muses. 'She asked for help and we tried to give it to her: that's what true friendship is.'

Iris chimes in: 'For a long time, I suspected Guinevere had a hand in all of this.'

'Ginny loved Natasha, more than I believe she knew,' reflects my mother. 'In legend, Guinevere has always been a mysterious character, angel or devil.'

'Like Eve,' Iris replies thoughtfully. 'More sinned against than sinning.'

'Lance had little time for his mother,' remarks Ren, threading another daisy through a loop and directing it towards the outstretched chubby fist of my daughter.

'But Lance found true love and fathered two beautiful babies,' said Iris pensively, glancing at me.

Trelly is looking up from a Chemistry text-book and regarding me sagely. After due consideration, he speaks very deliberately and matter-of-factly.

'Well, it's like this. In Arthurian legend, Guinevere took holy vows and so did Ginny. Tristan killed himself for love of Iseult, just like our Tristan and Lancelot was the bravest knight of them all.'

I look away, wondering why a woman called Belinda Fairfax was with Lance when he died. He was working freelance and alone, so he said. I had adored the man but could I ever have trusted him?

Demelza Lowe

THE END

Character List

Mel (Demelza) Lowe – Mel tells the story and sets out to investigate Natasha's death. She lives and works in London, at a clothing shop in Knightsbridge.

Ren (Kerensa) Lowe – her twin sister. Ren helps Mel with the investigation into Natasha's death. She works at a gym and lives with her mother Ruth, in Gulval, near Penzance in Cornwall. She also contributes to writing some of the story.

Ruth Lowe – Mel and Ren's mother. She lives in Gulval, in Cornwall, with her daughter Ren, and her cats, Piskey and Janis, and her dog, Growler. She owns a shop, Ruth's Remedies, selling crystals and colour therapies in Penzance.

Mac (Mackenzie Lowe) – Mel and Ren's father. He is a US citizen who now lives in New Orleans, where he was born. He lived with Ruth for many years, in Cornwall.

Sam (Isambard) – Mel's and Ren's older brother. Sam lives with his wife Joodee and their two children Bryony and Fern in Zennor, Cornwall. He runs a business, making Wendy Houses. Joodee makes jewellery, which she sells at craft fairs around the country.

Trelly (Trelawney) – is Mel and Ren's younger brother. He is nine years old and quite precocious.

Lamorna Trelawney – Ruth's elder sister. Lamorna is a lecturer at Exeter University and she lives on Exmoor, with her Newfoundland dog, Bedouin.

Arthur Trelawney – is a lecturer in Russian at London university, where he lives during term-time. In the holidays, he lives in Zennor, with his wife. He is father to Lamorna and Ruth.

Annie (Angharad) Davies – of Welsh heritage. She is wife to Arthur and mother to Lamorna and Ruth. She lives in Zennor. She is queen of malapropisms.

Natasha Lawson (née Rodomski) – She is married to BJ and lives near the Wash, in Lincolnshire. They have a large house and a butler, named Ferguson. Natasha has her own beauty company called *Oh-Naturel.*

BJ Lawson (Barry John) – Natasha's husband. He is older than Natasha and a landscape artist, specialising in the Fens of Lincolnshire. They have four children, Kai, Lance, Ginny and Tristan.

Kai Lawson – oldest child of Natasha and BJ Deceased, aged eleven.

Lance Lawson (Lancelot) – who is a journalist and lives in the Crystal Palace area of London.

Ginny Lawson (Guinevere) – who lives near to her brother, Lance, in Crystal Place, near to the Crystal Palace Park. She is an actress, frequently working in the West End and is married to Rick Morrison.

Tristan Lawson – lives in Devon near the River Teign with his partner, Izzie. Together, they run antiques and paintings galleries in Devon and Cornwall.

Izzie (Tom Isaacs) – born in Devon, is half Irish and from a wealthy family. He is interested in antiques and art.

Rick Morrison – Ginny's husband lives and works mostly in Zurich. His work involves animal testing. He and Ginny have a volatile marriage.

Ivan Rodomski – a Russian emigré. He moved to Finchley in London when his first wife, Galena and their son, Dimitri died. His second wife, Vera, is mother to their daughter, Natasha.

Minor characters

Marguerite – a care-worker, in the home where Mel is taken when she is suffering from amnesia.

Dr Emma Ridley – doctor and colleague of Marguerite. She is providing psychiatric support for Mel.

Felicia Galsworthy – owns a high-end clothing shop in Knightsbridge and employs Mel.

Vin (Vincent) – one-time partner to Mel. He runs a missing persons agency in London.

Jim Davy – a Cornishman and he is the Lowe's gardener.

Thirza – Jim Davy's mother.

Leigh – Ivan's live-in carer, who looks after Ivan when he is widowed and frail.

Reginald Ferguson – butler to the Lawsons.

Mike Mills – one-time boyfriend to Ren, who is friends with Natasha. He lives in Boston, Lincolnshire.

James – a pharmacist friend of Ren, who lives in Penzance.

Neil Macbeith – former lover of Ruth. He has a Chihuahua called Inez.

Daphne – Neil's sister.

Nathan – a school friend of Trelly.

Lois Shaw – mother of Nathan. She lives in Penzance and is friends with Ruth.

Gervaise – Nathan's school-friend.

Mark Banks – Izzie's gardener. He is besotted with Izzie.

Dora (also known as Robin) – a friend of Izzie and Tristan. He has lived in the US for most of his life.

Faye – Dora's half-sister. She has lived in the States for most of her life and is the mother of two daughters, Morgana and Joodee, Sam's wife.

Morgana – Faye's elder daughter. She has lived in the States with her mother for most of her life.

Vivienne Lowe – Mac's wife in New Orleans. She was born in Haiti. Vivienne practises voodoo and speaks French.

Raoul – Vivienne's friend, lives in New Orleans and speaks French.

Evangeline and Marie-Ghislaine (Evie and Emmie) – friendly twins who help at Mac's house in New Orleans.

Doc Donahue Jr – neighbour of Mac in New Orleans. He has many Rhode Island Red hens, of which he is very proud.

Iris - a good friend to the Lowe family. She is a member of the Coven and owns *The Bubbling Cauldron* bistro in Penzance.

Leila – partner to Iris. She helps to run *The Bubbling Cauldron.*

Zeus – Annie's Brazilian friend. He is a faith healer.

Adam – a private detective, working for Natasha. He lives in Boston, Lincolnshire.

Mila (Ludmila, also known as Rebecca) – Rachel and Godfrey's adopted daughter.

Rachel Dennis – Her husband Godfrey is deceased. She has a Mastiff for protection, as she lives in an isolated house on the Wash, in Lincolnshire, near to Natasha's home.

Mrs Ramsbotham – lives in the same block of apartments in South London as Lance.

Heinrich – concierge in Switzerland. He works in the apartment block Rick Morrison lives in.

Nils Ekelberg – an acquaintance of Rick Morrison.

Elaine Aston – former lover Lance. She worked for Abe Fischer in London, as a seamstress.

Abe Fischer – Elaine's boss. Owner of Goldstien's Tailors

Nancy and Clem – members of the Lincoln Animal Rights Association.

Joshua and Sarah Williams - parents to Regina Steinhart, Faye's mother.

Vladimir Rodomski – Ivan's father. He lived and died in Russia, during the time of the USSR.

Alexander Levitov – Russian connections of Vladimir.

Mishka – partner of Alexander Levitov.

Nikolai – son of Alexander, born in Russia but has moved to the US.

Belinda Fairfax – a close friend of Lance.

Coven Members – Past and Present

Levant Cooper – coven name, Hermes, communicator.

Tamara Killick – coven name, Demeter, specialist in growing herbs and pagan festivals.

Kerensa Lowe – coven name, Artemis, learner, under instruction in herbs and potions. Now a lapsed member.

Mackenzie Lowe – coven name, Merlin, specialist in ceremonial daggers and robes, one-time chief Warlock. Since his move back to the US, he is a lapsed member.

Abel Menheniot – coven name, Pendragon, Senior Druid.

Athena O'Shea – coven name, Brigid, specialist in domestic arts.

Morwenna (Wenna) Perran – coven name, Hecate, specialist in herbs, tisanes and omens. Wenna lives in Zennor, in an isolated cottage, at the bottom of a cliff, with her family of cats.

Natasha Rodomskai-Lawson – coven name, Tanith, healer.

Roisin Esther Jane Rose – coven name, Iris, specialist in meditation and the occult. She is in a relationship with Leila and lives with her in Penzance. She travels to New Orleans with Mel and Ren.

Faye Louise Steinhart – coven name, Morgan, Earth Mother. She has lived in the US with her two daughters, Morgana and Joodee but divides her time between there and the UK.

Ruth Trelawney-Lowe – coven name, Minerva, specialist in crystal healing.

About The Author

My interest in paganism and Arthurian legend has been long-standing. My first degree in French at King's College, London, included a module on French Arthurian legend written in Medieval French. Whilst studying for my second degree which was in English Literature at the University of East Anglia, I completed a thesis on Guinevere, having studied a module in Arthurian legend.

My love of the West Country began at a very early age. I spent many holidays in Cornwall with my Aunt Lorna, who had two friends living in Gulval, just outside Penzance. This is where Ruth, Mel's mother, lives in my story. One of my Aunt Lorna's friends, Dr Alice Gilbey, was a Cornish Druid, and took part in the annual Gorsedh. She spoke Cornish and used to take me, as a child, all around Cornwall in her car, a battered old Renault. We visited many of the ancient menhirs such as Lanyon Quoit, Chysauster and Carn Euny which feature in my story. We also drove to outlying villages on the coast. Zennor, I particularly loved. My ex-husband, Chris, to whom this book is dedicated, was born in Newton Abbot in Devon. His father was born in Shaldon and his mother in Teignmouth – both places are named and described in my story. We spent many holidays down there with our children. When Chris and I were first married, we lived in a Victorian house in a converted top-floor flat. This was located in the Crystal Palace, area of London. This is where Lance lives in my story. Chris, and I subsequently spent a day house-hunting, prior to moving up-country to a small village just outside Boston in Lincolnshire. It is where I drew my inspiration for Plumtree Hall, the home of Natasha and her family. We looked at a house similar, but less grand, at Freiston Shore, not far from the Wash.

I have a dear friend, an American, who still lives in the States, Tricia McCormack-Seybold. She and I have been friends since our school days. She was born in New Orleans. We went there together many years ago, shortly after Mardi Gras, just as Mel and Ren do. As well as visiting Marie-Lavaux's House of Voodoo, we also went to plantations outside the city, which became the Lowe residence in my story. New Orleans is where Mac and his wife, Vivienne, live in my story. Tulane Hospital is where Tricia's ex-husband trained as a doctor. This is where Ren fights for her life..

Friendship is of paramount importance to me and it is the main theme of my book. I am very fortunate to have many friends and to have lost very few.

However, all the characters in this story are totally fictitious and any who bear a resemblance to anybody I know is purely by chance.

Acknowledgements

Firstly, I would like to give huge thanks to the person who made this book possible, Abbirose Adey. Her support and encouragement, together with her editorial hints, have been invaluable.

Secondly, to my amazing husband, Dave, who has worked tirelessly on typesetting and on the cover of the book. He, too, has shown his support and love.

The theme of my book is friendship. I am fortunate to be blessed with an enormous number of friends, many of whom have been friends of a very long duration. One particular friend, and almost sister, Maureen, I thought of frequently when considering the close ties between Ruth and Natasha.

I would like to thank several friends who took time out of their busy lives to review chapters of the book for me and gave favourable feedback. They are all ardent readers, like me.

My thanks to Cas Smirthwaite for reading and commenting on the manuscript. Her help was much appreciated.

Last of all I would like to thank my four children for their encouragement and support, together with my ex-husband, Chris. Happy memories of our years together and family holidays in Devon and Cornwall have been incorporated into this book, not to mention the homes we made together in Crystal Palace and in Boston, Lincolnshire.

Wiccan Dates

Yule – 20th-23rd December (Officially 4 days).

A log is lit to drive back the darkness, for the light sleeps during these 12 sacred days. From 21st December to 1st January, a wreath rests upon an altar, adorned with nature´s offerings and candlelight.

Mistletoe and evergreens mark the season, as spicy soups and hearty stews warm the soul. A bird is shared at the table, and the old year is cleared away with bundles of sage, rosemary and pine cones.

The circle is cast around gifts given with intention, perhaps destined for charity, by the High Priestess, the Crone and the Maiden.

Imbolc – 1st February (24 hours until sundown the next day)

Imbolc (pronounced Imbol, with the c silent) is a festival of light and fertility, closely associated with St Brigid. Traditionally, bonfires are lit and small straw dolls are crafted as offerings, often tied to trees near scared wells.

This time is linked with rites of initiations, ritual cleansing baths and thorough house cleaning – symbolic acts to welcome renewal and growth.

Divination practices also play a role. One such method involves reading stones, thirteen in total, each marked with symbols representing the sun, moon, the seven classical planets, and the four elements: earth, air, fire and water. These stones are used similarly to tarot, offering insight and guidance through symbolic interpretation.

Ostara – 21st March

Easter and the Spring Equinox mark a time of balance, renewal and awakening. Traditions include baking hot cross buns, enjoying fresh asparagus and decorating honey-coloured eggs – symbols of fertility and new life. Bunnies, chicks and birds' nests woven from pussy willow, spring blossoms and willow branches to celebrate the season's rebirth.

Seeds are planted in ceremony, with a man and woman representing the spring god and goddess – embodying the union that brings forth life. At sunset, sage is burned over a fire, cleansing the space and honouring the turning of the wheel. Sage is burned over a fire at sunset.

Beltane – 1st May

Beltane is a fire festival, celebrating passion, fertility and the vibrant stirrings of life. A maypole wrapped in ribbons of green, red, white and silver stands at the heart of the celebration, while flower baskets and the presence of the Green Man symbolise nature in full bloom.

Couples leap over the fire together, sealing bonds and invoking blessings for the season ahead. Tiny faery houses are built from acorns, moss, bark and leaves – offerings for the unseen world.

It is a night for sleeping beneath the stars, deep in the woods. Hawthorn branches, sacred and protective, are welcomed into the home only during Beltane.

Children and dreamers craft wish boxes from shoeboxes and paper, filling them with sunflower seeds, rose petals and strips of willow bark – each one a silent hope tucked away to grow with the season. As the box is filled you make a wish for the coming season.

Litha – 21st June

Litha (pronounced Leetha) is at the height of summer, a time when the sun stands still at its peak. Celebrate with garlands of fresh herbs and wildflowers woven into hair or hung upon doorways. Crystals of green, gold and violet, precious stones such as garnets, amber, moonstone, jade, emerald and obsidian – are laid out to capture the season's radiant energy. The scents of honeysuckle, rose, chamomile and lavender fill the air. Honey and strawberries are savoured, alongside summer fruits and vegetables: sweet gifts of the sun. Mead is poured at the altar.

Lugnasadh / Lammas – 1st August.

Lugnasadh (pronounced Loo-nah-sah) is when the first harvest arrives, and with it, offerings of grain and gratitude. Ash trees are honoured, and sacred breads are baked – golden, round and filled with magic. Corn and wheat stalks are crafted into wheels, pentagrams and corn dollies, symbols of the earth's bounty. Herbal sachets filled with sage, rosemary and lavender are hung in doorways to cleanse and protect. The feast includes sweetcorn, ripe grapes and deep red wine, all shared in the spirit of thanks.

Mabon – 21st September

The balance of light and dark returns at the Autumn equinox. Named after an ancient Cornish figure, this festival honours the turning inward and the gathering in. The colours of the earth - orange, gold, red, brown and copper, surround gourds, apples and pumpkins piled high. Cider is poured and amber, citrine, sapphire and jasper, and cat's eye stones reflect the harvest light. Sunflowers, marigolds, thistles, and the joy of apple-picking mark this time of quiet abundance and farewell to warmth.

Samhain 31st October – 1st November

Samhain (pronounced sow-in or saw-in) is when the veil between worlds thins: the year darkens. It is the final harvest and a sacred time of remembrance. The barrier between worlds dissolves, allowing spirits to draw near. A place is set at the table for the unseen and silence is kept for the dumb supper – a moment of reverence and listening. Mulled wine, cider and mead warm the body while sweets and ale are left as offerings for the departed. Myths stir in the shadows: the shapeshifter, the headless woman, Lady Gwynn in white, followed by a black pig. Jack-o-Lanterns glow in the night and we dress in costume, stepping into the mystery as the wheel turns once more.

Significant Sites

The sites mentioned below represent some of the fascinating standing stones and ancient locations explored in this book. Each offers a unique opportunity for further study and discovery, inviting readers to delve deeper into the mysteries and stories that surround them.

Carn Euny

Carn Euny is an archaeological site, owned and managed by English Heritage near Sancreed on the Penwith Peninsular in Cornwall. There is evidence of an Iron Age settlement here, possibly abandoned circa 400 AD. Of special interest is the underground passage with a fogou – a monument specific to Cornwall.

Address: Sancreed, Penzance TR20 8RB

https://www.english-heritage.org.uk/visit/places/carn-euny-ancient-village/history/

Chysauster

This is a late Iron Age village, managed by English Heritage, overlooking the coast, near Penzance, Cornwall. The type of buildings here, still in evidence, are stone-walled and specifically West Cornish. It is believed that a community lived here between the 1st and 3rd centuries AD under Roman rule. The houses were arranged around a courtyard.

Address: Newmill, Penzance, Cornwall, TR20 8XA

https://www.english-heritage.org.uk/visit/places/chysauster-ancient-village/

Lanyon Quoit

This is a dolmen, to the south-east of Morvah in Cornwall, with three support stones and a capstone, Supposedly, high enough for a horse and rider to pass underneath during the 18th century. This is no longer the case. During a storm in the 19th century the dolmen fell down but was re-erected but, sadly, not to its former state.

Address: Madron, Cornwall

https://commons.wikimedia.org/wiki/Category:Lanyon_Quoit

St Michael's Mount

Karrek Loos yn Koos in Cornish (the grey rock in a wood) is a small tidal island off the coast of Marazion near Penzance with a fascinating history. At low tide, a causeway links the island to Marazion. St Michael's Mount's counterpart and with which it is has historical connections, is the famous Mont St Michel in Normandie, France. The island was probably inhabited during the Neolithic period and possibly the Mesolithic period when Britain was joined to the mainland of Europe. It was the site of a monastery in more recent times. It is partially managed by the St Aubyn family but the National Trust shares the management of the site.

Address: Harbour View, Marazion TR17 0HS

https://www.nationaltrust.org.uk/st-michaels-mount

Notes

Please use the following pages to jot down any thoughts, notes, questions, spells and general perusings about the story. I would love to hear from you. You can contact me at:

chrissieathomas@gmail.com

Thank you for reading *Deceit in Cornwall: Delmelza's Downfall.*

Chrissie

Notes

Notes

Notes

www.ingramcontent.com/pod-product-compliance
Ingram Content Group UK Ltd.
Pitfield, Milton Keynes, MK11 3LW, UK
UKHW051633231025
464243UK00001B/3

9 781919 231709